"*Burning Love* was a fabulous read from start to finish. From the serial arsonist turned killer to the growing attraction between the hero and heroine, it was hot, hot, hot! I loved it."
—*New York Times* bestselling author
Sharon Sala

* * *

"I've been working on three cases very similar to this. I think this is his fourth fire."

Jack's spine stiffened. "You're saying we have a serial arsonist?"

"I think so," Terra said, exhaling audibly.

"There haven't been any other fire deaths," he said bluntly. "I would've heard about that."

"If this is the same guy, last night was the first time he's killed."

"Why now? And why Harris Vaughn?"

"I have no idea." Her voice was even, but the glimmer of brightness in her eyes reminded him that the arsonist's first victim had also been her friend.

Dear Reader,

The days are hot and the reading is hotter here at Silhouette Intimate Moments. Linda Turner is back with the next of THOSE MARRYING McBRIDES! in *Always a McBride*. Taylor Bishop has only just found out about his familial connection—and he has no idea it's going to lead him straight to love.

In *Shooting Starr,* Kathleen Creighton ratchets up both the suspense and the romance in a story of torn loyalties you'll long remember. Carla Cassidy returns to CHEROKEE CORNERS in *Last Seen…,* a novel about two people whose circumstances ought to prevent them from falling in love but don't. *On Dean's Watch* is the latest from reader favorite Linda Winstead Jones, and it will keep you turning the pages as her federal marshal hero falls hard for the woman he's supposed to be keeping an undercover watch over. *Roses After Midnight,* by Linda Randall Wisdom, is a suspenseful look at the hunt for a serial rapist—and the blossoming of an unexpected romance. Finally, take a look at Debra Cowan's *Burning Love* and watch passion flare to life between a female arson investigator and the handsome cop who may be her prime suspect.

Enjoy them all—and come back next month for more of the best and most exciting romance reading around.

Yours,

Leslie J. Wainger
Executive Editor

Please address questions and book requests to:
Silhouette Reader Service
U.S.: 3010 Walden Ave., P.O. Box 1325, Buffalo, NY 14269
Canadian: P.O. Box 609, Fort Erie, Ont. L2A 5X3

Burning Love
DEBRA COWAN

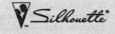

INTIMATE MOMENTS™

Published by Silhouette Books

America's Publisher of Contemporary Romance

If you purchased this book without a cover you should be aware
that this book is stolen property. It was reported as "unsold and
destroyed" to the publisher, and neither the author nor the
publisher has received any payment for this "stripped book."

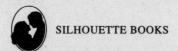 SILHOUETTE BOOKS

ISBN 0-373-27306-1

BURNING LOVE

Copyright © 2003 by Debra S. Cowan

All rights reserved. Except for use in any review, the reproduction
or utilization of this work in whole or in part in any form by any
electronic, mechanical or other means, now known or hereafter
invented, including xerography, photocopying and recording, or in
any information storage or retrieval system, is forbidden without
the written permission of the editorial office, Silhouette Books,
233 Broadway, New York, NY 10279 U.S.A.

All characters in this book have no existence outside the imagination of
the author and have no relation whatsoever to anyone bearing the same
name or names. They are not even distantly inspired by any individual
known or unknown to the author, and all incidents are pure invention.

This edition published by arrangement with Harlequin Books S.A.

® and TM are trademarks of Harlequin Books S.A., used under license.
Trademarks indicated with ® are registered in the United States Patent
and Trademark Office, the Canadian Trade Marks Office and in other
countries.

Visit Silhouette at www.eHarlequin.com

Printed in U.S.A.

Books by Debra Cowan

Silhouette Intimate Moments

Dare To Remember #774
The Rescue of Jenna West #858
One Silent Night #899
Special Report #1045
  "Cover Me!"
Still the One #1127
Burning Love #1236

DEBRA COWAN

Like many writers, Debra made up stories in her head as a child. Her B.A. in English was obtained with the intention of following family tradition and becoming a schoolteacher, but after she wrote her first novel, there was no looking back. After years of working another job in addition to writing, she now devotes herself full-time to penning both historical and contemporary romances. An avid history buff, Debra enjoys traveling. She has visited places as diverse as Europe and Honduras, where she and her husband served as part of a medical mission team. Born in the foothills of the Kiamichi Mountains, Debra still lives in her native Oklahoma with her husband and their two beagles, Maggie and Domino.

Debra invites her readers to contact her at P.O. Box 30123, Coffee Creek Station, Edmond, OK 73003-0003 or via e-mail at her Web site at http://www.oklahoma.net/~debcowan.

ACKNOWLEDGMENTS

I wish to acknowledge and thank
Jack Goldhorn, Public Information Officer,
Norfolk Fire Rescue, Norfolk, VA,
and David Wiist, Chief of Fire Prevention, Edmond, OK,
for their invaluable and generous assistance. You have
my word that my small arson knowledge will be used
only between the covers of a book.
All liberties taken in the name of fiction are my own.

Chapter 1

"Body found in blaze at one-sixteen Sorrel Lane."

The dispatcher's voice crackled across Terra August's car radio. As the sole fire investigator for Presley, Oklahoma, she was already on her way to the two-alarm fire in the established Hunter's Ridge subdivision, jarred out of a deep sleep minutes ago by her pager.

In the past ten years, the Oklahoma City suburb's population had grown to nearly fifty thousand. The police department had hired enough officers before the growth spurt, but not the fire department. These last few weeks had doubled Terra's wish for another investigator in her office, but until next year's budget was approved, she was it.

Her mentor lived on Sorrel Lane, but she didn't know the house number. Their frequent meetings had never taken place at his home or hers, and usually involved a meal somewhere. *Please, don't let it be Harris's house.*

After flashing her badge for the uniformed officer stationed at the neighborhood's entrance, she maneuvered her

Explorer down a neatly kept residential street. The older brick homes were bathed in a mix of moonlight and shadow. Red and blue lights strobed from a police cruiser at either end of the block. Fire trucks, engines, police cars and two vans bearing the names and logos of the nearby Oklahoma City television stations crowded both sides of the street. The frantic swirl of lights spiked her blood pressure. Less than five hours ago, she and Harris Vaughn had enjoyed a Sunday night dinner and put their heads together about a case that had her stumped.

Fighting to calm a sudden flicker of panic, Terra eased her SUV past three police cruisers, around Station One's rescue truck and squeezed to the curb just behind an ambulance. The paramedic raised a hand in greeting and shut the door. Terra glimpsed the empty gurney inside. No survivors.

Her heartbeat stuttered, but she uncurled her death grip from the steering wheel and stepped out. The blaze was out, but gray smoke streaked across the midnight-black sky. Water from the firefighters' hoses ran down the streets, gurgled into grates and glistened on trees, yards, nearby cars. Smoke still hung heavy in the air. Police and fire radios crackled into the night. Yellow crime scene tape squared off the house and yard. Officers stood guard at each of the four corners and probably in the back yard where Terra couldn't see.

At one time, the single story, traditional redbrick home had been inviting. Now it looked cold and bleak. Dead. Still mostly intact, the brick was streaked with soot, burned black on the west side of the house. The one front window on the west side was blown out; the trio of windows on the east side looked untouched except for the dripping ash and water as the firefighters from Stations One and Four, her old station house, stood amidst snaking hoses and a now soggy lawn. In a neighbor's yard, a firefighter stood videotaping the scene. Terra would get the tape from him later.

The blaze appeared to have burned only one area of the home before firefighters managed to douse it.

Urgency had her slamming her door and looking around for the police officer who held the log book to check people in and out of the scene.

The familiar sharp odor of burning wood and engine fumes wrapped around her like the wet midnight. This fire was different. It had taken more than a home, more than memories. It had taken a life. And she had to know whose.

Ash swirled through the air, clung to her cheeks. The Oklahoma County Medical Examiner's wagon eased past her and found a spot farther up the crowded street.

She opened the back door of her Explorer and grabbed her boots. Stumbling out of a dead sleep when her pager buzzed, she had automatically pulled on jeans and a heavy flannel shirt with sleeves she could roll up. She'd sleeked her shoulder-length hair into a ponytail. Hoping like crazy that the victim's identity would be someone other than the mentor whose company she'd enjoyed earlier in the evening, Terra toed off her tennis shoes and tugged on her rubber, steel-soled boots.

The ambulance pulled out and ambled down the block. Trying to steady her racing pulse, she grabbed her hard hat and slid it on.

Her thick, well-worn gloves were in her pockets. She slung her camera around her neck, picked up her shovel and a tackle box containing her hand tools. Stepping around the back of her truck, she racked her brain for any memory of Harris's house number. She came up empty, which only sharpened the dread pricking at her.

Her gaze swept the knots of people moving around the scene. Several uniformed officers wound through the crowd of reporters, cameramen and neighbors. At the sidewalk which led to the front door, Terra spotted a cop holding a clipboard. She started toward him, dodging the hood of a police car, stepping over a hydrant hose.

This neighborhood had probably never seen anything more traumatic than a bicycle wreck. Farther up the street, uniformed officers were directing passersby to keep moving and news vans to park at the end of the block.

As they'd finished dinner, Harris had mentioned taking in a movie after running some errands. Terra had grabbed a swim at her gym before heading home to turn in early. She hadn't been asleep two hours before her pager went off.

Four years as a fire investigator and nine years on the job had taught her to level out her emotions so she could objectively do her job, but tonight she failed. Tonight she was terrified of whose body the firefighters had found.

Her nerves snapped tight as she continued to walk toward the slightly built policeman with the clipboard, standing at the curb in front of the victim's mailbox. Water dripped from the mature maple trees in the front yard, their yellow and red leaves glimmering red and blue in the flashing lights from one of the police cruisers. Firefighters walked past dragging hoses back to their engines. Perhaps the officer in her sights would know the victim's identity.

"Hello, Luscious."

Ugh. Terra knew the smooth, practiced voice, but kept walking. Dane Reynolds was an investigative reporter for one of Oklahoma City's television stations and seemed to always beat her to the scene. "No time, Reynolds."

"Just one minute, Angel Face." The local newsman with spray-stiff hair hurried toward her. "Just one?"

Terra kept moving, drawing up sharply when the reporter suddenly appeared. Flashing too-perfect teeth, Dane Reynolds planted his impressively trim self in front of her. He probably spent hours at the gym, and more time on his hair than she did on hers.

She stepped around him. She wasn't about to let Reynolds see the cold sweat that clung to her nape. Or get a glimpse of nerves that were raw with uncertainty. Dane Reynolds would jump on that like a rat on a Cheetoh. "I'm working here, Dane."

"I know." He fell into easy step beside her as if he'd been invited. "Just wanted to ask if you'd talk to me about this case when you're finished here?"

"Station Four caught this one. Captain Maguire is around somewhere."

"But I want to talk to *you*." He lightly skimmed his fingers over her shoulder as if brushing away something. "You know you want to."

What she wanted was to pop him with her shovel. "I already told you—"

"And what about that interview we talked about? Surely you've changed your mind by now. The guy's set three fires and you're no closer to—"

"How's that camera working out, Investigator?" A pleasant male voice interrupted firmly.

"It's great, T.J." Terra smiled over at T. J. Coontz, Dane's cameraman, who had played the buffer before. A few months ago, she'd asked the cameraman to recommend a place to buy a good used camera for the advanced photography class she'd enrolled in this semester. The city's current budget didn't support further education so Terra had signed up on her own time and money. She would have borrowed a camera from Harris, but she needed to learn how to use a newer model. T.J. had generously offered one of his cameras in order to save Terra some expense. "Thanks for loaning it to me. I'll get it back to you as soon as the class ends."

"Keep it as long as you want."

She eyed his dark suit and tie. "You look nice."

"I was at my cousin's wedding when I got the page for the fire."

Dane shot T.J. a withering look before saying to Terra, "Come on, Luscious. What about that interview?"

"Dane, you're not helping your case," T.J. said.

"Good point." Terra stepped past the men. "Please excuse me."

She had to make sure it wasn't Harris inside that torched house.

"How about a drink tomorrow night?"

"Sorry," she called to Reynolds over her shoulder as she moved up to the cop. The guy couldn't take a hint. She'd refused every time he'd asked her out in the past two months. Just as she'd refused his requests for an interview.

"What about Thursday?"

Ignoring him, she flashed her badge at the thirty-something officer who stood eye-to-eye with her five-foot-nine frame. "Terra August, Fire Investigator."

He nodded and held the log out for her to sign her name and record the time.

Her gaze going to the brass nametag he wore, she swallowed around the painful knot in her throat. "Officer Lowe, do we know the victim's name?"

"Yes, ma'am." He skimmed a finger up to the top of the page. "Officer Farrell spoke to a neighbor who said a man named Harris Vaughn lived here and the neighbor saw him come home around nine-thirty."

No! A sharp pain pierced her chest and Terra struggled to absorb the shock, tried to keep her wits about her.

"Hey, you okay?" Lowe peered at her.

"Do they know for sure that it's him?"

"No, ma'am. Just that this is his residence."

She shook her head, urgency and dread fusing inside her. What had happened? Electrical fire? Arson? She could already rule out cigarettes. Harris didn't smoke, never had.

"Ma'am?" The policeman had lifted the tape and now waited expectantly.

Her knees wobbled, but she moved forward, partly out of reflex, partly out of denial. No, it wasn't Harris. It couldn't be.

Wait for facts. Harris's ingrained instruction played through her mind and she hung on to it with single-minded focus as she sidestepped the labyrinth of hoses on the sidewalk. Sooty water splashed over the toes of her thick rubber boots. The cops knew only that this was Harris's house. No one had identified *him,* only a male victim.

Out of habit, she reached for the camera around her neck, but rather than stop for her first set of pictures, she moved inside.

The smell of wet ash settled over her like a cloud of fog. Gripping her tackle box, she nodded to the firefighters coming toward her. The somber, whipped look on their faces sharpened the knot in her throat. They'd contained the fire, but lost someone. She knew from her nine years fighting fires that no one would sleep tonight.

In the living room to her right, Terra spotted Don LeBass and Rusty Ferguson from her old station house. Rusty's eyes were red rimmed and Terra knew it wasn't strictly due to the blaze he'd battled. The two men were deep in conversation with Captain Maguire.

She absently registered moving across slick tile then soggy carpet past a couple of firefighters, down a long hallway to her left. The wall's creamy paint was hidden beneath streaks of soot and ash. Wood and glass littered the floor. A clump of men and women stood in the doorway at the end of a hall and Terra knew the body was there. The bedroom door had been blown out from its hinges. Was this room the point-of-origin?

She'd need to check every room for that, ask if anyone had discovered any sign of forced entry, anything that might indicate arson, but all she cared about right now was seeing the body and making sure it wasn't Harris.

Three firemen stood against the wall just outside the door, nodding soberly as she reached them. She recognized the oldest of them, Jerry French, a twenty-year veteran from Station Four. She stepped into the room, leaning her shovel against the nearest wall.

The bedroom was now a skeleton of burned rafters and support beams, studs peering out from gouged and blackened Sheetrock. She automatically noted those details as her gaze went immediately to the body lying on the bed.

She drew in a deep breath and moved closer so she could see the body. The face was too severely heat-bloated to be recognizable, but her gaze snagged on the victim's cowboy boots. Water-gray, Australian sharkskin.

No! Her vision grayed. Dizzy and nauseous, she turned and stumbled blindly toward the door. Harris. Harris. Harris.

Her heart clenched painfully. Those boots had cost a pretty penny. Terra and the other Presley firefighters had pooled their money to buy Harris the pair for his retirement, along with an Alaskan fishing trip. The M.E. would have to use dental records for a positive identification of the body, but for Terra the boots were a macabre dog tag.

Trying to breathe without keeling over, she reached for the nearest wall, grabbed only air and pitched forward.

An arm, solid and thick, caught her at the waist. ''Easy there.''

The deep masculine voice commanded rather than soothed. Reflexively she clutched at the arm bracing her waist, her stomach rolling. For an instant, she let herself

lean into the steel-hard strength, tried to absorb the pain
slashing through her. Her entire body throbbed with it. In
another few seconds, her vision cleared and she registered
dark brown hair, hard blue eyes and a mouth that meant all
business.

Cop. She saw the gold badge clipped to the waistband of
his faded jeans at the same time she realized he still held
her. She felt steadier and managed a thank-you.

He frowned, his lips flattening. "This your first body at
a fire scene? Something like this isn't for a rookie."

Irritation flickered through the smothering pain. She
mumbled thanks only out of politeness and pushed her way
out into the hall.

"Cut her a break, man," Terra heard Jerry French say to
the cop. "The victim's a friend of hers."

She ducked into an empty bathroom, boots squishing
through ashy water and crunching over glass and splintered
wood. Wet smoke and the rotten smell of death weakened
her knees as she dragged in deep breaths of cold, rancid air.
The bloated, unrecognizable mass of Harris's face floated
through her mind. She closed her eyes, leaned her forehead
against the wall and focused on breathing. She'd thrown up
twice in her adult life; she battled to keep from doing it a
third time.

Tugging off one of her gloves, she pushed back her helmet and wiped at the cold sweat on her forehead, her nape.
Tears burned her throat and she thumbed off the strays falling down her cheeks. The cop's disapproval of her pricked,
but it didn't matter. What mattered was what had happened
to Harris and she meant to find out.

Despite how difficult this case was, fire investigation was
her job, what Harris had trained her to do. What she *would*
do. For him.

Terra waited there until her stomach settled. She had to

focus on her job, not Harris. *You can't make it personal.*
That had been one of the first things he'd taught her. A sob
ached in her throat, but she swallowed it. After another minute, she pulled her glove back on, adjusted her helmet more
comfortably and returned to the bedroom.

The medical examiner, Ken Mason, handled bodies for
Oklahoma County, which included the town of Presley. He
now stood beside the bed waving off a young man who
approached with a body bag. "Wait until Investigator August is finished."

Ken, who'd worked with Harris during his last year as
the fire investigator, turned to Terra with compassion in his
dark eyes. "Take your time."

She nodded, fighting down another swell of emotion. Her
mind still couldn't accept what her eyes had seen. For a
moment, she made herself stare at the body. There was nothing of the shy grin, the trimmed beard shot with gray, the
kind brown eyes. All traces of the man she knew—*loved*—
were gone. Except for the boots. Bit by bit, she let in the
pain until she felt she could control it. When she began to
tremble, she bit her lip and looked away.

Someone, probably Jerry and the guys from Station Four,
had set up her portable floodlights while she was gone. Putting herself on autopilot as best she could, Terra decided to
record the body first, get it over with. She lifted her camera
with shaking hands and snapped pictures from several angles. After each photo, she dictated a brief memo into her
microcassette recorder. Tears blurred her vision, but she had
a job to do. Harris, of all people, wouldn't have cut her any
slack.

She moved to the right side of the bed. The hallway, guest
bathroom and living room only had smoke damage, but fire
damage was severe in this room. Especially on the wall
beside the bed where destruction was the heaviest.

This could very well be the low point—the place where the fire started—for this room. There could be other origins. She would double-check and verify every room before making notes to that effect. Her initial guess was the bedroom as the point-of-origin, but she would make no conclusions until she finished her investigation.

"Where did you come from?" she murmured to the fire, staring at the charred wood that moved in an upward-spreading vee from the bedside table. "Here? Or another room?"

She forced herself to look a second time at Harris's body. She wanted to scream, to run, but she didn't. Her heartbeat thundered in her ears and her breathing went shallow, but after a minute, she was able to detach a bit. That's when she noticed his hands and feet were tied. She froze as the implication sunk in. He wouldn't have been able to escape.

She jerked her gaze away. Rage swept over her until she shook with it. She stared blankly at the blackened wall and counted to ten as she struggled to level out the tide of emotion battering her. *Do your job,* she mentally reminded herself. *Do your job.*

She should take measurements of the body's position, compare them later to the ones taken by the lab tech who'd already put away his tape measure. And as quickly as possible, she needed to determine what, if any, accelerant had been used before any remaining indication vanished due to the areas ventilated by the firefighters.

She'd always been able to scent kerosene or gasoline at a scene; she smelled neither here. She could call Vicki at the State Fire Marshal's office and request the use of their German shepherd. Pyro was trained to sniff out accelerants, but Terra didn't want to wait for the dog to arrive. Besides, her portable "sniffer," an instrument that detected combustible gases, would confirm the presence and identity of the accelerant. After that, she would take samples if necessary.

Urging herself to get started, Terra turned. For the first time, she noticed her tackle box at the foot of the bed and realized she must've dropped it upon first seeing Harris.

Jerry French picked it up and handed it to her. "You okay?"

"Yes, thanks. I just needed a little time."

He nodded, his smoke-reddened hazel eyes sympathetic. "The guys from Four and One are waiting to begin overhaul. That way, you can move them away from where you think the fire started."

"Great. That will save a lot of investigation time."

"The walk-around's finished. The structure appears sound enough for you to begin."

"Your guys were first on the scene, right?"

Jerry nodded. "We had some trouble putting out the blaze. It took a small spray pattern to finally do the trick."

Terra noted that in her tape recorder. If the typical wide or "fog pattern" spray was inefficient in putting out the fire, that was a clue to the type of accelerant used. "Thanks, Jerry. I'll come out in just a minute to talk to your crew, walk through overhaul with them. Right now, I need to check for accelerants before they evaporate."

"Gotcha."

Still off balance and slightly disoriented, she set her tackle box down on the soggy, debris-covered carpet.

Soot streaked Jerry's weathered, leather face. Concern darkened his eyes. "You sure you're okay?"

She nodded, giving him a small smile. "I can do this."

"I'll see you outside." He squeezed her shoulder and motioned to the two firefighters she'd barely noticed earlier. One woman, one man, both pale and wide-eyed. Probies. Had she ever been that green?

The cop who'd kept her from planting her face in the floor watched her coolly from a few feet away. Uneasy with the knowing steadiness in his eyes, her gaze slid away. She opened her tackle box and took out the small, boxlike "sniffer." The wooden footboard for the queen-size bed was still intact, but the headboard was a crumbling screen of ash. Charred mattress. Closed, scorched closet door.

Rubbing her temple where a headache had started, Terra walked to the far side of the bed. Bedroom fires were typically caused by three things: frayed lamp circuits, electric blankets or smokers. Harris had never smoked so she dismissed the possibility that he could've started the fire that way. Though fires due to frayed lamp circuits and electric blankets were rare, Terra checked anyway. There was no electric blanket on this bed. At the bedside table, she noticed a blackened brass lamp and knelt to check the electrical cord. No frayed lamp circuit here.

Intent on checking the same things on the opposite side, Terra edged around the foot of the bed. An identical bedside table held another brass lamp, now soot-black. This lamp's electrical cord wasn't frayed either. The fire hadn't been caused by faulty electric wiring. Glass fragments sprinkled the sodden carpet. The shattered base of a bulb still screwed into the lamp testified that at least some of the shards belonged to an exploding lightbulb.

"You the fire investigator?"

She remembered the rough velvet voice. Standing up, she had to tilt her head a bit to look him in the eye, something she didn't have to do with very many men. "Yes."

"Detective Jack Spencer. I'll be the primary on this case."

His gaze scoured her face. What was he looking for? She wasn't going to faint. In the harsh flood of the portable fluorescent lights, Terra noted fine lines fanning out from Detective Spencer's eyes. Very blue eyes. *Hard* blue eyes.

He stuck out his hand.

She shook it and released it quickly. "Terra August."

"I apologize for my comment earlier. I didn't know he was a friend of yours."

She tamped down the slash of pain. Presley was still small enough that all police, including the detectives, worked solo rather than with a partner. Except in fire death cases like this. Procedure between Presley's police and fire departments stated that when P.F.D. found a dead body in a fire, they worked to contain the blaze, then stopped and called Homicide. "I guess we'll be working together."

"Yes. Looks like murder."

Struggling to keep a rein on the emotions swirling inside her, she pressed her lips together and nodded. "The bound hands and feet of the victim also indicate the fire as a probable arson. But why?"

"That's what I intend to find out," Spencer said. "Do you have any ideas?"

"No. I'll concentrate first on confirming or eliminating arson. Then we'll have a solid starting place." She'd have to work with the detective until one of them proved the death was an accident, suicide or murder. If Harris's death was an accident, Terra would turn over her part of the investigation to the insurance company. Otherwise, she and Jack Spencer were in this together. She could interview and interrogate, but she couldn't arrest or serve warrants. Spencer could.

He glanced around the sooty, soggy room. "Can't you already tell if it's arson?"

"I approach all fires as if they are, but I need proof."

"Well, something's fishy. Why else would he have been tied?"

She curled her shaking hands into fists around the instrument she held. Her voice cracked as she asked, "Was he dead before the fire?"

"I don't know." Sympathy and an unidentifiable emotion flashed through his blue eyes before he turned toward the M.E. "Mason?"

"You know it's too soon for me to have anything for you yet, Jack."

Numb and still reeling, a part of her noted the cop's clean soap-and-water scent she caught beneath lingering smoke. Someone had tied up Harris, but why? So he couldn't escape the fire? Or for another reason?

This was too much. She couldn't process it all right now. She needed to test for accelerants and the firefighters from Stations Four and One were waiting. If she wanted to unravel this puzzle, she had to start somewhere. She turned to scan her instrument across the most burned part of the wall above the nightstand.

Jack Spencer snagged her elbow; she looked sharply at him.

He released her, but his gaze lasered into her. "Since the victim was a friend of yours, I'll need to interview you before I leave here."

The *victim* had a name. Terra bit off the sharp words, resisting the urge to rub the place where he'd touched her. The cop was doing what she should be doing—putting his emotions aside so he could do his job.

His features were just as exacting as his eyes. The stubborn chin, rough-hewn cheekbones and shadow of whiskers did nothing to soften a jaw that looked as if it could take a few blows.

"I'll also be conducting an investigation," she said.

"I'll notify the family, talk to the firefighter who found the body." He scribbled in the small notebook he held.

"That should give you time to do some things you need to do, then you and I can talk."

"Harris had only an ex-wife." Thinking about Cecily Vaughn unsettled Terra's stomach again. "His parents passed on some years ago."

"Thanks. That confirms what I learned from his neighbor." Jack Spencer tucked his notebook into the inside pocket of his lightweight tweed blazer. "Anything else you can tell me? Had he made anyone mad recently?"

She frowned. "He's retired."

Broad shoulders lifted in a shrug.

She shook her head. "I had dinner with him tonight. He was fine."

Spencer's gaze sharpened. "We can talk more about that when I see you again."

"All right." She flipped the switch on her "sniffer" and turned toward the charred wall.

"Should you be working this case? He was your friend, after all."

Having her doubts voiced only served to tighten her jaw. "I *am* working it."

"Look, I apologize for what I said when I first walked in, but seeing him obviously affected you. I don't want anything to jeopardize this case."

"Neither do I. And nothing will. What happened earlier was shock. I'm not used to seeing my friends burned to a crisp," she said sharply.

"I know you're the only fire investigator we have, but maybe someone else could help you out, give you some space."

"What I need to do is my job, and I will. Maybe you could do yours."

His lips flattened. "I'll be by to talk to you once I finish my preliminary interviews."

"You know where to find me."

She wondered if his blue eyes were that hard all the time, then she pushed the thoughts away and focused her attention on piecing together what had happened to her mentor.

Chapter 2

He wished he hadn't touched her, although he couldn't have let her fall flat on her face. That was where Terra August had been headed when he'd first seen her. Jack could still feel the taut curve of her waist, smell the hint of sweet woman beneath the acrid burn of smoke.

Late the afternoon following the fire, he scrubbed a hand over his face. The setting sun glared through the windshield of his pickup as he drove back to the fire scene. He'd stopped in town to interview a possible witness in a carjacking, one of his several active cases, but his thoughts were mainly on his newest case. A mix of appreciation and admiration still flared when he thought back to his earlier meeting with Presley's fire investigator. Professional admiration was where he should draw the line, so he did. She'd put her personal feelings aside and done her job. Despite the raw pain in her eyes, she'd been careful and attentive at the scene. Now he needed to know how much, if any, progress she'd made.

Jack bit off a curse.

Terra August had been on the fringes of his mind like a shadow, not keeping him from his job, but a distraction he'd been unable to dismiss. Was it the vulnerability in her face when he'd first seen her at the fire scene? The agony in those jade-green eyes when he'd stuck his foot in his mouth about her friend? He rubbed at his eyes, scratchy from lack of sleep.

The reason she lingered in his mind had to be because she was still on his suspect list. Until he'd interviewed and cleared her, she would be. Still, his gut told him she was innocent. Which didn't explain why he'd thought so much about her.

Why Terra August? What was different about *her?* Since Lori's death three and a half years ago, Jack hadn't noticed anything except work. Certainly not women. Not like this.

Some of his time today had been spent asking questions about Terra. She'd spent nine years fighting fires on the front line with Station Four. The last four had been spent as a fire investigator. Orphaned at age fifteen by the death of her parents in a car wreck, she'd moved in with her grandfather, a firefighter who'd died of smoke inhalation in a fire about ten years ago.

She was also divorced from Keith Garcia. Garcia was a sharp young defense attorney with a prestigious law firm making a name for himself in the state. Jack found himself wondering what had gone wrong between the two of them.

He turned into the Hunter's Ridge subdivision. As he reached the yard squared off with fluttering yellow police tape, he noted a lone police cruiser. It appeared the fire investigator had finished here.

He stopped and rolled down his window.

Pope, the officer at the scene, stepped up to Jack's truck. "Hey, Jack."

"Hey. The fire investigator still inside?"

"No, sir." The hefty, twenty-something officer checked his clipboard. "She left about noon. Said she'd probably be back later, though."

"Thanks." Jack waved and turned around in the neighbor's driveway, then drove out of the neighborhood. He wasn't wild about going to see her, but there was no way around it. They were as good as partners on this case. Even if Jack had argued about it, he would've been shut down.

Fire deaths were worked by both homicide and the fire investigator. He'd probably have to explain to a few people they interviewed that partnering up on this investigation was not only legal, but necessary. In cases like this, a fire investigator's knowledge was invaluable in asking all the right questions. Jack had already been told by the captain that the victim was the mayor's uncle. Mayor Griffin had called. He expected everyone to work in whatever capacity was needed. And probably twice as fast.

The more information Jack had, the quicker this case would be solved. Right now, Terra August had information. Regardless of the way she'd intruded on his thoughts all night and day, this was a job. *His job.* The one thing he could always count on.

Cool air streamed in from his open window, clearing out the cobweb of thoughts he'd been unable to escape all day. He was curious about her; that was all. Of course he'd known Presley's fire investigator was a woman, but if he'd heard anything about *her,* he sure didn't remember it.

Her picture could've been plastered on every billboard in town for the past three years running and he wouldn't have even noticed. His job commanded all his focus. In the first six months after his wife's death, his world had narrowed to minutes—making coffee, putting gas in his car, mowing the grass. Eventually, he functioned day by day, lead by lead, case by case.

Dating was a distant memory, just like sex. He knew what that said about him, but he didn't care. His attitude drove his sister crazy, but Jack had found a place where his head—and his heart—weren't stuck in the past.

He needed to get back on track. Once he interviewed Terra and got caught up on her investigation, he'd be able to go about his business, alone again.

He might admire the way she'd sucked it up at the crime scene, but that didn't mean he liked this new awareness sizzling in his blood. Still, he'd worked with dozens of women over the years, a few of them very beautiful. There was no reason he couldn't do it this time.

Jack pulled up in front of Presley's original fire station, which now housed the fire investigator's office. The red-brick firehouse, antiqued from years and wind, had held one fire engine and one rescue truck. A weather-scrubbed metal sign hung over the door identifying the old building as the Fire Investigator's Office. Newer, crisp black lettering repeated the same on the glass front door.

When the city had experienced a population explosion ten years ago, the fire investigator's office had been moved into the sturdy, but outdated, building. Recent renovations included new electrical wiring and plumbing, but no facelift to the exterior. Now Presley boasted four fire stations complete with engines and trucks.

Prodding himself to get out of his pickup truck, Jack gave himself a mental shake. Regret still flared that he'd made the crack about her reaction to Vaughn's body. Jack shouldn't have said what he did to her—he probably had less experience at fire deaths than she did—but she'd looked so out of it. Her peachy velvet skin had gone ash-white, making her green eyes even more vivid and huge.

He rubbed the taut stretch of muscle across his nape. There he went again. Thinking about her when he should be thinking only about what she could bring to this case.

Patting the pocket of his khaki sports jacket to make sure his notebook rested in its usual place, Jack pulled open the creaky glass door. The smell of chemicals and scorched air hit him full on, not overpowering, but strong and steady. The empty desk outfitted with a phone and neatly stacked files caused him to look at his watch. A little after six.

"Hello." His voice echoed off the flat concrete floor. He let the door shut behind him and moved past a worn oak secretary's desk.

Separated from the front area by glass walls was a small office. It was crammed with a squat oak desk, files piled ten-deep on its scarred top. Fresh, ruby-red roses spilled from a vase at the desk's center. The flowers looked frivolous and out of place in the midst of records and a computer. Two wooden armchairs faced one side of the desk and a stuffed leather chair sat on the other. Scratched gray filing cabinets lined the wall adjacent to the desk. Photographs, some framed, of fires and ancient fire engines covered the wall above the files.

Opposite the open door stood a dry-erase board on wheels. He stepped over to study the pictures stuck there in meticulous precision and recognized them as being from Harris Vaughn's bedroom. "Anyone here?"

When he received no answer, he whistled. Still nothing. He heard a muffled thud and peered down a short, dark hallway to a metal door. Seeing a thread of light beneath it, he made his way there.

A loud pop sounded, causing his pulse to spike. The burn of smoke filled the air. Panic stretched across his chest as he rushed the door and slammed down the metal tension bar. He sprinted inside and stopped dead in his tracks.

Terra August, wearing a turnout coat and hard hat, stood several feet away over the scorched base of a lamp. Jack could also see she had on safety goggles and gloves. Flames raced in a vee pattern up a large section of Sheetrock attached to wood, which was propped against the brick wall. As the fire spread, she made notes. Notes, for crying out loud!

Why would any man want to be involved with a woman in a job like this?

"What the hell are you doing?" he yelled. He couldn't help it. Just standing this close to flame caused his entire body to pucker, even if he wasn't about to become barbecue. A wave of heat rolled past him.

Terra jerked around at the sound of his voice. Grabbing an extinguisher from somewhere near her feet, she doused the fire.

Relief seeped through him. He hadn't been in danger, but he felt better with the fire out.

She set down the extinguisher, scribbled more notes on the yellow pad she held, then turned to him as she pulled off the hard hat. She wore the same ponytail she had at the crime scene. "I was right in the middle of something."

"I noticed." He'd forgotten that her gaze was nearly level with his, how long her legs were. "What happened?"

She frowned as she removed her goggles. "Nothing. I was testing my theory about how the fire started at Harris's."

"You've already figured that out?" The admiration he'd felt earlier slid up a notch.

She shrugged, sliding off the turnout coat and draping it over the back of a chair he only now noticed. A red-hot sweater snugged her full breasts, disappeared beneath the trim waistband of the faded blue jeans that gloved her long, lean legs.

Well. Presley's fire investigator could start a few fires of her own. His gaze tracked over the curve of her breasts and the sleek flare of her hips. Jack knew now why a man would be drawn to a woman in a dangerous job. Terra August had the kind of shoulda-been-a-stripper curves he'd seen only on the wrong side of a badge. Hell, a man could get whip-lash trying to look twice at her.

At his scrutiny, her chin lifted slightly. Her warning stare snapped him back to the job at hand.

Shake it off, man. He cleared his throat. "You have a theory about how the fire started?"

"Maybe." Cool wariness slid into her eyes. "I found a piece of evidence and wanted to test my theory."

"Wanna share? That's why I'm here." He could tell she wasn't wild about the idea, but after a brief hesitation, she nodded and walked past him, motioning for him to follow her out the door and back down the hall.

He did, trying to keep his gaze from tracing the slender lines of her back, the gentle rounding of hips his hands suddenly itched to span. A vague hint of woodsmoke drifted around her, but Jack was more aware of the scent of sweet, musky woman. Good hell, what was going on with him? "This building's in pretty good shape for its age."

"Yes. I like it—the history, the stories."

They walked into her small office where the scent of roses merged with a metallic whiff of chemicals. Behind her desk sat a pair of firefighter's boots, a shovel and a fire ax. Amid the stacked files on the cluttered desk were maps and newspaper clippings.

He gestured to the files. "Are you handling all this your-self?"

"My secretary, Darla, helps a lot."

Jack gestured to the photographs covering the opposite wall. "Did you take the pictures?"

She glanced at them as she walked around the corner of her cluttered desk. "I took a few. Harris actually took most of them. Like that one." She pointed at a framed black-and-white photograph in the middle of the wall. "That's Presley's first fire engine."

Terra moved aside the vase of full-blooming flowers and pulled on a pair of latex gloves. After opening a small paper bag, she shook into her palm a piece of glass about the diameter of a pencil eraser.

Jack leaned forward to get a better look.

She lifted her hand toward him. "Lightbulb glass."

"Yeah."

"See the tape?" The pleasure in her voice had him glancing up before directing his attention to her palm as she pointed at what he now determined was a piece of clear tape on the glass.

He nodded.

Reaching to her left, she flipped on a lamp then adjusted the shade so the light shot across her palm. She pointed again. "See this hole? You can make it out if you hold the piece of glass up to the light."

She did so gingerly.

"Someone drilled a hole in the lightbulb?" He frowned.

"Yes. The fire was deliberately set and this lightbulb plant is the incendiary device."

"Lightbulb plant?" He straightened, his pulse revving. "How does that work?"

"Our arsonist drilled a hole in the top of the bulb, probably used a syringe to fill it with accelerant, covered the hole with tape then screwed in the bulb. He connected the lamp to a clock timer—" she picked up a blackened piece of metal sprouting a short wire "—and he left."

"So the lamp wouldn't come on until the timer tripped the switch?"

"Right."

"The heat generated by the electricity caused the explosion."

"Yes." She smiled.

"And our guy was far away, establishing an alibi."

"Yeah. Lightbulbs distort at a thousand degrees and will hold that temperature for about ten minutes. The explosion would've happened once the temperature climbed higher."

"There was definitely an explosion? Not just a leak?"

"An explosion, probably close to what sounded a while ago back in the testing area. The bedroom door and windows were blown outward, not inward. That's a sure sign."

"So, it makes sense to think the victim was either immobilized or dead before the fire started."

"Absolutely. Whoever did this probably tied up Harris then set the plant."

"The killer and the arsonist might be two different people."

"Maybe, but I don't think so. Still, the M.E. will be able to tell us if Harris died before the fire or as a result."

Jack agreed. "Any ideas about the type of accelerant used?"

"Isopropyl alcohol. I think it was some type of cleaning fluid." After carefully returning the piece of bulb to its brown paper bag, she closed it. She gestured to the pictures around her office. "I was able to recover some traces of the accelerant. No other lightbulbs exploded at the burn site. I washed down the lamp with the blown bulb and the bedside table holding it, and found a fluid pattern at the base of the lamp. I also took some samples from Harris's darkroom. He was an avid photographer."

"Right. I noticed a lot of photographs in his house."

She nodded. "I scraped some samples from the charred

wall around his bed, also from the lamp base, and ran them through my gas chromatograph.''

"Do you have a full lab here?'' Jack glanced around, wondering if he'd missed another door.

"No. I have a few pieces of equipment, but until our budget gets a little more healthy, I have to use the lab in Oklahoma City for most of my analysis. My chromatograph showed an alcohol-based chemical.''

"So, none of the darkroom chemicals were used to start the fire?''

"No. A photo fixer in Harris's darkroom did contain glacial acetic acid, which is also highly flammable, but that isn't our accelerant.''

"This is great. You've really made some progress.''

"Unfortunately, I didn't have to start at the very beginning.''

"What do you mean?''

"I've seen this before. Three times, in fact.''

"What? The lightbulb thing?''

"The alcohol-based solvent, the lightbulb plant, the timer.''

The little nerve on the side of his neck twitched, as it always did at any sign of danger. He narrowed his gaze. "What are you saying, August?''

She exhaled and reached up to release her ponytail, funneling her fingers through the reddish-gold fall of hair as it tumbled to her shoulders. The thick satiny curtain was an equal mix of gold and red, a true strawberry blonde.

"I've been working on three cases very similar to this. I think this is his fourth fire.''

Jack's spine stiffened. "You're saying we have a serial arsonist?''

"I think so.''

"There have been no other fire deaths," he said bluntly. "I would've heard about that."

"You're right, but the other fires involved a janitorial supply store, a photography studio and a dental office."

"All places with the same accelerant?"

"Yes. The first fire was about ten weeks ago, mid-July. The photography studio was torched in August and the dental office about a month ago. Our guy is a professional. He uses as little accelerant as possible and something that might be used in the course of cleaning any building. If this is the same guy, last night was the first time he's killed."

"Why now?" Jack drummed his fingers on the edge of her desk. "And why Harris Vaughn?"

"I have no idea."

Her voice was even, but the glimmer of brightness in her eyes reminded him that the arsonist's first victim was also her friend. "I'm sorry."

"We've got to catch him."

"We will."

"I'm not sure if I'm—we're—dealing with an emotional firesetter or a pathological one. Revenge, attention, concealment of a crime are all motives I'm considering. I've eliminated juveniles, who often start fires out of curiosity or vandalism. And of course, these fires didn't start during a riot."

"What about insurance fraud?"

"That's also been ruled out. So far, I don't find that any fire was set in order to conceal a crime, but the revenge and attention angles will take more digging."

Jack nodded, surprised by a growing urge to offer some sort of comfort, a promise that went beyond his usual dedication. Since when had he even noticed anything about people besides how they fit into his investigation? "I got a call from Mayor Griffin."

"I thought you might."

"Since you know Mr. Vaughn was the mayor's uncle, you probably also got the same…encouragement about solving this case."

She nodded.

"A good start to that would be you answering my questions."

For a heartbeat, raw pain stressed her features then it disappeared. "Oh, yes, go ahead."

Jack swallowed the apology on the tip of his tongue. She wanted to get this slimeball as much as he did. Taking out his notebook, he flipped to a blank page. "How long did you know Mr. Vaughn?"

"Twenty years. He was a good friend of my grandfather's."

He searched her softly sculpted features. "So you knew Harris when *he* was the fire investigator?"

"Yes. He trained me. I apprenticed under him for two and a half years before he retired."

"And you had dinner with him last night?"

She nodded.

"Did you do that often?"

"Lately, we'd done it once a week."

"Lately? Does that mean the last month, the last year?"

"The last couple of months, I guess. Since the second serial fire. I was bouncing ideas off him about this arsonist."

"What time did you meet for dinner last night?"

"Seven. We left the restaurant about a quarter to nine."

"What restaurant was that?"

"Charlie's Steakhouse."

"Can anyone there vouch for you?"

"The waitress, I guess. Charlie, too. We always speak…spoke to Charlie."

She didn't react to her slip other than to swallow hard,

but Jack felt an unfamiliar burn in his chest. Despite her willowy height, he remembered how wobbly she'd felt in his hold last night and wondered how she was really doing. She put on a good front. "Is there anyone who saw you after you left the restaurant?"

"I went to my gym for a swim and when I got home, I called a friend. Robin Daly."

"*Lieutenant* Robin Daly, Presley P.D.?" Jack's eyebrows arched.

"Yes."

He jotted a note. Terra's friendship with one of the best female cops on the Presley P.D. was something he hadn't uncovered. "And then?"

"Another friend, Dr. Meredith Boren, called. We talked for about twenty minutes then I went to bed," she said in a wooden voice. "My pager went off a little before 1:00 a.m. You know where I was after that."

The crime scene. Discovering that the victim was her friend. She didn't lose her composure, but he saw the bleakness in her eyes. Jack gave her a moment. "You said Harris was divorced."

"For about six months now."

"And were the two of you more than friends?"

"No."

"Ever?"

Her jade gaze leveled into his, but her voice was tired, not angry. "Friends only, regardless of what you may have heard from Cecily."

Jack felt an unexpected relief upon learning Terra hadn't been romantically involved with the victim. "His ex-wife thought the two of you had something going on?"

"She thought Harris had something going on with a lot of women."

"Did he?"

''No.''

''There was no girlfriend at all, no other women?''

''He wasn't ready. Besides, he loved Cecily, despite her jealousy. If she hadn't been so obsessed, they would still be married. He just couldn't live with it anymore.''

''With what?''

''She followed him everywhere, accused him constantly of lying to her. That was *before* the divorce. Even afterwards, she wouldn't leave him alone.''

''Does she still believe you were involved with him?''

''I don't know.''

He flipped through his notebook unnecessarily, giving her a moment to control the emotion swimming in her eyes. Understandably, women might be jealous of Terra August's perfectly molded features, the classically straight nose and peach-tinted skin. Her moist, plump lips looked as if they could leave a man weak. ''Do you know what contact, if any, Harris had with Cecily recently?''

She hesitated, chewing on her bottom lip. ''He said she'd been calling, leaving messages on his answering machine. He'd also seen her following him.''

''Did she follow the two of you last night?''

''If she did, I didn't see her.'' She sighed, stroking nervous fingers down the long, elegant column of her neck. She had a beautiful neck.

''Did Cecily ever threaten you?''

''No.''

She paused and his eyes narrowed. ''It's better if I hear it from you rather than her.''

She contemplated a moment, then said, ''One time, she blamed me for their divorce. She never threatened me, but for a while after they split up, she would show up here or at my house. She also left messages on my answering machine.''

"Saying what?"

"Just…none of it was true."

He stared at her.

Protest flared in her eyes, but she finally spoke. "Saying I couldn't have him, that he didn't want me, things like that. There were never any threats against me. And she stopped bothering me altogether about a month ago. Didn't she tell you this herself?"

"I haven't been able to talk to her yet." Sounded like Terra had a motive to kill Harris's ex-wife, but so far, Jack hadn't found one to explain why she would want to kill Harris. "When I stopped by her house, she'd taken a sedative."

Terra's gaze held his. "When you go back, I'd like to go with you."

Which was perfectly legal and within her rights as the fire investigator on this case. He had no grounds to refuse, but he wished he did. "Okay. I plan to try again after I leave here."

"Great."

He wondered if she would confirm the information he'd learned about her earlier. Watching her closely, Jack said, "I thought firefighters who were interested in investigations could move into the job with a lot less years on the job than you had."

She arched a brow. "How many was that?"

"Nine."

She cocked her head. "You've been checking up on me."

He could read nothing in the midnight-soft voice. He wondered what she was thinking, then asked himself why he cared. "It's my job."

She crossed her arms, putting an invisible wall between them. "You're right. Firefighters can move into investigation whenever they pass the tests. I wasn't sure until then that I wanted to be a fire cop.''

There was a story there; he could read it in the way her eyes shuttered against him. That old familiar itch to solve a puzzle, dig out every secret kicked in.

What kind of training had she had? From what he remembered, there were no formal courses for fire investigation offered at their local universities, just on-the-job training. Jack found himself wanting to ask Terra questions that had no direct bearing on the case, only on *her*. The realization irritated him as did the anticipation thrumming in his blood. He felt as if he were losing his focus and his voice came out hard.

''Is there anyone else who could be jealous of you seeing Mr. Vaughn?''

She stiffened. ''I already told you about Cecily.''

She still looked a little disoriented. Again, he felt the same clench in his gut that he'd felt upon seeing her so torn up at the crime scene. He knew this had to be hard on her, but didn't think she would appreciate the observation.

''I meant whoever *you're* seeing.'' For some reason, he really wanted to know who that man was. Jack fingered the velvet-soft petals of the rose nearest him. ''Like whoever gave you these flowers.''

Her gaze skipped away and she rubbed at a spot just below her collarbone. Jack found his gaze trailing down the sweet line of her neck, the hollow in her throat where her pulse fluttered softly.

''I don't know who those are from. I've got a…secret admirer.''

''A secret admirer?'' He couldn't keep the surprise from his voice. ''These aren't from someone you're dating?''

''I'm not dating anyone at the moment.''

He ignored the sharp jab of adrenalin that hit his system.

"So you can't think of anyone who might be upset by your seeing too much of Harris Vaughn?"

"No."

"What about your ex-husband, Keith Garcia?"

"Only if it interfered with something he wanted to do."

Whoa, he'd hit a nerve there. "How long have you been divorced?"

"Two years. As if you didn't know."

He wondered if her quiet anger was due to pain over the breakup of her marriage or his blatant digging into her past.

"That's a long time to go without dating." Not that he had any room to talk.

"I didn't say I hadn't dated," she responded coolly. "Just that I wasn't dating anyone now."

A grin tugged at his lips. "Did your relationship with Vaughn have anything to do with your marriage breaking up?"

"No."

Her curt answer indicated that was all he'd get on the subject. Good thing he believed her. "Any ideas about the identity of your secret admirer?"

"I think it's one of the local news reporters. I figure if I ignore him, he'll eventually give up."

Shifting his weight to the other foot, Jack squashed an unexpected—and unwanted—flare of jealousy. Maybe her divorce had been caused by Garcia's having another woman. Or if not, could their breakup have been related to the dangers of her job?

He supposed some men might find a woman exciting who battled fire, who risked her life, but Jack didn't. Women in perilous jobs were as unappealing to him as working as a crossing guard.

He didn't have a problem with women in dangerous jobs—combat, police work, fire fighting. He just had a problem with *his* woman being in such a line of work. His wife's job had seemed low-risk and she'd been gunned down by a pissed-off social work client. Since her death, his work had been his world. Not much penetrated, but Terra August certainly had.

"What about you, Detective?"

"What about me?" He stuffed his notebook into the inside pocket of his khaki jacket.

"Are you dating anyone?"

Sliding his hands into the pockets of his navy slacks, he arched a brow. *He* was the one who asked the questions.

"Not married, are you?"

This was a job, not *The Dating Game*. Jaw tight, his gaze locked with hers. "I'm heading over to talk to Cecily Vaughn. Are you coming?"

Her gaze measured him, sending a lick of fire through his belly. She tucked her hair behind her ears, the movement stretching the red sweater taut across her lush breasts.

Jack looked away, trying to ignore the way his body hardened from his shoulders to his calves.

She walked around the desk toward him. "Before I left the burn site, I picked up the videotape."

"Of the scene?" He opened the door, then followed her out. As his mother would say, Terra August was a handful.

"Yes, inside and out. Also the ones from the other three fires. An arsonist almost always returns to the scene."

"Wants to see what he's done?"

"Yes."

Again he caught a faint whiff of smoke, overlaid by the clean sweetness of her skin. His pulse drummed low and hard. Clenching a fist, he tried to stem the awareness shifting through him. "I'd like to watch those tapes with you later."

"Sure."

Her agreement came readily enough, but he sensed the

same reticence he'd had all during his visit. Maybe it was due to the wariness that had clouded her eyes since he'd first met her. And maybe he was imagining things. Hell, his mind had certainly worked overtime doing just that since he'd met her.

That had to stop. Now. The only reason his awareness of her was a big deal was because she was the first woman he'd given more than passing attention to in three years. And more important, because Terra August represented everything he didn't want.

Forget those are-you-man-enough eyes and killer lips. The woman chased fire for a living. No thanks. No way. No how.

Chapter 3

No man had ever made Terra's head spin. It was spinning now. Jack Spencer looked at her as if he wanted to get inside her head, inside *her.*

His penetrating, midnight-blue gaze gave her the same spine zap she got at a fire. Except she understood fire. She did not understand this at all. When she'd taken off her turnout coat and caught his gaze on her breasts, a sizzling awareness of him, of her own body, had hit her fast and hard. The force and heat of it exploded like a fire that had fed for hours.

At the crime scene, she'd been too numb to register anything except shock and grief, but she did so now. During the ride to Cecily's, sitting only a foot away from the hollow-eyed cop, Terra had to admit Jack affected her. Even Keith had never gotten to her like this.

She breathed in the scent of clean male, a tang of aftershave. His heat settled over her like a second skin. She gripped the armrest, fighting to push away the thoughts. She should be thinking about Cecily and the questions she needed to ask, but this guy crowded out everything else.

Her gaze followed the slant of streetlight across a chiseled jaw and cheekbone. Huge hands palmed the steering wheel and Terra felt a flutter in the pit of her stomach.

She and Keith had enjoyed good sex and wonderful intimacy, but getting there had been a process. Two years of distance and resentment about her job had whittled away the closeness of their marriage. Since the divorce, she hadn't come close to wanting that again. Wanting, period. She'd learned she couldn't trust what she thought she knew, *who* she thought she knew. Which meant she absolutely couldn't trust this quick flare of attraction.

She'd never been this curious about a man. Or this aware. She wanted to know whether the shoulders beneath Jack's khaki jacket were as broad as they appeared to be, whether the thighs covered by neat navy slacks were as powerful as his stride hinted as they walked from the car to Cecily's door.

His not answering the personal questions she'd lobbed earlier only made her want to figure him out the same way she figured out the burn path of a fire.

Whether or not he was married was none of her business and it bothered her to admit it, but she hadn't stopped wondering about that either. The desire to know more was like an itch she couldn't reach.

Whatever a woman had with him wouldn't be casual and probably not brief. Harris and Granddad had always urged her to listen to her instincts. Right now those instincts screamed at her to nip this fascination with Jack in the bud, and focus on finding the arsonist and whoever had murdered Harris.

Jack Spencer was the man who could help her do that. She couldn't, *wouldn't,* let things get personal between them. *Do your job.* Keith had always said she did that to the exclusion of everything else. She wondered if Jack Spencer would feel the same.

Telling herself to knock it off, Terra slid her gaze to the tall man standing beside her on Cecily Vaughn's sweeping porch.

Jack jabbed the doorbell button, shoving his other hand through his thick, seal-brown hair. While darkness edged the sides of the house, light glowing from fixtures flanking the door highlighted the whisker stubble that shadowed his jaw, giving him a rumpled, dangerously sexy look. A woman would have a hard time resisting him when the lights went out. She knew *she* would have a hard time.

She had an investigation to run and information about Jack Spencer was not pertinent to that. She needed to think about the coming interview with Harris's ex. "I need to warn you, Cecily probably won't be too happy to see me."

Jack slanted her a look just as the door opened.

Cecily Vaughn, wrapped in a candy-pink peignoir, stared dully at Terra and Jack for a moment. Her unfocused brown gaze told Terra the woman was still under the influence of the sedative Jack said she'd taken earlier.

Pulling together the thin edges of her robe, Cecily's gaze registered recognition. "I guess I should've expected *you.*"

"I'm sorry we have to meet again under these circumstances, Cecily." Terra's throat tightened as a fresh wave of pain rolled through her. Shoot, she couldn't lose it now.

Jack stepped into the pool of light, flashing his badge. "My condolences, Ms. Vaughn. I'm Detective Spencer and we need to ask you a few questions."

She studied his badge for a moment, then cut her gaze to Terra. "Is she with you? Is that allowed?"

"Yes, ma'am. Investigator August is working this case

with me, so her being here is perfectly legal. And expected,'' he added.

''Remember that Harris used to work with the police from time to time?'' Terra asked quietly.

The other woman's stare flattened, but she stepped back to allow them grudging access. Her filmy pink robe trailing, she led them into a small, formal sitting area with matching moire Queen Anne love seats and a high-sheen cherrywood coffee table. She stopped behind one of the love seats, her long manicured nails curving onto the muted tan-and-black striped fabric. ''How did the fire start?''

''We're not sure yet,'' Jack answered.

Dark shadows ringed Cecily's eyes. Her usually flawless makeup couldn't hide her wan skin or the tight lines around her mouth. She looked at Terra. ''Maybe that's where you need to be.''

Terra told herself the woman was upset. Who wouldn't be? For the moment, she let Jack take the lead. Cecily was on the edge. Easing into asking questions of her own seemed the best idea to Terra.

Jack flipped open his small notebook. ''Harris Vaughn was your ex-husband?''

''Yes.''

''How long were you divorced?''

''Six months.''

''Any children?''

Terra noted that Jack kept his voice low and soothing. Evidently he had plenty of practice with distraught people. She wondered how long he'd been a detective.

''No children.'' Tears welled in Cecily's heavily made-up eyes and she grabbed a tissue from a box on the glass-topped end table next to the love seat.

Jack gave her a minute before continuing in the same soft tone. ''When was the last time you saw him?''

"A week ago Sunday. Our divorce was final and I wanted to talk to him."

"About getting back together?"

"Yes."

"Did you see him here?"

"At his house." She dabbed her eyes again with the tissue.

Terra planned to confirm that with Harris's neighbors. Edging a step away from Jack and the power he exuded like heat, she asked, "Did he indicate he was worried or upset about anything?"

Cecily stared at her flatly. "He was upset about our divorce."

Anger streamed through her, but Terra reminded herself that staying calm was the only way she and Jack would get anywhere. She focused her gaze on Cecily's diamond ring, a huge butterfly. Terra had never liked that ring. It was gaudy.

"Ms. Vaughn?" Jack drew Cecily's attention back to himself. "Was there anything else that might have upset him?"

"He really didn't talk to *me* about other things," she answered with a meaningful look at Terra.

"Do you know anyone he'd argued with or might've been angry with? Did he talk about anything like that?"

"No."

"He never mentioned any enemies at all? Anyone who may have threatened him or had a reason to harm him?"

Cecily frowned, crumpling the tissue in nervous hands. "Wasn't this fire an accident? What's going on?" She seemed to struggle to focus, her gaze bobbing from Terra to Jack. "Are you a homicide detective?"

"I do investigate homicides."

"Was he murdered?" she shrieked.

"Ma'am, please try to stay calm." Jack stepped around the love seat toward Cecily.

Despite her feelings about Harris's ex, Terra's heart ached for the agony she read in the woman's eyes. "Cecily, can I get you something?"

Hatred flashed across her face and she pushed past Jack to stalk around the love seat toward Terra. "He told me he was helping you on a case. That's why he's dead, isn't it? It's *your* fault."

"Ma'am." Before Terra even saw him move, Jack planted himself in front of Cecily, his face and voice stern. "We don't know that Ms. August's job has anything to do with this."

"I do." She glared, stepping around him. "Harris wouldn't be my ex if it weren't for you, Terra. He wouldn't be dead if it weren't for you, because he would've been with me. All I ever wanted was to take care of him."

There was a difference between taking care of someone and smothering them, Terra thought. "Cecily, I didn't come here to upset you. We're trying to find out who would do this to Harris."

"My marriage was fine until he started spending so much time with you." She poked a finger in Terra's chest.

Fury erupted, but Terra stepped back, fighting to rein in the hurt and anger crashing through her. Her hands curled into fists. "Don't do that again, Cecily."

Jack firmly gripped the woman's elbow. "Ms. Vaughn, please try and calm down."

"You're the reason he left me in the first place." The woman's voice rose high and brittle with anger.

Terra wasn't going to be drawn into an argument, but she let out a sigh of relief when Jack guided Cecily to the love seat. "Here, take a seat. Let me get you a glass of water or something."

"No." She glared through her tears at Terra.

He studied her for a moment, then walked over to Terra. Keeping his back to Cecily, he pitched his voice low. "How do you want to play this?"

His shoulder brushed hers, sparking an unexpected warmth. She forced herself to read his eyes, appreciating the earnestness in the blue depths. "I don't want her calling a lawyer. I'll wait for you outside."

"You don't have to."

"It's for the best. She'll talk to you. I'm only upsetting her."

"You sure?"

"Yes." She kept her voice low, her stomach knotting at the sound of Cecily's sobs. Terra felt like doing the same thing. The whole situation was horrible enough. Antagonizing Harris's ex would only prolong things.

She moved toward the door.

"Where's she going?" Cecily demanded.

"Outside—"

Terra closed the door on Jack's soothing tone. As she made her way down the sidewalk toward his pickup truck, anger at Cecily and whoever had killed Harris burned through Terra. She paced from the hood of the blue pickup to the tailgate.

She had to calm down, shake it off. Leaving Cecily's house was the best thing for the investigation. Terra would be no good to anyone if she were angry. After a few minutes, her anger subsided. The cool night air skipped over her, raising goose bumps on her arms.

She hugged herself against the chill.

Crossing her arms, she walked the sidewalk to the end of the block, then back. She hoped Jack was getting somewhere with Cecily.

A sudden vibration at her hip had Terra grabbing for the cell phone clipped there. "August."

"Hey, it's me." Robin Daly's normally sunny voice was subdued. "How are you doing today?"

"Okay." Terra leaned against the truck's door, grateful for such a good friend.

"Did you eat?"

"Yes, Mom." Terra laughed, though she couldn't remember how long ago she'd finished the cheese and crackers she'd grabbed on her way to the office earlier that day.

"Were you able to stop by your place and shower?"

"Yes. I was at the office until just a while ago."

"I'm off duty and so is Meredith. She doesn't have to be back at the hospital until tomorrow night. Want to meet us for dinner?"

"I wish I could, but I'm still working." She, Robin and Meredith Boren had been friends since both the other girls had moved to Presley in junior high. "I came over to interview Harris's ex."

"Ugh. How's that going?"

"I'm outside and she's inside. What does that tell you?"

"So, who's interviewing her?"

"Jack Spencer."

"You're with Detective Yummy?" Robin squeaked.

It wasn't her friend's incredulity, but the nickname, that had Terra grinning. "Detective Yummy? I guess I can see that."

"I should hope so, since you're female and still breathing. Well, well, no wonder you don't want to meet your two best friends for dinner."

"Hardly." Terra would rather be with them. She knew what to expect from the two women who'd been her closest friends since eighth grade, who'd seen her through the deaths of her parents and her grandfather, and had been there for her immediately upon hearing about Harris last night.

"...pretty sad."

"What's that?" Terra snapped back to Robin's conversation.

"His wife. She was murdered by one of her social work cases."

"Murdered? How awful." An image of Jack's impenetrable blue gaze flashed in her mind. Was the loss of his wife the reason his eyes were so hard, so old? "When was this?"

"Three or four years ago, I think. He hasn't dated since then. At least not that anyone knows about."

"Can't say I blame him." Terra's divorce had left her raw and skittish. The only reason she dated was to keep Robin and Meredith from pulling any matchmaking stunts. She made sure to date men who were interested in temporary fun, just like she was. The instincts she'd honed over the years told her Jack Spencer would be no casual dinner or last-minute movie.

At the sound of a masculine voice, Terra straightened. "Here comes the detective now. Gotta go."

"Call me when you get home," Robin said.

"Okay." Terra disconnected and clipped the phone to the waistband of her jeans.

The light from Cecily's porch haloed Jack from behind, a hazy outline of broad shoulders and long legs. He moved down the sidewalk toward her, shadows shading the hollows of his cheeks, making his eyes dark and intense.

As he rounded the hood of his truck and opened the driver's side door, Terra glanced back at Cecily. The woman stood in the doorway. Even from here, Terra could feel the heat of her glare.

Terra climbed into Jack's truck. Only then did Cecily go

inside and close her front door. Terra looked at Jack, jolted by the penetrating stare he aimed past her. "What did you find out?"

"She has my favorite alibi." That laser-sharp gaze shifted to Terra and she was glad she had nothing to hide. "She was home alone all night."

"So, we'll check out her story about her last meeting with Harris."

"Do you know anything about it?"

"No, but hopefully his neighbors do."

"We can go there now, if that's all right."

"Yes."

He turned out of the subdivision and headed north on Keller Avenue.

"What else did you learn?"

"Just like you said, she was obsessed with the man."

"Do you consider her a suspect?"

He paused. "I got a definite read of 'if I can't have him, no one can.' Do you agree?"

"Yes, but do you think *she'd* kill him?"

"Nothing surprises me anymore," he said in a weary voice.

Terra now understood the bleakness in his eyes. The loss. Knowing what had happened to his wife tangled something deep inside her.

Keeping things professional was going to be a lot harder than she'd thought. He rattled her and she couldn't pretend otherwise.

A cell phone chirped and Jack slid it out of his jacket pocket. "Spencer. Hi, Lieutenant."

After a brief conversation, he hung up. "We just got a call that there's a homicide about three blocks from here, just south of Tenth."

"I thought you were off duty."

"I am, but the other detective on call just started a case on the east side of town by the water tower. I'm next on the on-call list. I really need to check this out. Do you mind?"

She wasn't about to tell him that she'd welcome anything that got him out of the truck and farther away than the foot that separated them right now. "No, not at all."

"Thanks."

As they made a U-turn in the middle of Keller and headed through the light at Tenth, Terra shifted her gaze out the window.

Two police cruisers, lights flashing, marked the apartment complex's parking lot where Jack parked his pickup truck. Terra got out when he did, wanting some fresh air and some distance between her and the warm scent of him lingering in the cab.

The news vans were already parked a few yards away and setting up. From the corner of her eye, Terra saw Dane Reynolds head for her. Brother.

Jack moved in front of her, paused. "If it looks like I'm going to be a while, one of the patrolmen can take you back to your office."

"Thanks." She wrapped her arms around herself to ward off the cool night air. Reynolds moved up next to Jack, who cut him a sharp look.

The news reporter kept on moving and Terra bit back a smile. T. J. Coontz settled a large camera on his shoulder and gave her a thumbs-up as he hustled to catch Reynolds.

Jack's gaze bored deep into hers. "Are you okay?"

"Sure." Was that concern in his eyes? "I don't mind."

"I meant about Cecily Vaughn. She was brutal back there."

Taken aback, Terra found herself unable to look away. "I'm all right. Thanks for asking."

"He was your friend. I can only imagine how hard this is," he murmured.

The connection she had felt to him snapped tight. Was he thinking about his own experience when his wife had died? How difficult not only to lose her, but to be a cop and not be able to prevent something like that.

"I just want to find whoever killed him." A shiver shot up Terra's spine and she hugged herself tighter. "If I have to deal with Cecily, so be it."

Jack nodded, taking off his khaki jacket. Surprising her again, he slipped it around her shoulders. "Here, wear this."

"I'm okay. Really." The jacket smelled of him, clean and male and mysterious. She reached to take it off.

His hands covered hers, keeping the jacket in place. "It's starting to get cold out here. Wear it, okay?"

She nodded, blinking at the slow spread of warmth in her belly. She wanted to tell him to stop touching her, but she couldn't get her voice to work. Or anything else, for that matter.

"I'll be back as soon as I can."

"Sure." Her voice was a raspy whisper.

He released her, but his gaze stayed locked on hers. A long moment arced between them and Terra swallowed around a knot in her throat. She was suddenly aware of gripping the edges of his jacket with unsteady hands.

"See ya."

"See ya." She watched him walk away, power and purpose in his smooth, long strides. Trouble. Big trouble.

Hadn't she told herself not to let things get personal? When he touched her, it was nothing *but* personal. She'd never backed away from a challenge. Joining a profession that traditionally employed only men didn't allow for it, but she wanted to back away now. She wanted to run.

Chapter 4

Late the next morning, Jack walked into the fire investigator's office as they'd agreed on last night. The trim blonde sitting behind the oak desk looked up from her computer. This must be Darla, Terra's secretary. The woman, who Jack judged to be in her late-twenties, gave a smile that didn't quite warm the sadness in her eyes and asked if she could help him.

He flashed his badge and told her he was supposed to meet with Investigator August. Anticipation that he'd been trying to ignore tightened his body. This was a job, he reminded himself. That's all it would be.

Just as the secretary rose, Terra walked out of her office and said, "Darla Howell, this is Detective Spencer."

Jack shook her hand, noting that the lush flowers he'd seen in Terra's office yesterday had been moved out to the secretary's desk.

"You're working with Terra on Harris's murder?" Darla asked quietly.

"Yes."

"I was Harris's secretary for a year before he retired. If there's anything I can do to help you guys find this sicko, just ask."

"All right. Thanks." Jack smiled, noting the affection in the squeeze Terra gave the other woman's shoulder.

His gaze shifted to the leggy fire cop and he wondered how she was holding up. "How's it going today?"

"Busy." As she stepped back into her office, she smiled tiredly and waved him in behind her. "You've got good timing. I just returned from a safety inspection so as soon as Darla brings me the last videotape, we'll be ready to go."

"Okay." Moving inside Terra's space-at-a-premium office, he hitched a thumb over his shoulder. "I noticed you moved the flowers from your secret admirer."

"It seems a little strange to keep them when I'm not interested."

"Between safety inspections and fire investigations, you must have your hands full."

"Yes, and then some. The city also provides fire safety classes for the public and I teach training classes whenever they're needed." She moved around her desk and picked up a jacket from the back of her chair. His jacket.

She handed it to him. "Thanks for letting me borrow this last night. I hope you didn't freeze after I left."

"I was fine." Immediately the delicate scent of flowers and soft woman drifted to him. He remembered the slight shiver in her shoulders when he'd draped the jacket across them. Remembered, too, the way he'd wanted to curve his hands around them and pull her closer. His fingers clenched on the camel hair and he asked gruffly, "Were you warm enough?"

"Oh, yes. It was great. Were you at the scene late?"

"About three hours." He'd had a patrolman drive her

back here, but that hadn't meant she'd been out of his thoughts. Standing this close to her, inhaling her warmth, brought back the uncomfortable reminder that her green eyes had been the last image in his mind last night before going to sleep. And the first when he woke up. His nerves pinged.

"Can you talk about what happened there?" she asked.

"A shooting, the result of a domestic dispute." Jack rubbed his neck, not liking the tension that settled there. Trying to ignore the provocative scent stealing up from his jacket, he kept talking. "A neighbor heard the victim threatening his wife and came over after calling the police. The neighbor walked in on the victim beating his wife and jumped him. He wrestled the gun away from the victim and it went off."

"Will charges be filed?"

"No, the wife declined. Said she knew her husband would've killed her if the neighbor hadn't stepped in."

Darla appeared in the doorway with a videocassette and a green folder. "Here you go. Want me to shut the door?"

"Thanks." Terra took the items and checked the date on the labeled tape case. She placed the cassette atop four others, which all sat on a filing cabinet tucked into the corner of the full office. Perched on top of the metal filing cabinet was a television with a built-in VCR.

The anticipation that had coiled in Jack's gut earlier now settled tightly in his shoulders. Terra's hair was pulled back in a sleek ponytail, revealing the elegant curve of her neck. Today she wore the long-sleeved, white shirt and navy pants of her uniform. A red-and-white patch, embroidered with the words Presley Fire Prevention, was sewn over her left breast.

The regulation clothing emphasized her long legs and trim waist. Not that they needed emphasizing. Her arms and legs, lean and slender, were perfectly suited to a swimmer. She walked with a flowing grace reminiscent of skimming through water. Jack had no trouble at all imagining her in a swimsuit, those legs bare and wet and glistening.

He hadn't seen her in uniform before, had seen only her badge. Nor, for that matter, had he noticed a fire department insignia on her vehicle. "You drive the red SUV, don't you?"

She nodded.

"Don't you have a fire department vehicle?"

"No, just my red truck. It's not marked, in case I need to go stealth in an investigation."

"Go stealth?"

"Undercover."

"Or a stakeout?"

"Yes."

He grinned, getting a mental picture of her skulking around in the dark. Skulking was not what he would want to do with her in the dark. The thought darted in and out, but he didn't need this kind of distraction. They had a case to work.

As she made a notation in a file, his gaze rested on a framed photo on the wall. He recognized her and Harris Vaughn in full turnout gear, appearing to walk straight out of a fire. Blood-orange flames swallowed the sky and walls of black smoke billowed around and behind them. Jack could almost feel heat pulsing from the picture.

At the sight of her walking out of those flames, a cold knot congealed in his gut. Jack didn't need the photo to remind himself that he wasn't interested in a woman in a high-risk job, but he sure wished his body would get the message.

"I stopped by your gym on the way over here," he announced. He had no intention of acting on any of the damn crazy impulses that shot through him whenever she was around. "Your swim two nights ago checked out."

"So, you're marking me off your suspect list?"

"Yeah." He grinned. He hadn't really considered her a suspect, but he was glad to have his instincts backed up. "Records from the phone company detailed the times of your phone calls, and both the waitress and owner at Charlie's Steakhouse confirmed the time you were there night before last. Three gym employees also remembered seeing you enter the gym or leave the pool. Now we can focus on who really did this."

"Great." She pulled over one of the chairs in front of her desk and turned it to face the television in the corner behind him. "Have a seat here and we can get started."

She flipped on the set and slid in a videotape. The picture flickered then images filled the space—flames and smoke and a storefront. "This is the janitorial supply store," Terra explained.

Just then the door opened and Darla stuck her head in. "Sorry to interrupt, but I think you should see this, Terra."

"What's going on?"

"I found a card with those flowers."

"The ones delivered yesterday?" Terra frowned. "I didn't see a card. There's never been one before."

"It was stuck down inside the stems and greenery. If I hadn't started to water it, I wouldn't have seen it either."

"Is it signed?"

"No."

Jack's lips twisted. "Guess your secret admirer still isn't ready to 'fess up."

Terra sighed. "Just throw it away."

"I really think you should take a look," Darla insisted.

Jack noted the strain around the secretary's mouth, the worry in her eyes. And the fact that Darla had on a pair of latex gloves. Evidently, Terra noticed that, too, because she rose quickly from her chair beside him.

He stood as well, his shoulder grazing hers. From the corner of her desk behind him, she plucked up a pair of gloves and pulled them on before handing him a pair to don, as well.

Darla reached across and handed the card to Terra, who took it carefully. She glanced down at it and Jack saw her lips tighten.

Were the flowers from Dane Reynolds? Jack recalled the homicide scene last night when the pretty-boy reporter, his faithful cameraman on his heels, had headed straight for Terra. At Jack's flat look, Reynolds had possessed the good sense to steer a course away from the willowy fire investigator, but Jack had seen the glint of emotion in his eyes. Avid interest. Or was it obsession?

Just thinking about the hungry look the reporter had aimed at Terra and the lush roses she'd removed from her desk put a hard knot in Jack's chest. The same knot he'd felt the night before when he'd draped his jacket around her slender shoulders.

Something in him had responded to the vulnerability in her face, a vulnerability she hid pretty well. That's what it was about Terra August which drew him to her. That, plus he'd been in a similar situation once—called on to do a job after losing a loved one. Called on to be a cop while the man, the husband in him, nearly shattered.

He suspected Terra had at least some of those feelings. Torn between trying to do her job and not give in to the grief.

She passed the note to him and Jack noticed that her hands were unsteady. This time it was concern that had him wanting to reassure her.

The words jumped out at him first. ''This is between you

and me.'' But it was the flames drawn around the words that had him narrowing his eyes.

An instinct he'd only ever felt for his mom, his sister and his late wife roared to life—a fierce possessiveness. He told himself to rein it in even as his jaw tightened.

''How did I miss this?'' Irritation etched Terra's voice.

''I didn't see it either,'' Darla said. ''Besides, this is the first time there's been a note. It didn't occur to me to check for one.''

''Do you have an evidence bag?'' Jack asked.

Darla nodded and retrieved a plastic baggie from a shelf behind her desk, then gave it to Jack.

Jack gestured for Terra to carefully slide the card inside. ''Before now, there have been no cards with the flower deliveries. There also haven't been any murders.''

''You think this is related to the arsons?'' Shock widened Terra's eyes.

''Well, the murder shows the arsonist's acts are escalating. You said so yourself. Why not a note, too? This could definitely be meant as a threat.''

''It sounds like a threat to me,'' Darla agreed. The phone rang and she hurried back to her desk.

Terra's green eyes clouded. ''Could *all* the flowers I've received been sent by the arsonist?''

''Good question. Can you remember when the other deliveries were made? We know you received the latest one yesterday.''

''The day following the fire at Harris's.'' A slow horror unfolded across her refined features. ''I received the others on the day after each fire set by the serial arsonist.''

''Are you sure?''

She closed her eyes for a moment. ''Yes, fairly certain. That's about the time Dane Reynolds started showing interest. I assumed all the bouquets were from him. I didn't connect them to the arsons at all!''

"They still might be from him," Jack pointed out quietly. Terra froze. "Are you kidding?"

"Isn't it possible Reynolds could be the arsonist?"

"Anything's possible, but…yuk." She shivered. "Why? What would be his motivation?"

"Didn't you say the desire for attention was a motive?"

She nodded, her fingers stroking down her throat in what Jack was beginning to recognize as a sign of nervousness. Was he the one making her nervous? Or the topic?

Darla stepped back into the doorway. "Excuse me for interrupting, but that was Mayor Griffin's office on the phone. He wants you to meet him in an hour for lunch and bring him up to speed on Harris's case."

"All right. Thanks, Darla."

As Darla walked away, Jack steered Terra back on track, knowing his captain was probably next on the mayor's list for a call. "So what about Reynolds? Any thoughts?"

"I started getting flowers right after the first fire, but Reynolds didn't approach me about an interview until after the second arson. If he is the arsonist, don't you think he would've started asking right away?"

"Not necessarily. Maybe he didn't ask for the interview until he was sure *you* knew you were dealing with a serial arsonist."

"So as not to tip his hand?"

"Maybe."

She glanced at the evidence bag he held. "Whoever sent this bouquet killed Harris. Shouldn't I have noticed the pattern before?"

"Why? Until now, the arsonist has given no clues except what you've found at the fire scenes. Plus the flowers seem unrelated until you examine the deliveries in relation to the dates of the fires.''

"I guess so. I don't like missing things, though. What if I'm missing something bigger right now?''

"We'll figure it out. Listen, since you need to see the mayor, I'm going to take this florist's card over to the lab and run it for prints. On my way, I'll drop by and ask if the florist has a record of the sale. I also want to do some checking into Reynolds' background. Are both yours and Darla's prints on file?''

"Yes.''

"There's also someone else I want to check out.''

"Another suspect? Who?''

"Someone who has an obvious grudge against you.''

She frowned, shaking her head. "You're coming up with a lot more than I am.''

"She's extremely jealous.''

"Cecily?'' Terra exclaimed. "She couldn't possibly have the knowledge to be an arsonist, to set those lightbulb plants and the timers.''

Jack shrugged. "She could've picked up any number of things being married to a fire investigator.''

"But she wouldn't kill Harris. She loved him. To the point of suffocation, yes, but she did love him. You saw her last night. She was devastated about his death.''

"The grieving widow act could be just that.''

A sick look flashed across her face. "I guess so.''

"It gives us a place to start. Her motive could be revenge.''

"On me?''

"Or Harris for dumping her.''

"But why would she set fire to the other places? Or why would Dane Reynolds, for that matter?''

"That's why they call it an investigation.''

Her face paled and Jack caught a glimpse of that same vulnerability he'd seen in her eyes last night. The same vulnerability that had put a hard-boiled knot in his chest.

"What about viewing the tapes?" he asked. "I won't be free until after five. I'm on call for court."

Her gaze skimmed over him, sparking a hum in his blood. "Don't you have to wear a tie?"

He patted the pocket of his navy suit coat. "It's in here. I could meet you back here around six or so."

She looked uncertain. "I was going to take the tapes home and watch them. My heater conked out a couple of days ago and I have a repairman coming."

Thanks to the repairman, he and Terra wouldn't be alone. "Mind if I drop by your place? I'd really like to view the tapes with you in case I have questions about fire scene procedure."

She hesitated then nodded. "That would be fine. What about seven o'clock?"

"Sure." He jotted down her address and slipped his notebook back into his coat pocket. Going to her house, seeing how she lived, wasn't blurring the lines he wanted to draw between them. The tapes they would be watching were business, not porn. Besides, the quicker they moved on this case, the faster they could get it in the can and go their separate ways. "I'll see you later then."

"All right." She was already turning away, going through a folder on her desk.

He didn't want to feel anything for her, but last night he had. Something hotly unsettling, something primal and damn tempting. Desire.

He didn't like it. She tweaked all of his senses—just a notch, just enough to feel an uncomfortable stretch across his chest. No one had done that since Lori. And he certainly didn't need to feel this way about a woman who walked through flames, a woman who was supposed to be strictly his partner on this case.

He needed to keep a lid on these feelings, but he certainly hadn't counted on it being this challenging.

He told Darla goodbye as he walked out the door. He'd wanted to believe the protective instinct that had nagged him like a hangover since last night had been a result of Cecily Vaughn's brutal words to Terra. He understood how hard it was to do your job when someone you loved was the victim.

But he wasn't into lying to himself. He was interested in Terra August—at least his body was—but he wasn't going to act on the little buzz he got just by being in the same room with her. A murder investigation was at stake here and he knew neither of them wanted or could afford to be distracted.

Jack Spencer would be here any minute. And the repairman had just left. Terra prowled around her oversized leather chair and ottoman, rounded the matching chestnut sofa, trying to calm the shimmer in her nerves. She'd wanted to ask Lefty to stay, tried to think of something besides the heater he could check, but that was silly.

Earlier in her office, the concern and flare of fierce protectiveness in Jack's eyes when she'd handed him the card Darla had discovered had made her stomach do a funny flip. She knew that flip had nothing at all to do with the case, only the man.

Something insistent and strong stirred between them, something she hadn't been able to ignore last night when his hands had lingered on her shoulders. Something she hadn't been able to completely channel out of her mind today. Terra knew she should run from the man who was reawakening feelings in her she'd sworn to never trust again, feelings that had filled her with a sense of safety and confidence. Feelings that had been based on a relationship that was an illusion. What she needed from Jack Spencer was distance, but there was no chance she'd walk away from the man who could help her find the arsonist who'd murdered Harris.

Ditching Spencer wasn't an option. Her instincts were blaring at her to watch her step with him, and she would. She could do whatever was necessary in order to find Harris's murderer, even if it meant ignoring her emotions and spending twenty hours a day with Detective Yummy.

She needed to keep her focus on the investigation.

Wondering if Jack had eaten yet, she had just checked the refrigerator to see if she had anything to offer for supper when her doorbell rang.

She opened the door, her pulse skipping slightly at the six-foot-plus hunk of man leaning against her doorjamb, balancing a steaming pizza box on one hand.

He'd looked handsome earlier today in his navy suit and now he looked…rugged. Delicious. Her pulse hitched at the intensity of his blue eyes. His white button-down shirt was unbuttoned at the throat, showing tanned skin and the faint shadow of hair. His patterned tie was gone, as was his suit coat. His shirtsleeves were rolled back just enough to show the dark hair on his wrists. He had strong, broad hands with blunt, clean nails.

She invited him in. She didn't need to be thinking about his hands or his piercing blue eyes. Jack was coming to her house only to work. Even if they'd met at her office, they'd still be alone together. And she'd still feel this acute flare of interest whenever she saw him. A degree of interest and curiosity she hadn't felt since Keith. Even worse, her ambivalence about it was underlaid by a hard throb of awareness.

He stepped inside and shut the door. "I didn't see a repairman's truck. Were you stood up?"

"He left a few minutes ago." Heat flushed her cheeks, but she refused to let on about the way her nerves jumped when Jack's gaze lasered into hers.

"So, your heater's working now?"

"Lefty says yes." She smiled, but the words felt stilted and heavy. Jack didn't look any more comfortable than she felt.

He lifted the box. "I brought pizza. Hope you haven't eaten."

"No, I was just looking for something."

"You like pepperoni?"

"Love it, but you didn't have to do that."

"Hey, you brought the movies. It was the least I could do."

She knew cops, like firefighters, dealt with death by putting it right out there. He wasn't making light of Harris's death or the reason he was here. He was getting the subject out in the open so she could talk about it if she wanted. She didn't, but her heart did that funny flip again at his thoughtfulness.

"Want a beer?" she asked.

"Better pass. I need to be clear when we're watching these videos, try to grasp what you tell me as you lead me through the crime scenes."

"How about iced tea?"

"Great." He followed her across the living room carpet and into the kitchen, placing the pizza box on her small rectangular table.

Conscious of the man who watched her steadily, she moved the teak bowl filled with decorative fruit from the center of the pecan table and turned toward her cabinets. Even though Jack looked relaxed and the most unguarded she'd seen him, she felt an urge to smooth her fingertips over the deep furrow between his brows, try to erase the tinge of sadness that accompanied the fatigue in his eyes.

Good grief. They were here to work, period. Terra put two plates on the table along with napkins. They both dug in and didn't speak for several minutes. She hadn't realized how hungry she was. Or how on edge she felt about being alone with him. But he was all business and that would help her to do the same.

"How was your meeting with the mayor?" Jack reached for his third piece of pizza.

"Fine. I brought him up to speed on the investigation, confirmed this latest fire was started by the same person who started the other three with lightbulb plants."

"Did you tell him about the card with the most recent delivery of flowers?"

"Yes." She'd been trying to keep her pulse even all afternoon. Her appetite suddenly gone, Terra put her second slice of pizza, half-eaten, back on her plate. "Did the florist have a record of the sale?"

"Yes. The flowers were paid for in cash, but the owner's teenage daughter handled the transaction. She couldn't remember if the customer was male or female."

There was no sense getting tied up in knots until she had more information, but she had a bad feeling all the same. She couldn't discount Jack's theories about Cecily or Reynolds. Today when she'd seen that card, she'd been swallowed up by a vulnerability that locked her breath in her chest. A gaping uncertainty she hadn't felt since the day her grandfather had died. She'd needed reassurance, steadying, and Spencer had given it without her asking, taken quick charge of the evidence and the situation.

"I had to testify in court this afternoon, but I sent a lab guy to take the florist's prints and her daughter's."

"And?"

"Both were on the card. So were Darla's, but that was all."

A shiver rippled across her shoulders and she rubbed her arms. "I was hoping we might get lucky."

"So was I." He pointed at the last piece of pizza and raised his brows.

She nodded, indicating he could have it. The apprehension she'd felt upon reading the arsonist's message flooded her again. The words and the flames drawn around them had been a statement. She'd tried all day to consider the card as nothing more than a lead, but it was too creepy. "You know, now that you've connected the flower deliveries to the arsonist, I can't get past the feeling that these fires are about something personal. About me."

His gaze sliced to her. "Is there something you need to tell me?"

"No. I mean, if there is, I don't know it. I have absolutely no evidence that these arsons are related to me any more than they're related to anyone else. I'm just being paranoid."

"Understandable. The connection between your roses and the fire dates surprised me. I imagine it did you, too."

She nodded. "The card is another clue, another pattern we can track." She hoped she was convincing him; she didn't think she was convincing herself.

She'd thought the fires hadn't turned personal until Harris's death, but was it possible the arsonist had targeted *her,* that he or she was setting fires to make a statement to Terra? It was another angle to check.

"Have you heard from the mayor?" She picked up her uneaten pizza.

"My lieutenant has, and we're supposed to meet at Griffin's office tomorrow morning. Any word from the M.E.?"

"Ken called about an hour ago and said he needs at least one more day before he's finished."

"Does he think he'll be able to release the body in another forty-eight hours?"

"Probably sooner." A knot of pain lodged in her throat.

As she rose to get him more tea, he gave her a satisfied smile and pushed back his chair, patting his stomach. "I'd better stop eating or I'll have to buy a new suit."

He had plenty of room in that suit. His flat stomach was probably hard enough to bounce a quarter.

"Anything on Reynolds?" She tried to finish her pizza, but now it tasted like lumpy dough.

Jack drained his glass of tea. "Nothing suspicious yet. I'm digging deeper."

The arsonist's message today had rocked her with the first sense of personal danger she'd felt in these cases.

She was also rattled by how drawn she felt to Jack Spencer. The way something in him—his confidence, perhaps—had reached inside her and calmed the shimmer of nerves in her belly at the realization that every one of those bouquets had been delivered after a fire that met her serial arsonist's pattern.

"Hey, you okay?" Jack's voice quietly penetrated her thoughts.

She looked over her shoulder to find him standing several feet away, concern turning his eyes to cobalt. "Yes."

She tried to shake off the apprehension crawling through her. The card was a lead. What Terra had to do was view it that way and work the case. "Let's start those videos."

After she plugged in the video from the first fire scene, they settled on her leather sofa. Punching Play, Terra explained, "We video about eighty percent of our fires, especially if they're suspicious. I can't do them all, so some firefighters are trained to help me."

"Do you video so you'll have a record of exactly how things were found and left by the firefighters?"

"Mainly so we can train others in investigation and also to keep the chain of evidence in our control. That way, it can't be enhanced or altered."

"What are we looking for first?" Jack sat a foot away from her, but it was close enough to remind her of the way his jacket had felt on her. Had smelled.

"Faces. We want to determine if there's anyone who showed up at more than one of the fires. Arsonists like to watch their handiwork so they'll return to their burn scene."

He nodded.

"This is the janitorial supply store," she said as they watched flames explode from the front window of a small store.

Next to her, Jack scanned the people in the crowd as intently as she did. The second video showed the fire at the photography studio. Neither of them recognized a person there as being from the first scene. Except Dane Reynolds.

Since the reporter had already made their suspect list, Terra simply pointed as the camera panned past him.

Jack muttered, "Expected to see him. Is he in all of them?"

"Yes, but his regular cameraman, T. J. Coontz, isn't." She reached for her notebook on the coffee table in front of them and thumbed to a tabbed place. "The night of the arson at the photography he was out of town at a training seminar."

Jack checked his own notes. "And the night of the fire at Harris's, he came from his cousin's wedding. He showed me pictures of him with the bride and groom."

"So he checks out."

During the third video which showed the dental office

fire, Jack asked her to pause. "That firefighter. The one on the left? This is the second fire scene where I've seen him."

"Don LeBass," Terra answered. "He's with Station Four."

"Isn't Station Four assigned to the quadrant on the south side of town?"

"Yes, and the dental office is in the city's east quadrant. I checked that out." She smiled. "LeBass filled in for a sick firefighter on that shift. Captain Maguire confirmed Station One was shorthanded and he okayed LeBass to work."

"All right, but Station Four also worked the fire over at Mr. Vaughn's in the east quadrant. Why not just Station One?"

"Captain Maguire knew the address belonged to Harris and called for backup." Somehow Terra managed to keep her voice from cracking.

Jack nodded, admiration flaring in his eyes before he looked back at the screen.

They made a good team, she thought, so the sooner they wrapped up this investigation, the better. She found herself wanting to touch Jack Spencer, soak in some of his power, that seeming invincibility. She didn't want to believe the hard ache in her chest was the result of just plain lust, but that's exactly what it was.

She finally put in the last tape, the video of Harris's house. Her nerves crackled and she realized her hands were clenched in a death grip on the remote as they viewed the flames snaking out of the front, west window of his house. The scene pried open the fresh wound of losing her friend, but she forced herself to mentally replay Harris's instructions through the years, to focus on the case and work around the raw place inside her as best she could.

Jack sat beside her, leaning forward, his gaze trained intently on the television screen. Despite the unwanted smolder Terra felt between them, his presence was surprisingly comforting. Just as it had been earlier in her office when he'd taken decisive action with the card from the arsonist.

Except for Dane Reynolds, Terra didn't match any faces in the crowd around Harris's house with people they'd observed at the other scenes, but she felt she'd missed something. She rewound the tape and started it again.

"What did you see?" Jack scooted closer, the hard length of his thigh burning against hers.

"I don't know. Something's bugging me."

Trying to concentrate on the screen with Jack's leg melded to hers and his woodsy scent sliding into her lungs was like trying to douse a bonfire with a garden sprinkler and she struggled to stay focused. She rewound the tape again, her gaze probing flames and faces in the crowd, trees, darkened corners of the house. Shadows.

"There!" Hitting Pause with one hand, she grabbed Jack's thigh with the other. "Look! Do you see that? Someone in the shadows on the west end of the house? I think it's a woman. Is it? Do you see?"

He didn't answer.

She glanced over and saw that he wasn't looking at her, but down. At her hand on his thigh.

Her heart thumped hard. Shoot. Slowly, she removed her hand, tried to cover the sudden spike of her blood pressure by gripping the remote with both hands and forcing her gaze to the television. She asked unevenly, "Do you see her?"

"Yes." His voice slid over her, trailing a luscious bite of sharp pleasure down her spine. "I see her."

She couldn't help herself. Her gaze shifted, locked with his. He wasn't looking at the television screen. He was looking at her.

Chapter 5

Dammit, why couldn't he focus? It was just her hand. On his thigh. Big deal. And it wasn't even there anymore.

Jack's skin burned like she'd stroked her fingers up the inside of his bare leg. He clenched his fist in an effort to keep from reaching for her, running *his* hand up her leg, kissing that luscious mouth until they both turned inside out. He wanted to touch, to taste. To take.

Her eyes darkened to the color of wet moss; the pulse jumped in her throat. Just looking at her made his skin pull taut. Hell, he liked her hand on him, wanted more. A lot more. Which was not going to happen.

He didn't make any sudden moves, which he considered damn amazing. Torn between bolting off the couch and jumping her bones, he managed to drag his gaze back to the screen, though for a few seconds the picture was only a blur.

He had to stop thinking like this.

After a long moment, he said in a rusty voice, "Yes, I

think it's a woman, but the picture is too dark and grainy for me to really tell.''

"I know. Now I'm not sure if it's a man *or* a woman, but it's someone who doesn't want to be seen.''

"I agree.'' He scrubbed a hand over his face, trying to clear the fog from his mind. His blood still pounded hard through his veins. He needed to get out of here. Now. "I can take the video to the police lab for enhancement. Unless you have someone who can do it?''

"That's where I'd take it, too.'' With the remote, she rewound the tape to the desired spot and ejected it from the VCR. She got up to retrieve the cassette. "How long do you think that will take?''

"It depends on how much the lab techs have going on. I'll tell them it's priority. We'll probably know something by noon tomorrow. I'll let you know once I have an idea.''

"Okay.'' She remained standing over by the television, keeping plenty of distance between them.

She had to feel it as much as he did. The look he'd seen in her eyes, surprise mixed with desire, still twisted his gut. "I'll talk to you tomorrow then. Let me know if you hear from the M.E.''

"Will you take the tape to the lab in the morning?''

"Yes.'' He stood, moving toward the door. "On my way to the mayor's office.''

"Sounds good. Do you want to update him about the tape or do you want me to?''

He shrugged. "I'll do it since I'll be there.''

"Okay.'' Terra handed him the tape cassette marked with the date and name of the Vaughn fire. Careful to keep distance between them, she walked him to the door.

"I'll talk to you tomorrow then.''

She nodded, looking as dazed as he felt.

He got into his truck, his whole body tight and vibrating.

Just because he was attracted to her didn't mean his brains had fallen out. He'd enjoy having sex with her, no doubt about that, but he wasn't interested in anything else. *Wouldn't* be interested in anything more with a woman in such a dangerous job. And he just wasn't cut out for mindless, meaningless sex, though he'd tried it a couple of times since Lori had died.

As much as he was tempted, he wasn't getting involved with a woman whose job was a tightwire between danger and more danger. Jack drove out of Terra's subdivision, past the newer, small homes then found himself heading east toward the police station.

He'd gotten more than distracted in there. He'd gotten personal. Too personal. She'd touched him out of excitement at finding someone hiding at the fire scene. Jack had just gotten excited, period. And he was still buzzed. He had to dial it back. Steer clear of any lustful thoughts about Presley's female fire investigator, regardless of her torturously long legs and you-want-to lips.

It helped that he didn't have to see her again until the tape was ready for viewing or another lead surfaced. Still, he wouldn't get any sleep tonight unless he sweated out the soft, teasing scent of her, the want. He headed for the police gym and the punching bag.

Last night, Jack Spencer had thought about kissing her. Terra had wanted him to, wanted to know what it would be like. Her response had been pure instinct—fast and hard and certain. Late the next evening, a thrill shot through her as she recalled the way his eyes had darkened with a fierceness that spiked her pulse.

Thoughts of the frank, male interest in Spencer's face, the imprint of rock-hard thigh still warming her palm had hovered all day, during her building inspections up until several minutes ago while wrangling over code enforcement with a difficult building owner. The sun had long set. A crisp velvety night settled around her as she walked to her truck.

The smoldering desire in Jack's eyes had touched—and shattered—a hard place inside her. A place she hadn't had until her divorce. For that instant, looking into the heat of Jack's gaze, she'd melted. Ached. The reaction had thrown her. She hadn't responded to a man like that since Keith, and hadn't expected to. That's all it was. She'd touched Jack strictly out of reflex, but after that she'd barely been able to concentrate on the video from Harris's house. She'd felt numb one minute, charged the next. Despite the regret needling her about that almost-kiss, it was good Detective Yummy had left when he had.

She couldn't allow the lines to blur between her job and her personal life, especially not on this investigation. Her friendship with Harris should be her *only* personal interest in this case, not the detective who acted as gun-shy as she was.

On her own today, both she and Jack were dealing with job details that couldn't be ignored, and Terra was glad for the space. Her emotions skipped between relief at not seeing the steely-eyed cop to disappointment. She had to get back on track, streamline her thoughts to include only those about the arsons.

Darla would be long gone from the office by now. While letting her truck warm up, Terra called in to check her voice mail. She had four messages, two from Jack. The first time he called to give her his cell phone number and ask her to call him; the second time, to tell her he would be at the police gym until eight-thirty that evening. She glanced at the digital clock on her dash. Seven-thirty. He had news; so did she. She'd catch him at the gym.

Maybe his news concerned the videotape. This morning,

he'd phoned to let her know that the equipment in the police
lab was being serviced and he'd been told not to expect to
hear anything from the techs until at least tomorrow. But
maybe they'd been able to get things working quicker than
they'd thought. Hopefully, the lab boys had been able to
clear up the picture on the tape enough to show some usable
detail about the person hiding in the shadows of Harris's
house.

Terra leaned against the headrest for a moment. She welcomed a break from the long day of safety inspections she'd
performed. She'd gone round and round with a building
owner whom she'd finally hit with a fine for not bringing
up to code everything she'd listed. She'd previously given
him three months longer than she normally would've because he'd told her he was having problems with financing,
but today she realized he wasn't going to comply with Presley's fire codes. Pulling away from the building on the outer
western edge of town, one of the faster growing areas in
town, she headed east toward downtown and the police gym.

She was tired and on the edge of cranky. A root beer float
sounded great after her tough day. Terra loved ice cream
year-round. Granddad had always pulled out the treat after
a bad day or for a special occasion.

Thinking about Granddad made her think about Harris,
which put a darker cloud on her less-than-sunny mood. The
sooner she got that ice cream, the better she'd feel.

It took her only about ten minutes to reach the gym, lo-
cated across the street from the police department in downtown Presley. She hoped Spencer had encouraging news
about that videotape. Her news from the M.E., combined
with the day she'd had, wasn't encouraging in the least.

Finding a place close to the door, she parked and headed
inside the football-field-size metal building. Earlier temper-
atures had been pleasant, but now a sharp wind bit at her

and she huddled into her fleece-lined department jacket. Since she could wear socks rather than hose with her uniform boots, at least her feet were warm. The gym provided a welcome respite from the chill. Terra paused in the doorway, her gaze scanning the large, high-ceilinged room.

Only a few people populated the workout area, which was divided into sections with machines, treadmills and bikes, free weights and punching bags.

Music from Eric Clapton played through speakers set high overhead. Weights clanged as three people worked on machines and in the free weight area. The smells of sweat, cologne and perfume mingled. Terra became aware of a wiry, muscled man watching her from a weight machine to her right.

Shaken out of her thoughts, she moved across the lightly padded floor, passing machines that worked everything from abs to calves. In the free weight area, she recognized Officer Lowe, but not the trim brunette who lifted weights with him.

She spotted Jack in a corner across the gym, going at a punching bag with quick one-two jabs, leashed power evident in the hard lines of his body, the razor-sharp focus in his face. It was a view that had her stopping in her tracks a few feet away. A loose gray tank shirt bared bronzed biceps sheened with sweat. Black shorts hit him a couple of inches above the knees and for a moment, Terra simply stared. With each blow to the bag, muscle flowed into muscle, a ripple of rock-hard sinew and flesh.

She'd never panted over a man in her life, but she came close. Jack Spencer was one gorgeous package. Her gaze traveled over him again, noting the dark hair on a chest broad enough to stop a truck. Muscular, hair-dusted legs were well sculpted. Good grief, the P.D. should start putting out a calendar. Spencer alone could sell thousands.

Her gaze backtracked, pausing on the strong calves, then

the two inches of rigid abdomen he exposed when he lifted up his shirt to wipe his face. A breath finally eased out of her. Her gaze met his and—uh-oh.

He stared right at her, one dark eyebrow arched questioningly. Shoot. He steadied the punching bag then let go. Heat flushed her cheeks, but she forced a smile, as if she hadn't just been ready to gobble him up. He smelled tangy and wild and her pulse skittered.

"You're…boxing."

"Yeah." His dark hair was wet, spiked up in front as if he'd shoved his fingers through it. "With my nephew."

A young boy, whom Terra judged to be ten or eleven, stepped out from behind the punching bag. "Hi."

"Hi." Terra reached out to shake his hand. "I'm Terra."

"Connor."

She smiled. "Nice to meet you." He was a good-looking kid, favoring his uncle with the same blue eyes, dark hair and solid jaw. He also wore shorts and a shirt identical to his uncle, but where Jack's sneakers were white, Connor's were red.

"My sister's boy," Jack offered. "Connor Heath."

"Do you guys box often?" she asked the boy.

"Twice a week. I think I can just about whip him."

Terra laughed. "I'd like to see that."

Jack grabbed the kid around the neck and jokingly wrestled him close. "Watch out, buddy. You might have to back up those words."

"I'm ready, Uncle Jack. I'm ready to go into the ring."

"Not quite." Jack squeezed the kid's shoulder. "Would you get us some water, Con? I could use some."

"Sure." He turned to Terra. "Do you want anything?"

Just your uncle. The thought jumped into Terra's mind. She shook her head, astounded at herself. "No, thanks. I appreciate it, though."

"Sure. Be right back." Connor darted around her, and as she turned to watch him go, she caught him giving Jack two big thumbs-up.

About her? Amused, she looked back at Jack, surprised to see a flush crawl up his neck.

"Thanks for stopping by," he said gruffly. "I found out something I think you'll be real interested in."

"Are the lab guys ahead of schedule? Were they able to enhance the video so we can see who's in the shadows?"

"They haven't called me yet. This concerns some information I got from one of Mr. Vaughn's neighbors."

"Oh." She frowned. "I thought you talked to all of them the night of the fire."

"The Emersons, who live two houses down, were in Texas last weekend. I checked on them again this afternoon and they were home."

"If they weren't here at the time of the fire, what information could they have?"

Connor walked up just then, carefully balancing two full cups of water. "Here ya go, Uncle Jack."

"Thanks, Con." Jack took the cup, his hand dwarfing the large foam cup. He downed its contents in three swallows.

Terra couldn't pull her gaze from the strong column of his neck, trailing a trickle of sweat into the hollow of his throat and down the middle of his chest. The gray shirt molded to nicely defined pectorals, sleeked over the flat abs that looked hard enough to deflect steel.

Good ever-lovin' grief. Her temperature must've gone up ten degrees since she'd first walked in here. She shifted her attention to the nephew, who was a lot less dangerous. "What else do you like besides boxing, Connor?"

"Fishing and paintball."

"He's good at both of them, too." Jack beamed. "He

won a paintball tournament in Oklahoma City about two weeks ago.''

Their obvious affection made Terra smile. ''Do you like school?''

''It's all right.'' His blue eyes shone with curiosity. ''My uncle said you're a fire investigator. Do you fight fires?''

''If I need to. I also enforce safety codes and investigate fires to determine the cause.'' She smiled, feeling rather than seeing Jack's smile dim somewhat. ''Plus some double-o-seven secret spy stuff I can't talk about.''

''Awesome.'' Connor's eyes shone with admiration.

Jack handed Connor his cup, now empty. ''Hey, Con, can you give me a minute alone with Investigator August? I need to talk to her about a case we're working on.''

''Sure. I'll go jump some rope.''

''Great.'' Jack's fond smile triggered a small pain beneath Terra's rib cage. When she'd divorced Keith, she'd lost more than a husband. She'd lost the people who'd become her second family. And the opportunity, at least in her foreseeable future, to have a family of her own.

''You're pretty good with kids.'' Jack grabbed a towel from a hook on the wall behind the punching bag.

''My ex had several nieces and nephews. I always enjoyed them.''

''Do you have any nieces or nephews of your own?''

''No, I'm an only child.''

''Did you and your ex ever talk about having kids?'' His blue gaze seemed to sear right through her.

She hadn't come here to discuss personal issues. She stroked a nervous hand down her neck. ''For a while, then he changed his mind. It was for the best.''

It really had been. She wouldn't have wanted to put a child through their divorce, but there were times when she wished for some family Keith couldn't have taken away from her. His parents hadn't blamed her for the failed marriage, but they kept their distance. Sometimes it hurt all over again.

Pushing away the sting, Terra said, "You were telling me about Harris's neighbors, the Emersons."

"Yeah. Let's go sit down."

She followed him several yards toward a cushioned bench next to the wall. He glanced at the weight area where Connor jumped rope and gave his nephew a thumbs-up. The kid's smile was blinding even at this distance.

"He's a cutie." Terra's lips curved. "How old is he?"

"Twelve. He's got a nine-year-old brother at home, but he wanted to play Game Boy tonight instead of sweating it out at the gym."

Jack's obvious attachment to his nephews made her wonder if he had any children, but she didn't ask. "How'd your meeting with the mayor go?"

"Fine. He's anxious to hear what, if anything, we find on that video."

"Take a number," she said dryly.

"Exactly what I told him."

Terra smiled, knowing he hadn't done any such thing.

Jack took a seat on the bench. Uncomfortably aware of her intense interest in the way his shoulders flexed, Terra thought perhaps she should remain standing. She wouldn't be here all that long.

He looked up, his eyes a vivid blue in the light. "How's it been going?"

"I've had better days. I had to fine someone and it didn't go over well."

"Sometimes people don't understand you're just doing your job, enforcing laws already in place for their own safety."

Of course, Jack would understand. His job involved the

same thing, didn't it? "Making people toe the line is why we're called the 'black sheep' of the fire department."

He nodded, scrubbing at his face with the towel.

She tore her gaze from the ripple of steel bicep. "So, how about your news?"

He glanced at the space where she would've sat beside him. "The Emersons told me that late one night about three weeks ago, they heard screaming and went outside to find a woman on Harris's porch. This happened four nights in a row. The husband went over to check on Harris and Harris told him the woman was his ex-wife."

"Cecily?" Terra had no trouble imagining Cecily screaming, but she did have trouble imagining Cecily embarrassing Harris like that. Besides, Harris hadn't mentioned that particular incident.

Jack nodded. "Harris told the husband he was planning to get a V.P.O."

"A victim's protective order? Did he get one? When?"

"I called the court clerk and found out that Harris filed for, and was issued a V.P.O. two weeks ago. It was served within twenty-four hours."

"For what offenses?"

"Stalking and trespassing."

Hurt sliced through her. "He never said anything to me."

"I figured if he had, you would've told me." Jack ran the towel over his face again.

"Did he use an attorney?"

"No. You don't have to."

Terra felt as if the room had tilted and she couldn't get her balance. "What do you think of this?"

"Maybe the ex got really angry when she found out about the protective order."

"Angry enough to kill him?" Some of Terra's numbness wore off.

"People have killed for less. I think we need to look pretty hard at her."

"Did anyone else know about Harris getting the order?"

"I was hoping you could tell me."

"Sorry." Stunned, she sank down on the bench. Despite the cold shock of Jack's announcement, doubts flared like a flash fire inside her. How many secrets had Harris kept from her? Cecily had blamed Terra for Harris's violent death. Could she be right?

She wasn't touching Jack, but his heat pressed against her. Even through her jacket she could feel him and it comforted her somehow. She studied his strong hands, the towel loosely dangling between his knees.

"Maybe Harris's good friends would know something. Judge Bob Seat was a fishing buddy. And Frank Massey is a firefighter who went through the academy with Harris and retired at the same time."

"Maybe his judge buddy told him how to go about getting a V.P.O."

"Could be." She shook her head. "I'm sorry I'm not more help. I had no idea Cecily had gotten this bad. She had to have been following him and showing up a lot more than I knew about."

"Yeah." Jack leaned forward, elbows on his knees.

She tried to keep her gaze from wandering over him and stared blankly at the floor as she absorbed the bombshell he'd dropped. Learning about the victim's protective order notched up Terra's unease. Cecily had been more of a threat than she'd realized.

"Hey, you okay?" Jack's voice quietly penetrated her thoughts.

The strong male scent of him, the tang of sweat and a faint hint of cologne slid into her lungs. Her stomach fluttered. "Sure."

Doubt spread through her, making her feel unprepared for what she might learn next, what might *happen* next. Thank goodness, Jack Spencer didn't seem to be falling apart. The V.P.O. was another lead, regardless of whether Harris had told her about it.

"You said you had some news?"

"Oh, yes." Terra dismissed the butterflies in her stomach, determined not to be sidetracked by a silly attraction. "The M.E. found large quantities of Halcion in Harris's tox screen."

"Halcion? Isn't that a sleeping pill?"

"Yes. Overdoses can cause unconsciousness, and often death."

"So someone drugged Mr. Vaughn, then tied him up?"

"Or tied him up first." Terra laced her fingers together, working to keep her voice steady. "Ken can't determine which."

"So this just strengthens our case for premeditated murder."

"Yes." She found herself wanting to grab his hand and hold on tight, to cling to something immovable and rock steady. "Ken released Harris's body today and the funeral will be Saturday."

His gaze slid to hers and held. "I'm sorry."

"Thanks."

"Is his ex-wife planning the service?"

"No. Harris had already arranged to have what he wanted."

"That's good. I don't think the ex is in any shape to plan anything."

Emotion tightened her throat. She struggled not to give in to it, even though right now she felt like throwing herself against Jack Spencer's broad chest and having a good cry. "You're planning to talk to Cecily, aren't you?"

"You bet. I plan to ask her about that V.P.O."

"I want to be there."

"No problem. I also want to talk to Mr. Vaughn's friends, anyone who might've known about this V.P.O. against his ex. Any other names you can give me?"

"Maybe the mayor's mother, Harris's sister."

"Okay, that's a place to start. What about any friends of Cecily's I can talk to?"

Terra thought for a moment. "She and Harris were good friends with Rod and Janet Engel. Rod was a firefighter. From what Harris told me, Cecily and Janet remained friends after the divorce."

"Okay, I'll put them on my list. I don't want to talk to the ex-Mrs. Vaughn until after we talk to some other people, see if her info matches up with what we get."

"Good idea. Tomorrow?" She rose, her nerves raw, the massive gym space closing in on her.

Jack stood, too, seeming suddenly very close. Very big.

She rubbed her arms, struggling to hold back the frustration biting at her. Harris didn't have to tell her everything, but she'd thought he had. To file for a V.P.O., he must've felt in real danger from his ex-wife, yet he hadn't said a word. "Shall we meet in the morning at my office?"

"Eight o'clock all right?"

She nodded.

Concern darkened his eyes. "You sure you're okay?"

"I'll be fine. It's just a bit of a shock."

"The V.P.O.?"

"Yes. I thought Harris would've told me."

"So did I. Is there any reason you can think of that he would keep it to himself?"

She shrugged. "Maybe to keep from embarrassing Cecily. He was a real gentleman about stuff like that."

Jack edged closer, his heat wrapping around her like a

hug. "He was probably protecting you, too. First instinct. I'm sure he didn't keep silent because he didn't trust you."

She searched his eyes, saw compassion and sincerity. "Thanks."

He smiled, a gentle, barely there smile that caused her heart to turn over.

Just then, Connor ran up. "Uncle Jack?"

"I'm watching the time, bud." He flashed Terra a grin. "We're going for hamburgers."

"Ask for ice cream, too," Terra whispered loudly.

"Hey, don't gang up on me!" Jack put up his hands in mock self-defense before pointing a finger at Connor. "I counted only a hundred jumps."

"How do you do that?" the boy exclaimed. "You weren't even looking at me!"

Jack laughed and threw an air punch, which Connor dodged, then threw his own.

Terra smiled in spite of the ache inside her. "Connor, it was nice to meet you."

"Yeah. Maybe I'll see you again sometime."

"Maybe so." Doubtful. Terra pulled her keys out of her jacket pocket. "I'll see you in the morning, Spencer."

"Eight sharp."

Jack Spencer was someone a woman could rely on. As shocked and off balance as she'd felt at the news about Harris's V.P.O., Spencer had steadied her. Reassured her.

She had to be careful. She wasn't going to let her hormones or loneliness or the fact that she liked Jack more all the time get in the way of justice for Harris. Seeing him with his nephew brought home the fact that Jack Spencer was a man, with wants and needs just like any other. She'd seen more evidence of that last night when he'd thought about kissing her.

The blue-eyed detective opened a place inside her that

had closed up when she and Keith divorced, a deep, secret place that urged her to invite someone in. But she wasn't ready to get cut off at the knees again. She might never be.

Her thoughts and emotions swirled together. So far, their investigation had yielded tons of questions and no answers. The day had been capped off by disturbing information learned by both of them—the V.P.O. he'd obtained against his ex-wife, the drugs found in Harris's system. Terra's throat tightened.

This whole day had been a series of unsettling revelations, starting with her regret over not being kissed by Jack. She should be thinking platonic, professional thoughts, *not* about getting naked with him.

All her energy needed to be focused on the arsons, on her job. She could not let Jack Spencer go to her head.

Chapter 6

The day of Harris's funeral dawned bright and crisp, but by one o'clock that Saturday afternoon, the October temperature had grown unseasonably mild. The service was held at Presley Memorial Gardens in the larger of two chapels on the cemetery grounds. Terra, Meredith and Robin walked into a lovely stone building with arched doorways and polished mahogany floors. Plush area rugs in deep burgundy muffled footsteps and led into the carpeted auditorium where the service would be held.

Seated between her two friends, Terra was grateful for their support. She wore her fire department dress uniform and Robin wore her police blues. Meredith, her wild blond curls pulled into a chic twist, wore a black suit. Though numb, Terra was determined to hold herself together today and function as best she could. If she started crying, she was afraid she'd break down. Since the night of Harris's death, she hadn't let herself dwell on the personal aspect of the investigation. Thank goodness, Robin and Meredith had come with her today.

Pastor Goolsby, from Harris's church, gave a lovely service. The casket remained closed, for which Terra was grateful. She didn't think she could handle seeing Harris the way she had that night nearly a week ago. Even though the horrific image of his burned body would stay with her a long time, she wanted to remember him the way she always knew him. The time they'd spent with her grandfather, the fires they'd fought together, the first door he'd let her hack through. He'd been a constant support after she'd lost Granddad, a shoulder during her divorce from Keith, a model of strength in the days they'd helped work the Murrah building bombing.

And now he was gone. Gone. All because of some twisted pyromaniac who also murdered.

A heaviness pressed against her ribs. She couldn't believe this service was for Harris. That she'd come to say goodbye to the man who'd always been there for her.

After several eulogies, the pastor invited everyone outside to attend a short graveside memorial. Terra had put a shell around her heart and her thoughts, not allowing herself to think about what this investigation really meant, the finality of what was now happening. As she walked out of the chapel and across the paved drive toward the tent set up for the graveside service, she felt that shell crack. Harris was truly gone. She looped her arms through those of both her friends to keep herself steady.

The fire chief, Al Wheat, walked ahead of her with the police chief. She recognized the councilwoman who made her way with the city manager across the fall-dry grass to the waiting tent. Terra saw Dane Reynolds along with his cameraman, T. J. Coontz, hanging back from the crowd, quietly setting up T.J.'s camera against a row of cars. They weren't intrusive, but neither were they invisible.

Reynolds's presence wasn't suspicious on the surface; every news channel had sent a crew and they, too, set up their equipment a respectable distance away. Harris Vaughn had been first a decorated firefighter for fourteen years, then the fire investigator for more than ten. His funeral service would've received media attention even if his death hadn't been so grisly.

Soon, everyone was gathered under the open-sided tent. Ten chairs had been provided. Terra took a place behind the row of chairs, leaving the seats for family or those unable to stand comfortably. A quick flutter of wind made her glad she'd worn her uniform's dress jacket.

She scanned the chairs, three of them filled by Cecily, her mother and her brother. The next four chairs were taken by the mayor, his wife, father and mother, who was Harris's sister. Rod and Janet Elder used two chairs, which left one empty. Terra counted firefighters from every station house as well as several police officers in dress uniform. Pain and loss stabbed through her and she battled to level out her breathing. She couldn't lose it now.

Plenty of Presley's brass had turned out to pay their respects, but was the arsonist also here?

Arsonists returned to scenes of their fires, not funerals, but Terra couldn't take her gaze from Cecily. Or stop wondering if Jack had come up with anything else on Dane Reynolds. Afraid the shaky rein on her emotions would snap if she listened too closely to the pastor's final words about Harris, she let her mind drift over the investigation.

Jack had learned that Dane Reynolds abruptly left a news anchor job in Denver before coming to Oklahoma City. Upon talking to Denver police yesterday, Jack had unearthed the fact that a restraining order had been issued against the pretty-boy reporter. He was attempting to contact the woman who'd filed the restraining order.

Terra had spent most of Thursday with Jack, talking to friends of both Harris and Cecily. Harris had told his friend, Judge Bob Seat, about seeking a protective order against his ex-wife and asked how to proceed. Neither Terra nor Harris's retired firefighter buddy, Frank Massey, had known about the V.P.O. Terra didn't understand why Harris hadn't told her about his V.P.O. against Cecily, but the fact that he'd also kept it from Massey helped lessen the sting. According to Judge Seat, Harris had remained silent out of embarrassment for both himself and Cecily.

If only Terra and Jack could get a break in this case. They might get one from the videotape, *if* it could ever be enhanced. The equipment at the police lab had been repaired, but yesterday when the techs tried to analyze the videotape from the fire at Harris's, the machine shorted out. Jack had driven the cassette down to the lab at the Oklahoma State Bureau of Investigation. They would call when it was ready.

Terra's gaze traveled over Cecily's black hat trimmed with a half veil and her slender black suit. The woman's shoulders shook noticeably. The pastor stepped aside and a petite blond woman sang beautifully about "The Sweet By and By." Terra lost track of the words, fighting an intense sense of suffocation, a slow rip of pain through her chest. She tried to gauge Cecily's reaction. Was it too over the top? Too restrained? Was she still taking Valium?

Cecily's friend, Janet Elder, had uncomfortably admitted to Jack and Terra that she knew about the victim's protective order Harris had obtained, but that was all she'd said. Same for her husband, Rod.

Cecily's brother, Barry Mullins, had answered Terra and Jack's questions, but refused to let them talk to his mother. Watching the frail, tiny woman who leaned heavily on Cecily's shoulder during the service, Terra could understand why.

Mullins had an arm around both mother and sister, trying to offer what support he could. Cecily sobbed quietly into a mascara-splotched handkerchief. Terra and Jack hadn't spoken to her yet about the victim's protective order and certainly wouldn't do it here.

As the pastor's voice soothingly read a passage from the Bible, Terra closed her eyes, reaching deep inside for the strength to stifle her emotions. She couldn't fall apart, couldn't lose control. She wanted to get whoever had done this to Harris, no matter what it took or how long.

She and the other firefighters had planned to meet at Harris's favorite bar, Hotshots, after the funeral to say goodbye to their colleague in their own way. She would stop by for a little while before heading home. She was exhausted and grief had begun chipping through her defenses with sly, knifelike pricks.

During the short service, she felt someone's gaze on her and glanced back straight into Jack's blue eyes. He gave a slight nod and she responded with the barest of smiles. No doubt he was there to see if he spotted anyone on their suspect list, but she felt a warmth steal through her, almost a calming.

She didn't have the strength to push it away even though she'd made her decision yesterday about Jack Spencer and the crazy dance her hormones had done two nights ago while visiting with him at the police gym. Today was about Harris and tomorrow would be about searching for the murdering arsonist who'd killed him.

Jack didn't appear to want to be involved with her any more than she did with him, at least not romantically. Which was good.

Terra felt shaky inside, but she locked her knees and remained at rigid attention as the flag was folded and presented to Harris's sister, Jeannie Griffin. The pastor said a final prayer and, on behalf of the family, thanked everyone for coming. People had said their goodbyes to Harris inside the chapel so the crowd broke up quickly and dissolved into smaller groups.

When the mayor and his mother walked with their families toward the waiting limousines that would take them back to the funeral home, Terra made her way over to them. They stopped when they saw her and she held out her hands to Jeannie. The two women embraced and Terra whispered her condolences. She shook hands with Harris's brother-in-law, Bill, then with the mayor, expressing her sorrow.

As Jeannie and Bill walked off, the mayor turned. "Will you be able to find this monster, Terra?"

"Yes." Her voice cracked, but her gaze didn't waver. Neither did her belief.

"Do it."

He walked away and she turned to find Meredith and Robin just behind her.

Meredith hugged her. "You okay?"

"Yes. I just can't believe this is real."

Two male police officers walked up to Robin and she introduced them. Terra made small talk, but wasn't really aware of what she said. She *was* aware that someone was watching her. Her skin prickled and she looked over her shoulder to again find Jack Spencer's attention on her.

From his distance of several yards, she read a shared pain in his eyes and face. He studied her as if he could see the small cracks beneath the surface. But she was working hard to make sure no one could see them. At his knowing look, she turned away, struggling to keep her mental balance. Jack understood what she felt right now, how desperate she was to maintain control. His knowing weakened Terra's defenses, made her long to be closer to him.

Meredith and Robin talked quietly to the police officers. As Terra tried to ignore the hollow ache in her belly, someone touched her elbow.

She turned, stiffening when she saw Cecily.

"May I talk to you?" Gripping her handkerchief in one hand, Harris's ex lightly touched Terra's arm, then drew her away from her friends.

Though wary, Terra looked into Cecily's red-rimmed eyes and didn't have the heart to refuse. They stopped several yards away from Robin and Meredith. Terra's gaze followed Cecily as she flashed her mother a reassuring smile. Looking as though it took all her energy to stand, the woman tottered along beside Cecily's brother. Her pale, delicate hand was closed tightly on his arm.

Cecily turned back to Terra, but instead of releasing her, Cecily gripped her tighter. The woman's manicured fingernails dug through Terra's uniform jacket. Cecily somehow managed to keep her face blank, but her eyes glittered with a hatred Terra had rarely seen.

"I'm warning you to back off."

Terra's eyes narrowed. "Off what?"

"I know you've been telling lies about me all over town."

"Hardly—"

"You've been telling people that Harris was afraid of me. How ridiculous. Harris would never have taken out a protective order against me. He didn't need to be protected from me." Cecily kept her voice low and glanced over at her mother with a sweet smile.

She signaled she'd be finished shortly then said to Terra with low venom, "He needed to be protected from *you*. *You* killed him. You and your stupid cases, your investigations.

You put him up to getting that protective order. He would never have done something like that if you hadn't interfered."

"Listen." Terra jerked her arm away from the woman's surprisingly strong grip. "I didn't know anything about that protective order until a couple of nights ago."

But Harris's ex wasn't listening. Terra felt brittle inside, battered. She tried to realize that Cecily was in pain, just as she was, but she was in no mood for Cecily's accusations.

"I still have friends."

"What does that mean?" It sounded like a vague threat.

"I can talk to Mayor Griffin. Do you think Harris's nephew will let you get away with treating me like this? I'm his widow and it doesn't matter how much you hate that fact. You can't change it. If you don't leave me alone, I'll make you sorry you started these lies."

"I know you're having a horrid day, Cecily. This isn't easy for any of us."

"Harris would never have left me if it hadn't been for you. His involvement with you got him killed. You might as well have set that fire yourself."

Hurt and fury exploded through Terra, but before she could turn away, T. J. Coontz was there. The cameraman slipped between her and the other woman.

"Ma'am," he said to Cecily. "May I please walk you to your car?"

"Who are you?" She blinked at him, her voice indignant.

Terra was a little surprised herself. Just then, a deep familiar voice chimed in over Terra's shoulder. "Mr. Coontz is right, Ms. Vaughn. Your family is waiting for you."

Jack didn't even wait for Cecily to speak, just took her arm and escorted her over to where her brother and mother now looked on with concern.

"Are you all right?" Worry darkened T.J.'s hazel eyes.

''Yes.'' She patted his arm. ''Thanks. I had no idea she was going to do that.''

''I saw her heading for you. She looked like trouble.''

Terra nodded, her gaze going over T.J.'s shoulder as she watched Jack firmly guiding Cecily toward a gray sedan.

Dane Reynolds sauntered up, his smoothly pitched voice shrieking over Terra like nails on a chalkboard. ''Was there about to be a catfight?''

T.J. gave him a withering look.

''Would you like to comment?'' the reporter asked.

''About what? That I was talking to Harris's ex-wife?'' The wall she had managed to erect after finding Harris, the wall she'd needed so she could do her job, began to crumble.

''You could make a statement.''

''Not one that's fit to be repeated on television.''

Robin and Meredith rushed up.

''What happened, Terra?'' Robin asked. ''Are you okay?''

She nodded, feeling a tremble start in her legs. She had to get away from here before she unraveled completely.

Robin smiled at T.J. ''Quick moves there.''

''I'm glad I could help.''

''Yes, thank you again, T.J.,'' Terra said. ''Thank you so much.''

''You're welcome.'' The cameraman paused for a moment then said shyly, ''I'm sorry for your loss, Investigator. I know Mr. Vaughn was a friend of yours.''

''Yeah, rough day,'' Reynolds added, eyeing her with a probing curiosity.

Why was he looking at her that way? To see if she was in pain? Tears burned the back of her throat. She reached out and squeezed T.J.'s hand with another thank-you before he walked away with the reporter.

Meredith looked hard into her eyes. "You're not in shock. You need a drink."

Robin jerked a thumb over her shoulder. "I'm going to talk to that witch, Cecily."

"No." Terra grabbed Robin's hand, then Meredith's. The self-protective fog that had enveloped her since arriving at the funeral was swept away on a sharp jab of pain and grief. She'd been trained to work around her emotions, but the funeral, combined with Cecily's verbal bullying, took its toll. "Just get me out of here. Now."

Meredith slipped an arm around her shoulders. "Let's go."

The three of them walked back toward the chapel and across the paved drive to Terra's Explorer. Panic nibbled at her. She felt fragile and empty and on the verge of breaking down. Her two friends were the only reason she didn't dissolve into a useless puddle.

Wondering what the hell Cecily Vaughn had said to Terra, Jack impatiently stuffed the woman into her brother's car with a terse warning that he'd be by to talk to her later. He tried to shrug off the wish that he'd gotten to Terra before the cameraman had.

He stepped back onto the grass, intent on getting to her now and making sure she was all right, but as his gaze shot to the place where she'd been standing, he saw she was gone. He scanned the perimeter of the cemetery. No sign of her.

Glancing around, he noted the news van carrying Reynolds and Coontz as it drove off slowly behind the other two local news channel vans. White limousines carrying the family pulled away from the chapel and down the black-topped drive. Terra's red Explorer was absent. She was most likely with her friends. She'd be fine.

He believed that, but it didn't squelch the disappointment that he'd missed her. Or the growing sense of urgency he felt to check on her himself. A misplaced need if ever there'd been one.

After the heated interest in her eyes that night at the gym, he'd told himself to forget her, told himself to think only about doing his job, but the case wasn't what he was thinking about. It was the stark pain in Terra's green eyes when he'd hustled Cecily away.

The glint of self-satisfaction Jack had caught in Ms. Vaughn's eyes a few minutes ago had been too blatant for him to believe nothing explosive had gone on between the two women. He needed to focus on other things, but until he saw Terra, he knew he wouldn't. She'd shot out of here like a spooked rabbit. Even knowing he might not be welcome, he had to know she was okay.

It wasn't so long ago that he'd experienced a suffocating sense of aloneness, the rippling shock of grief that grew until it froze out every other emotion. Those emotions had swamped him after the death of his wife. If the bleak grief he'd recognized in Terra's eyes earlier was any indication, she was feeling the same. And she'd been given the added bonus of dealing with Harris's ex.

The desperate, almost defiant look he'd seen in her eyes told him Terra was struggling to keep her emotions under tight leash. He could talk to her tomorrow, let her know that he'd received word the fire scene videotape was ready to view. Jack told himself she needed time alone, but that nagging urgency pushed at him to call and check on her. When she didn't answer her cell phone, he said the hell with it and called dispatch for Robin Daly's cell phone number.

The policewoman acted surprised to hear from him, but politely told him that Terra was no longer with her. She had gone to a small gathering in Harris's honor. If Jack couldn't reach Terra on her cell phone, she was at Hotshots with the other firefighters.

He didn't know what Cecily Vaughn had said to her, but Jack did know the aching loss, the look of trapped desperation he'd seen in Terra's eyes. He'd felt it himself the day of his wife's funeral, trying to hold it together for everyone else. He could just imagine the hell it would've been if he'd had to investigate Lori's death as Terra was having to do for her close friend.

He drove north from the cemetery, then turned east onto Tenth Street. He'd told himself at the service that he should be concerned with everyone *but* Terra. Yet she was the one his gaze kept finding, the one he kept wondering about. He'd watched both Cecily and Reynolds during the funeral service, and hadn't really noticed anything suspicious unless you counted the way Reynolds ogled Terra during the whole thing. For that, Jack wanted to haul the guy off and stuff him in the trunk of his unmarked police cruiser.

He rolled his shoulders. The service must've affected him more than he'd realized. His emotions were seesawing all over the place, and most of them were about Terra August.

Besides Reynolds's avid interest in Terra, the reporter's behavior had been insignificant. The only conclusion to be drawn from the reporter's presence at the funeral service was that he'd been assigned to cover the passing of a prominent city servant, the same conclusion Jack could draw about the other reporters in attendance.

As for Cecily, Jack couldn't dismiss her inaudible exchange with Terra. By the pain he'd recognized in Terra's green eyes and the tautness of her body, he'd bet his Oklahoma University football season tickets that Cecily hadn't been offering sympathy.

Still sunny and mild, it was after three-thirty when Jack arrived at Hotshots. Trucks and cars packed the bar's parking lot. He spotted Terra's SUV next to a light pole and parked a few spaces down the row in the nearest spot. The flat-roofed brick building with red-trimmed eaves sat between a wooded lot and a self-serve carwash. Twin oversize hydrants flanked a short sidewalk leading up to a covered patio.

A red neon sign flashed Hotshots over the double front doors. He stepped inside to a haze of cigarette smoke and the cracking of pool balls.

The old brick building had once housed a paint company warehouse. Retired firefighter Dean Schulze had converted it and now ran the place. As far as bars went, the police made few calls here, so Jack figured Schulze was doing something right.

A doorway separated the rectangular entry from the bar area. A collection of miniature fire engines lined a built-in shelf which ran high along the top of all four walls. Well-used firefighter's gear, including a scarred helmet and turnout coat bearing Schulze's name, hung on the wall next to the door. A pair of black rubber boots sat underneath in mock preparation for a fire call. The well-waxed bar, trimmed in brass with a matching foot rail and fitted with black leather stools, looked as if it measured at least thirty feet. Liquor bottles and glasses sparkled in the mirrored wall behind the counter.

Jack stepped aside to make room for a couple coming arm-in-arm through the door behind him. His gaze scanned the haze of smoke, roaming over circular tables for four, booths, a grizzly-bear-size stuffed Dalmatian in the corner. He noticed scrawls on the rough wall and upon closer inspection saw that firefighters from each station house in town had signed their names.

Finally Jack spotted a glint of red-gold hair in the far corner and headed that way. Upon confirming it was Terra, some of the urgency inside him eased. She stood next to the wall, surrounded by a group of about twenty firefighters— men and women. He recognized some of the faces from the funeral. As he made his way through the crowd toward her, he saw a big picture of Harris Vaughn, whom he recognized from photos at the funeral service, propped up on the table to her left.

Vaughn hadn't been a handsome man, but his brown eyes were kind and mischievous, as if he always had a joke to tell. Jack watched Terra closely. She hadn't seen him yet. If it hadn't been for the way she white-knuckled the drink in her hand, he would've thought she was all right. As it was, she looked as if she might be on her last nerve. The whole day of Lori's funeral, Jack sure had been.

"You go first, Ace." A male voice called out and Terra nodded.

Ace? Jack would have to ask her about the nickname. Standing in the back of the crowd, he watched Terra and listened with only half an ear to a joke about a little girl who'd tied her fire wagon to a cat's testicles so she'd have a siren.

Everyone laughed, but Jack's attention centered on the tightness of Terra's mouth, the strain around her eyes that belied the smile she gave at the end of the joke. Someone elbowed him in the ribs and he turned sharply as a guy built like a bulldog jostled his way through the crowd.

Even if the man hadn't been carrying a full beer in one hand and a near-empty one in the other, Jack would've known he was drunk. He didn't slur his speech, but his gaze was unfocused and he teetered with each step.

"I've got one." A red-haired fireman stepped to the front of the circle.

"Go, Ferguson," someone in the crowd yelled.

"A fireman came home from work one day and told his

wife, 'You know, we have a wonderful system at the fire station. Bell One rings and we all put on our jackets. Bell Two rings and we all slide down the pole. Bell Three rings and we're on the fire truck ready to go. From now on when I say 'Bell One,' I want you to strip naked. When I say 'Bell Two,' I want you to jump in bed. And when I say 'Bell Three,' we're going to make love all night.'''

Some in the audience snickered. Terra's mouth curved into a bare smile.

''The next night, the fireman came home from work and yelled, 'Bell One!' The wife promptly took all her clothes off. When he yelled 'Bell Two!' the wife jumped into bed. When he yelled 'Bell Three!' they began making love.

''After a few minutes, the wife yelled, 'Bell Four!' 'What the hell is Bell Four?' asked the husband? 'Roll out more hose,' she said. 'You're nowhere near the fire!'''

Roars of laughter followed Ferguson's joke and Jack noted that even though Terra's smile widened, it was wobbly. He doubted she'd stay much longer. He'd say hello and ask how she was doing, then leave.

The burly fireman who'd rammed into Jack a few minutes ago pushed his way to the front of the circle and glared over at Terra.

''Don't start anything, LeBass.'' Ferguson reached out and clamped a hand on the bulldog's shoulder.

''Shut up.'' LeBass shrugged off the man's hand and leaned toward Terra.

There was enough malice in his voice that Jack took an involuntary step toward her.

''Ya know, August, seems to me like it's taking you a long time to figure out who torched Harris. If I were the fire investigator, I'd already know. You might as well have torched him yourself for all the good you're doing.''

Even in the dim lighting, Jack saw Terra's face pale. He

pressed his way between two men who were as tall as he was.

"If you were worth anything as a fire cop, these serial arsons would already be solved and Harris would still be alive."

"Hell, LeBass," said a man nearby.

Her body rigid, Terra stared flatly at the red-faced fireman.

Probably all of those in the intimate community of firefighters knew there was a serial arsonist out there. It wasn't LeBass's knowledge of the nonpublicized connections between the fires that had Jack's eyes narrowing. It was the hatred in his voice.

"If I'd gotten that job instead of you," the man lashed out, "I would've already nailed this firebug."

A heavy silence fell over the group.

After a long, awkward moment, a petite, dark-haired woman stepped up. A firefighter, too? "Stick a sock in it, Don."

"It's okay, Shelby." Terra's gaze didn't waver from LeBass.

"Don't you have anything to say for yourself, August?" he taunted.

She stared at him with no expression on her face, but Jack saw a slight tremor when she reached down to grip the edge of the table next to her.

"What does the mayor say about how long it's taking you to find his uncle's killer?" LeBass yelled.

"Shut the hell up, you idiot." Ferguson grabbed one of LeBass's arms. An older man Jack recognized from the Vaughn fire scene grabbed his other arm and together they hauled him through the crowd while he blustered more of the same.

"Ignore him, Ace," someone advised. "He's drunk."

"And an ass," someone else added.

Terra nodded, her features composed. Coldly composed. Jack sensed she was tethering her emotions with everything she had left. He watched as she smiled emptily at those around her and calmly placed her still-full drink glass on the table. He tried to catch her eye, but she turned, wove her way through several people to a side exit, and disappeared.

Throat tight, Jack followed. If Terra had indeed beat out Don LeBass for the fire investigator job, he could be setting the fires to make her look bad. The guy sure seemed to have enough hatred in him to do it. The fireman who so obviously resented Terra had put himself on Jack's suspect list; he'd be the next to check out.

Jack found Terra outside at the far east corner of the building. She stood with her back to him, one shoulder braced against the brick wall. "Terra?"

She jerked around, eyes wide. "What are *you* doing here?"

"Sorry. Didn't mean to startle you." He moved slowly, trying to show her he wouldn't crowd. "I didn't like how the Demented Widow cornered you earlier."

"The Demented Widow? That's good." She gave a small laugh, brushing at her cheeks.

Was she crying? She'd certainly taken her share of hits today, first with Cecily, then the firefighter inside. He eased closer. "Want to talk about it?"

"Cecily made some threats, nothing physical. Just that she'd make me lose my job. She's mad that we've been asking questions about the V.P.O."

"I meant, did you want to talk about Harris?" Jack asked quietly.

Her eyes filled with tears and his heart clenched. She looked fragile and lost. But when she spoke, she jerked a thumb toward the bar and said dryly, "Don't you want to ask me about LeBass?"

"Are you okay?"

"Yes."

"We can talk about him later."

"Surely you have questions about Cecily."

"I'm not *all* about work." He smiled into her eyes though what he wanted was to take her hand, touch her in some way.

"I thought…shouldn't we talk about the case?" In the shade of the building, her eyes were dark and troubled.

"I came to check on *you*. We can talk about whatever you want."

Tears spilled onto her cheeks and she brushed at them angrily. "I can't believe Harris is gone. How can he be gone?"

"I'm sorry."

Her gaze, raw and vulnerable and lost, met his. The last of her composure slipped and she buried her face in her hands. Her shoulders shook violently.

Jack wrapped his arms around her and pulled her to him. He wasn't sure if he should. Hell, he wasn't sure of anything when he was near her.

She stood stiffly in his embrace for a long moment, then her arms went around him, clutching at him as if he were the only thing holding her up. Hot tears burned through the shoulder of his suit jacket where her head rested.

Sobs racked her body and he felt her tense up in an effort to stop them. "It's all right, sweetheart. You've been working nonstop on this case and haven't given yourself a break. Harris was your friend. It's okay to think of him that way."

After Lori had died, Jack had reacted exactly the same way—throwing himself into work. Trying to remain professional.

A choked sob escaped Terra and Jack's heart ached. "I really admire how you've investigated this case. I know it's difficult to draw a line when the victim is someone close to you."

She relaxed a fraction, the entire length of her body seeking contact with his. Her breasts, her hips, her thighs.

His hold tightened. He'd been in this kind of anguish before and there were no words that could ease the pain. He cradled her close, his lips against her hair. Breathing in the sweet fragrance of her shampoo, the scent of woman made his pulse throb, but he refused to give attention to the way his body hardened. She needed someone, the way he'd needed someone after Lori's death. His parents and sister had been there for him. Who did Terra have? Right now, only him.

Her sobs quieted. He continued to hold her, relieved when she exhaled a deep breath.

"I can't believe he's gone," she said into his jacket. "Can't believe we're not further along in finding his killer."

"It all takes time, and being patient is the hardest part. But we'll get this slimeball, Terra. We will."

She lifted her head, lashes spiky with tears. "Promise?"

"Yes." He stared deep into her eyes.

She gave him a ghost of a smile. "I'm gonna hold you to that, Spencer."

"Good." He rubbed her arms, forcing himself to step back slightly and put a little distance between their bodies. "Sometimes you have to vent that emotion churning inside you. You've been working solid on Harris's case, not allowing yourself to think about anything other than the job. I know, because I've been there."

"I guess you have." Her eyes reflected the knowledge of his wife's death, a dark compassion he wanted to share. If she'd let him.

Emotion shifted across her face. Even in the shadows of wavering sunlight, he could read a gratefulness. And the same hunger he'd seen a couple of nights ago in the police gym.

Her gaze drifted to his lips, back to his eyes. "You called me sweetheart."

"I did?" Had he? He must have. "Yeah."

She leaned slightly forward, inviting yet tentative. Warm, moist breath washed against his lips and her breasts teased his chest. Desire ignited inside him in a quicksilver molten stream, but he moved slowly. Giving her time to realize what he meant to do, to step away if she didn't want this. Trying to give himself time to do the same thing.

The only sensation he registered was the hard beating of his pulse in his head, his groin. He had to taste her. Wanted to put *his* taste on her. He gently caressed her now trembling lips with one finger, lightly dragged his hand down her silky throat. How long had he wanted to touch that creamy skin? He couldn't mistake the plea in her eyes, the invitation when her lashes fluttered half-shut. Beneath his touch, her pulse skittered.

His skin burned. He rested his thumb in the hollow of her throat, his pulse racing as wildly as hers. He claimed her lips and took what he wanted, what he'd denied wanting. He sipped at her, touching her with his tongue only when she made a tiny sound in the back of her throat, when her shaking hands framed his face to hold him to her.

Jack had the fleeting thought that his knees might give out. He backed her into the wall, savoring the rich, dark taste of her, the velvet heat of her tongue against his. Every wicked curve of her body fit him. He slid a hand down to her breast, hit with a savage need to take her. Here. Now.

She moaned, pressing into him. Her arms gripped him tighter, growing more frantic. He stilled her by gently cupping her nape, tilting her head back so he controlled the kiss. Agonizing in its deliberation, yet giving the sharpest, purest kind of pleasure. She clung to him, wild desperation in her touch.

Only his wife had ever sparked this kind of fierce want fused with need. It had been so long since he'd felt anything for a woman. Was that all this was? A connection with someone for the first time since his wife's death? Terra ignited an all-consuming slow burn that somehow seared away the scars from Lori's death.

Jack broke the kiss and lifted his head, breathing hard. His muscles strained at the command to stop.

Terra's eyes opened, dazed and clouded with passion. The raw hunger in her face nearly had him pulling her to him again, taking harder this time, rougher.

She sagged against the wall. "Wow."

He briefly closed his eyes, swallowed a string of curses as he clenched his fists to keep them at his sides. He couldn't get involved with this woman. With Terra's job, risk was a fact of life. Daily. Just like being a cop. He'd lost his wife to violence. No way could he put his heart on the line again for a woman who walked a high-wire for a living. He and Terra were partners on this case, but nowhere else. He couldn't forget that again.

"Jack?" She sounded confused, her voice raspy with longing.

Slowly, reason seeped back, past the lust roaring through him. He backed up a step, his voice ragged. "This is a mistake. It isn't smart. For either of us."

She touched her lips, looked as if she might kiss him again. And he'd let her, dammit.

"You're right," she said, her chest rising and falling as rapidly as his.

He wanted to press her against that wall and take what

she'd offered just seconds ago. So he turned to leave. "Talk to you tomorrow."

"Did you have some news about the case?"

It was then that he realized he hadn't given a single thought to the investigation from the minute he'd laid eyes on her in the bar. Even the shadows couldn't hide the dark circles under her eyes, the fatigue etching her face. "Nothing that can't wait until tomorrow. Get some rest."

She nodded. "Thanks for coming, Jack. To the funeral."

"You're welcome." He saw no regret, just the remnants of desire he'd felt minutes ago. And wanted to feel again. Damn.

His body tightened as he forced himself away from the circle of her heat. That kiss was the best thing to hit him in years and it couldn't happen again. Not with her.

He didn't go back inside, but walked around the building and across the lot to his car.

Why did the woman who finally tripped his trigger have to be a fire chaser? Fire was as dangerous a weapon as Jack had ever seen or used. There was more potential for jeopardy in her job than had ever been in Lori's and his wife had been gunned down.

The feel of Terra's lips still burned his. What the hell had he done?

What he'd wanted to do for quite some time now, he admitted. And he didn't regret it. But he couldn't let it go any further, either.

Chapter 7

A mistake.

Jack had called that consensual, bone-melting liplock a *mistake.*

The words every woman longed to hear, Terra thought wryly the next morning. Even after a good night's sleep, the memory of Jack's seductive taste, the want that had streamed through her like hot silk had her clenching her hands on the steering wheel as she headed to the police station to view the now enhanced videotape. She'd kissed him back as if she were trying to give him some competition for the world kissing title.

A mistake.

Hmmph. Could she pick 'em or what? First Keith, now Jack. She could tell when a man wanted to kiss her and Jack Spencer had wanted to. But then he'd pulled away.

Through the haze of building desire, Terra had registered the look of shock, then agony that had sharpened his features. Something had definitely gone through his mind, but what?

Had she misread him? It was possible. She'd been running on pure emotion. Drowning in it. Harris's funeral had brought to the surface all the grief and anger Terra had managed to work around during the past week. The service was the first time she'd let herself *feel* anything since finding him.

The final goodbye to her friend, her dealings with Cecily and LeBass's accusations had blurred the line she'd drawn between personal and professional. The kiss with Jack Spencer had erased the line. Still, her pride wouldn't have been so wounded if she hadn't almost puddled at his feet. The man had nearly melted her socks off.

She'd wanted to sink into his kisses and forget about the investigation for a while, but thank goodness she hadn't. Jack had made it plain he regretted what had happened between them. Dismissing a sharp stab of disappointment, Terra determined she'd be all business from now on. She could forget that kiss. In about twenty years.

Pulling up to the police station, she nosed her SUV into a spot in front of the door. She needed to focus on catching the serial arsonist. Jack Spencer was going to help her do that and that was *all* he was going to do with her.

At least she'd gotten some sleep. Though still fatigued, as she would be until they caught this torch, she had enough clarity to realize she'd needed comfort last night and Jack Spencer had given it to her. She wouldn't make more of it than that.

As she walked into the police department, she felt a little awkward about her upcoming meeting with Jack, but he'd never know it. Hell would freeze over before she'd bring up the *mistake* that had rocked her to her toes.

Since it was a Sunday, only a skeletal crew manned the

station. She thanked the officer who'd led her through the vinyl-floored squad room and around several desks assigned to homicide detectives. The instant she set eyes on Jack in the small windowless room where they would view the tape, her stomach gave its usual funny flip.

He stood in the center of what looked like a break room. A metal table along the wall to her left held a coffeemaker, foam cups and a television set. An old refrigerator squatted in the corner.

At Terra's approach, he looked up from a file. "Hey." His cool blue gaze flicked over her, setting off a shimmer in her nerves. "How are you today?"

"Fine." She couldn't help giving him the once-over. Before, she'd always seen him in slacks and a suit coat. Today worn, faded jeans gloved the muscular thighs she'd glimpsed at the gym and he wore weathered black cowboy boots. His broad chest was covered by a long-sleeved denim shirt. Her gaze drifted to his hands. She recalled their gentle touch on her face and the way he'd leisurely ravaged her mouth, as if she were the only one who could quench his thirst. Her heartbeat tripped. "How…are you?"

"Good. Thanks." He gestured to the opposite corner. "This is Denny Larkin. He's one of our lab techs."

The lanky man had to be at least six foot seven and Terra hadn't noticed him, which sent a jolt of irritation through her. She walked over and extended her hand. "Hi. Terra August."

"Hello." His soft-spoken tone matched his sandy, ragged hair and dark puppy dog eyes.

"Thanks for helping us out with the video."

"Happy to. Hopefully, you'll get something you can use." A slight flush colored his neck. "It's ready when you are."

Jack looked at Terra. "I asked Denny to stay in case you had questions or wanted something further done."

Maybe he had also asked the lab tech to sit in so he wouldn't have to be alone with the woman who'd practically climbed him like a tree last night. Which was fine with Terra.

"Great," she said cheerily, determined to forget last night had ever happened.

Jack's gaze searched hers for a moment before he walked over to what she now saw was a combination TV/VCR.

Sliding her purse strap off her shoulder, she moved around the small table where Jack stood. She placed her bag on the table and glanced at the medium-size television set in front of her. Sinking down into a folding chair behind the table, she tensed when Jack pushed the door shut.

"Denny said there would be less glare if we closed the door."

She nodded, chiding herself for being so jumpy. She dreaded seeing the torched remains of Harris's house, that was all. Even though she hoped they found something useful on the videotape, she was ready to be finished with it.

Closeted as they were, the room seemed to shrink even more. Or maybe it was just that Jack looked huge in the small space, his shoulders as wide as the door frame. Considering that she'd literally cried on those shoulders last night, Terra knew firsthand how broad they were, how naturally her head rested on his chest. She slashed the thought from her mind, forcing her attention to the videotape as Jack plugged it into the VCR. "Have you looked at the tape yet?"

"No, I wanted to wait for you."

"Thanks." She wouldn't have viewed it without him either.

He watched her carefully, his gaze softly probing. "You ready?"

Needing to be as objective as possible, she tried to filter out her swirling emotions until her primary thought was the video. At least they would view only the outdoor shots. Still, she struggled to keep the interior images out of her mind. Since learning of the large dosage of drugs in Harris's system, Terra felt a new horror at the thought of the murderer's premeditation. The Halcion had been an obvious attempt to disable him so he couldn't escape the fire at all. The viciousness of the act turned her stomach.

Biting her lip, she nodded. "Ready."

Jack picked up the remote and leaned against the table, his long legs stretched out in front of him. He sat only inches from her, close enough that she could feel his warmth, smell the woodsy scent that lingered in her memory from last night. She laced her fingers together on the table and forced back the anxiety crawling up her throat.

He punched a button and the screen flickered to life. The video started at a point nearly a minute before the shadowy figure became visible.

In the background, Terra heard the muted voices of firefighters and police officers issuing orders, offering aid. Her gaze stayed glued to the scorched scene as the camera panned across the front of the yard. In the strobe of police lights, water glistened on leaves; tree trunks shone darkly wet. Charred scraps of wood, twisted metal and pieces of glass littered the grass.

The west side of Harris's house came into view and Terra swallowed past a catch in her throat, squeezing her hands tight. The edge of the front porch. A yawning hole that had once been a window. The brick corner of the house. Then…there she was. A woman.

Terra leaned forward, straining to make out the mystery

woman's features in the shadows. The face was grainy, too blurry to identify. Terra searched for any recognizable feature, hair color or style, anything. But the harder she looked, the more scratchy the picture seemed to become. She blinked to refocus her gaze.

"What's that?" Jack pointed, pausing the tape. "A ring?"

"I can enlarge it if you need me to," Denny said, startling Terra, who'd forgotten all about him.

She shifted her gaze downward, following the direction of Jack's finger. The woman in the video wore dark clothes and except for her pale face, neck and hands, she melted into the tree she huddled against. Her arms were crossed in front of her, as though holding herself. Her right hand, resting in the crook of her left arm, was almost completely visible. Terra's gaze snagged on the ring Jack had seen.

"Yes—" Adrenaline pumped through her and she surged out of her seat.

"What is it?" He straightened with a frown.

Terra leaned forward. "Ring on the third finger."

"Right."

"It's…it looks like…." She stepped back and studied hard, making certain her eyes weren't playing tricks on her.

"What?" Impatience scored Jack's voice. He squinted at the screen. "What, dammit?"

She was sure. Her gaze met Jack's. "That ring is shaped like a butterfly. A diamond butterfly."

"That's what I thought, too," Denny said.

"And?" Jack prodded.

"Cecily Vaughn has a ring just like that."

Jack stared at her for a long minute, then glanced back at the television. "Are you sure?"

"Yes. She had it on the other day when we were there."

Jack frowned. "I remember a big ring, not a butterfly ring."

"Trust me." Terra looked again at the picture. "I'm sure. If it's not her ring, then someone has one just like it."

"If it *is* her ring, it means she was at Harris's house the night of the fire," Jack pointed out.

"And not home alone." Terra tried not to sound too excited, but they'd finally gotten a lead. "Her alibi is busted."

"With the victim's protective order in place, she would've been in violation if she'd been caught anywhere near his house."

"And if she were angry enough about that V.P.O. to go to his house…"

"And set fire to it—"

Jack's words made nausea boil up in Terra's throat, but she nodded. "We've got motive and opportunity."

"It's time to pay Ms. Vaughn another visit. You up for it?"

"You bet." She glanced over her shoulder at Denny. "Can we get a print of that shot?"

"Sure. Just give me a minute."

The lab tech retrieved the tape from the VCR and stepped out of the room. Terra paced the few steps to the refrigerator and back. She knew that had to be Cecily's ring.

Terra was taking the interview this time, even though the anger boiling through her made her want to wrap her hands around Cecily's neck and shake the truth out of her. It was probably a good thing Jack was going with her. "Grieving widow, my Aunt Fanny," Terra muttered.

"It'll take Denny a few minutes," Jack said. "Can I get you anything? Coffee or water? Although I don't recommend the coffee."

She smiled, telling herself they weren't really alone. The intimacy of the space was deceptive. The lab tech was only

a few feet away. So was the sergeant who'd shown her back
to the break room. "I'm fine. Thanks."

His gaze searched her face.

If he was looking for signs of her breathless response to
his kiss, he'd be out of luck. "What is it?"

"Did you get any sleep?"

"Do I look that bad?"

"You looked pretty beat last night."

Last night. Her pulse skipped. Was he asking if she'd
stayed awake because of that kiss? Had *he?* "I slept fine."

"You sure?"

She nodded, wondering at his concern. "Did you?"

"Me? Sure." He raked a hand through his dark hair.
"You had a pretty tough day yesterday. Cecily's little out-
burst, then the firefighter at Hotshots."

"LeBass is a jerk. I've learned to live with it."

"What's the story there?"

"He applied for the fire investigator position when I did."

"He's obviously resentful about not getting the job. I
hope you didn't let him upset you. He seems like a hothead.
Or is he like that only when he's drinking?"

"He's like that when he's *breathing.* That's one reason
he wasn't promoted."

"Do you think he could be setting these fires to make
you look bad?"

Terra's eyes widened. "That hadn't occurred to me. Do
you think so?"

"He's boiling over with bad blood toward you. Who better than a firefighter to get away with setting fires? Plus he'd
have the added attraction of making you look bad for not
solving them."

Terra had never considered it. "You could have a point,
but the job promotion happened four years ago. If the motive is revenge, why would he wait until now?"

"I don't know. I just know it's another angle we should check."

"If we're going to consider firefighters as suspects, it could be someone besides LeBass."

"Got any other enemies?"

"Not that I know of." She grimaced. "That's an ugly thought."

"Having enemies?"

"Yes. Plus the whole idea of a firefighter arsonist is creepy. Although I did read a story last year about two firefighters in New York state who were arrested for starting fires. They were trying to ensure their jobs."

"There was also the firefighter in Colorado and the one in Arizona."

"True."

Denny stepped inside the room and handed Jack an eight-by-ten photo. "Here ya go, Detective."

"Thanks, Denny."

The man nodded, his gaze going to Terra. "Nice to meet you, Investigator."

"You really helped us out here, Denny. We appreciate it."

"You're welcome." He smiled shyly then left.

Jack passed the photo to her. Terra thought the woman's features no more clear in the picture than they were on the screen, but the diamond clusters and shape of the butterfly ring were unmistakable. How could Jack have spied this before she had? *She* was the one familiar with this ring.

"Ready?" he asked.

She nodded, looking up to find him watching her steadily. Carefully.

"You sure you're up for this? She won't be happy to see us."

"You mean she won't be happy to see *me*. I'm ready."

He'd asked twice if she were all right. Why was he being so solicitous? Did he want to make certain she was steady enough to deal with the upcoming interview and the nasty turn it was sure to take when they showed Cecily this photograph? "I can handle it, Jack."

"I know, but if we need to take some time before we go talk to her, we can. If you want to regroup, we don't have to do anything until you're ready."

"I'm okay." He wasn't patronizing her; he was being sincerely considerate. The same way he'd been last night when he had followed her out of Hotshots to check on her. And look where that had led. To a big mistake, according to him.

"I'll be interested to see what Cecily has to say about the V.P.O.," she said. "And the fact that this is probably her standing outside Harris's house while it's burning."

"Yeah, it should be interesting." That too-intense edge still lit his eyes.

Heat crawled under her skin, but she ignored it. "Should we call to tell her we're coming?"

"No."

She wove her way among the detectives' desks and started down the stairs.

He followed. "So, why do the firefighters call you 'Ace'?"

She glanced at him over her shoulder. "The guys in my class gave me that nickname because I was the first girl to ax my way through a door during a drill."

"Really?" He sounded impressed.

She didn't turn to see. Once outside, he offered to drive.

"I'll take my Explorer," she said. "Just in case I get a call or something." It was a legitimate reason, but she could tell that he understood she didn't want to ride with him.

"Okay, I'll see you there."

It took less than fifteen minutes to reach Cecily's house. Terra worked hard to keep all thoughts of Jack and that kiss out of her mind. Instead, she concentrated on tamping down the urge to strong-arm the woman when she came to the door, looking fragile and small in a shell pink sweater and slacks.

"Detective?" She acknowledged Terra only with a glance.

"Cecily, we've got some questions we need to ask you." Considering the steam building in her blood, Terra thought she sounded amazingly calm.

"What kind of questions?" The woman's brown gaze shot daggers at Terra.

Jack shifted so that his shoulder slightly blocked Cecily's view. "First, I need to read you your rights, Ms. Vaughn."

"What! Exactly what are you doing here?"

"Just asking questions," Jack said. "Ms. Vaughn, you have the right to remain silent."

Terra barely kept from tapping her foot impatiently as he read Cecily her rights. She knew he was smart to do it. They didn't want any technicalities that Cecily might use later to get off.

"Do you understand these rights as I have read them to you?"

"Yes." The woman crossed her arms and smiled smugly. "You can ask whatever you want. I have nothing to say."

"Not even about the victim's protective order Harris had issued against you?" Terra clenched and unclenched her fist in an effort to keep her voice level.

Cecily stabbed an accusing finger at her. "He never would have done that if not for you."

"We have proof you were outside Harris's house while it burned." Seething, Terra stepped up, her shoulder brushing Jack's.

Shock flashed through the other woman's eyes, followed by panic.

Terra thrust the picture at her. "You don't want to explain this?"

Cecily glanced at the photo then looked at Jack, her lips firming. "I have nothing to say."

Anger swept through Terra, hot enough to put a painful throb in her temple.

Calmly, Jack said, "You'll have to come with me, ma'am. We need to talk to you at the station."

"I already told you, I won't talk."

"Fine, that's your right, but you will come with me." His voice turned hard and even Terra admitted he was intimidating. "Call your lawyer and have him or her meet you there."

Cecily glared at Terra. "I'm not going anywhere with her."

"No, ma'am. You're going with me."

Terra had never wanted to drag someone by their hair, until now. The urge passed quickly, but she decided it was best to head for her SUV while Jack waited for the other woman to call her lawyer.

She couldn't let Cecily upset her. She couldn't allow Jack Spencer to either.

A couple of minutes later, Terra heard the front door slam and she turned to see Cecily walk sedately down the porch steps with Jack and quietly get into his unmarked police cruiser.

"Meet you at the station?" He looked concerned, probably because he thought she was about to explode.

"Yes. I'm right behind you." She slid behind the wheel of her Explorer and followed him out of the subdivision.

She used the drive time to calm herself. If she were upset, she'd be no good during the interview. Thank goodness Jack was calm. He was a good partner. He had been the one to spot that ring, after all. Which bothered her, Terra admitted.

She should've been the one to see it on the videotape. The kiss she'd shared with Jack must have distracted her more than she realized. Which was a good reason to forget it had ever happened. She wasn't letting hormones come between her and finding the serial arsonist who'd murdered her friend.

She hadn't been able to compromise her job for Keith. She wasn't doing it for another man either.

Terra August was getting under his skin. He liked looking at her, liked listening to her, pretty much liked every damn thing about her. Despite the fact that he could tell she was teed off about last night. She wasn't rude toward him, but she was guarded. Jack hated that even though he knew better than to try and rectify it. Distance was good. If she were the one imposing it, all the better. He obviously couldn't be counted on to use *his* common sense.

Cecily Vaughn didn't break her silence on the way to the police station. Which gave Jack too much time to think about Terra. Since that kiss last night, all he'd done was think. About the taste of her, the feel of her. When she'd shown up to view the videotape, he had barely been able to keep from staring at the long sleek legs encased in denim, the firm curve of her bottom. He had put the mental brakes on hard during the watching of that videotape. Her sweet musky scent drifted softly around him, torturing and inviting at the same time.

And he wanted to *take*. He wanted her with a fierceness he couldn't ever remember feeling before. Hell. His hand had clenched on the remote more than once when her scent slid into his lungs. When memories flashed through his mind of the feel of her breast in his palm, the urge to run his hands up under the cinnamon-colored sweater she wore today had him breaking out in a sweat.

He might—*might*—be able to get past physically wanting her, but she intrigued him as well. She was a good investigator. She was the one who kept things professional between them, even while he was trying to figure out how. She hadn't let on about that kiss at all, not in the deep green of her eyes that had turned jade with passion last night, not in the skitter of her pulse. She'd been calm, businesslike. And wary.

Jack knew that was for the best. It also annoyed the hell out of him. He didn't like the distance between them, even though he should've been the one to put it there. In the harsh light of day, Terra might feel he'd taken advantage of her last night. Maybe he had, but just the memory of the way she'd met him kiss for kiss made his body harden. Still, she'd been through an emotional shredder yesterday.

He remembered being filled with a rawness after Lori's death, the desperation to feel something. *Anything.* That was probably why Terra had kissed him with such abandon, such surrender.

With a jolt, he realized he had reached the police station. He parked and led Cecily to the front door where Terra met them. Neither woman spoke, which didn't surprise Jack, but it did underscore how different things were between him and Terra today. Not exactly awkward, but definitely not comfortable.

Still, she partnered up with him during the interview with no hint that anything was wrong. As though they'd done this before, she let him lead, putting the pressure on Cecily exactly when he would have, backing off when he would have. His respect for her grew and Jack knew he could be in serious trouble if she showed the slightest interest in pursuing what had happened between them last night.

The cool remoteness in her eyes when she looked at him made it clear she wasn't pursuing it.

Professional distance was one thing. Distrust was another. He had to find out exactly which one he was dealing with. Judging by the glint of stubbornness he'd seen in her eyes more than once, he knew he would have to be the one to clear the air between them. To investigate this case, they had become a team.

While they were boxed into the interview room with Cecily and her attorney, Terra managed admirable control. Despite the emotion trembling beneath her questions, she kept her voice even. But two hours later, Cecily had given them nothing new. Terra held it together, but he could read the anger swirling in her eyes, turning them a deep stormy green.

How could she not be upset? They'd caught Harris's ex-wife violating a protective order *and* busted her alibi, but they couldn't prove she had anything to do with his murder or the fire. A couple of times, he had wanted to smash his fist through a wall. Terra had to feel the same level of frustration.

Finally they were forced to allow Cecily to leave with her attorney. A few minutes later, Terra said her goodbyes as well.

He walked with her out to the parking lot, noting the fury in her clipped strides. In the short time they had been left alone, Jack had picked up on an unmistakable skittishness in his fire investigator. She stayed several feet away from him and the rigid set of her shoulders told him she expected him to respect the invisible barrier she'd put between them.

"Well, that was like spitting into a high wind," she said with disgust. "The only thing Cecily admitted was violating the protective order, and that was just because we had a picture of her doing it."

"We'll keep digging. We'll find something."

"I hope you're right. Even knowing she was there, I have a hard time believing she could do this to Harris." Her voice shook. "How anyone could."

She took out her keys and turned when she reached her vehicle. The midafternoon sun burnished her hair to golden fire. "If she doesn't have anything to hide, then why doesn't she talk?"

He shook his head. "We can't hold her, but we can keep asking questions. Like does she have a prescription for Halcion?"

"And did anyone ever hear her threaten to kill Harris?"

"Right."

"The thing that really bugs me is that she stayed in the shadows while Harris's house burned."

"If she loved him as much as she says, why didn't she run for help? Try to call 9-1-1?"

Terra nodded. "Or why didn't she panic?"

"Maybe she didn't know Harris was inside."

"Still, I'm a trained firefighter and I had to learn to remain calm around a blaze. I know she explained that she arrived after the firefighters were already on the scene, but she just stood there. It's pretty convenient that she arrived just before the video camera was set up."

"I agree, but we can't *prove* she didn't."

"Right." Her features darkened.

"There's a whole lot about her I don't like. We'll keep after her until we find something."

"Do you think we will?"

"That's our job." He grinned, hoping to coax a smile out of her. Maybe get her to relax her guard just a bit. He didn't get either.

She was wound tight, from the top of that gorgeous head to the soles of her leather loafers. Tension pulsed from her.

"I thought you were going to blow a gasket in there," he said. "You sure you're okay about all this?"

"I don't like it, but I'm dealing with it." She opened her door and he decided to just go for it.

"Terra, there's something we need to talk about."

She stopped, frowning as if she really had no idea what he could want.

"About last night?" he prodded.

In a heartbeat, her face changed from animated and slightly flushed to cool, composed. Her eyes went flat. "Oh, the *mistake?*"

Ouch. "I shouldn't have put it that way."

"If that's the way you feel—"

"It isn't. It is. Wait." He held up a hand. "I wasn't trying to take advantage of you."

"I didn't think you were," she said firmly, carefully. Stepping away from her vehicle, she shut the door. "I did kiss you back, remember?"

As if he could ever forget. "That kiss wasn't a mistake because of you."

Her eyebrows arched.

He tried again. "I liked it. More than liked it. You aren't the problem."

"I didn't see anyone else standing there."

His gaze slid over her. Even now, he wanted to reach out and take more of what he'd had last night. "It's me. I'm the problem."

"Really?" She folded her arms and leaned against her truck with a this-had-better-be-good look on her face.

"I have a problem with your…"

"With what?"

He waited, long enough to put suspicion in her eyes. "Too distracting. *You're* damn distracting."

"Back at you."

Silhouette authors will refresh you

Silhouette ROMANCE®

DIANA PALMER

MERCENARY
WOMAN
SOLDIERS OF FORTUNE

The Family & Adventure Collection...

We'd like to introduce you to the
Family & Adventure collection, a wonderful
combination of Silhouette Special Edition® and
Silhouette Intimate Moments® books.
Your 2 FREE books will include 1 book from
each series in the collection:

**SILHOUETTE
SPECIAL EDITION®:**
*Stories that capture
the intensity of life,
love and family.*

**SILHOUETTE
INTIMATE
MOMENTS®:**
*Roller-Coaster
reads that deliver
fast-paced
romantic
adventures.*

Your 2 FREE BOOKS have a combined cover price
of $9.50 in the U.S. and $11.50 in Canada, but
they're yours FREE!

We can't tell
you what it is...but
we're sure you'll like it!
A FREE gift just for giving
the Silhouette Reader
Service™ Program
a try!

SPECIAL
FREE GIFT!

Visit us online at
www.eHarlequin.com

Your FREE Gifts include:

- 1 Silhouette Special Edition® book!
- 1 Silhouette Intimate Moments® book!
- An exciting mystery gift!

▼ **DETACH AND MAIL CARD TODAY!** ▼

©2001 HARLEQUIN ENTERPRISES LTD. ® and TM are trademarks owned by Harlequin Books S.A. used under license.

(S-SI-07/03)

Scratch off the silver area to see what the Silhouette Reader Service™ Program has for you.

FREE BOOKS

Silhouette®
Where love comes alive®

YES!

I have scratched off the silver area above. Please send me the **2 FREE** books and gift for which I qualify. I understand I am under no obligation to purchase any books, as explained on the back and on the opposite page.

329 SDL DU33   229 SDL DU4K

FIRST NAME	LAST NAME

ADDRESS

APT.#	CITY

STATE/PROV.	ZIP/POSTAL CODE

Offer limited to one per household. Subscribers may not receive free books from a series in which they are currently enrolled. All orders subject to approval. Books received may vary. Credit or debit balances in a customer's account(s) may be offset by any other outstanding balance owed by or to the customer.

THE SILHOUETTE READER SERVICE™ PROGRAM—Here's how it works:

Accepting your 2 free books and gift places you under no obligation to buy anything. You may keep the books and gift and return the shipping statement marked "cancel." If you do not cancel, about a month later we'll send you 6 additional books from the Family & Adventure collection–3 Silhouette Special Edition books and 3 Silhouette Intimate Moments books, and bill you just $23.94 in the U.S., or $28.44 in Canada, plus 25¢ shipping and handling per book. That's a total saving of 15% or more off the cover price! You may cancel at any time, but if you choose to continue, every month we'll send you 6 more books from the Family & Adventure collection, which you may either purchase at the discount price or return to us and cancel your subscription.

*Terms and prices subject to change without notice. Sales tax applicable in N.Y. Canadian residents will be charged applicable provincial taxes and GST.

If offer card is missing write to: Silhouette Reader Service, 3010 Walden Ave., P.O. Box 1867, Buffalo NY 14240-1867

DETACH AND MAIL CARD TODAY!

BUSINESS REPLY MAIL
FIRST-CLASS MAIL   PERMIT NO. 717-003   BUFFALO, NY

POSTAGE WILL BE PAID BY ADDRESSEE

SILHOUETTE READER SERVICE
3010 WALDEN AVE
PO BOX 1867
BUFFALO NY 14240-9952

NO POSTAGE
NECESSARY
IF MAILED
IN THE
UNITED STATES

He grinned, then shook his head. "So what are we going to do?"

She didn't answer immediately. Instead her gaze shifted, focused on the empty parking lot. "Our jobs?"

"Yeah?"

"Look, you're a good cop and I like working with you. I want you to help me catch this torch." She met his gaze straight on. "But I don't want things to be weird. If that…if what happened last night is going to be something you can't handle, just let me know."

"No, I can handle it. Even if I couldn't, it's not like either of us can bail now."

"That's right. So, let's keep things professional."

"Just partners." He wished like hell he could stop thinking about the sweet dark taste of her. The hot satin feel of her mouth on his. The weight of her breast in his hand.

"Just partners," she said.

"Okay, deal."

They shook on it and she got in her vehicle to drive away. Jack stood watching until her taillights faded from view. He should have told her about Lori, should've told Terra why he couldn't get involved with another woman in a dangerous profession.

But she had said business only, and he agreed. Last night, it had been the vulnerability in her eyes, the raw loss that had moved him to take her in his arms, but it was the feel of her body against his that had scrambled his brains. He'd shifted into a mode where he cared only about easing the trembling in her body, finally tasting the lips that he'd wanted to taste the first time they'd met. His body had taken over, but it hadn't been long before his head caught up. He couldn't risk opening his heart to another woman whose chances for risk were higher than the wife he'd lost.

Terra August was the one woman who tempted him to

do it. The need she'd ignited in him had made Jack question his own rules about getting involved with a woman in a dangerous job. From now on, he had to keep his hands to himself.

Chapter 8

Jack had managed to keep his hands off Terra for four days. He hadn't actually *seen* her during those four days, but as far as he was concerned, he got points for not touching her.

As he drove to the Channel Four studios in Oklahoma City to meet her, he told himself he could stick to the agreement they'd made on Sunday at the police station. Business only. Still, he couldn't deny that the urge to nudge things over the line to personal chipped away at his reservations about the risks of her job. Spending time together had shown Jack that the risks Terra faced were about equal to his.

Which only made the desire burn hotter. In fact, respect and passion overlapped too much for his peace of mind.

She was a good investigator, despite the added baggage of knowing and being close to the murder victim. She thought things through, kept her mind open to all possibilities. The trouble she'd had controlling her anger toward Cecily Vaughn's antagonism would've been experienced by anyone. Jack knew plenty of cops who wouldn't have been able to keep their cool as well as she had. Maybe himself included.

Besides looking like something he'd dreamed up, she was sharp, intelligent and levelheaded. It would take a better man than him to keep his thoughts strictly on business.

The memory of that kiss constantly tiptoed around his thoughts and now it hit him again, hardening his body. Before it could flower into full-blown fantasy, he squelched the thought and pulled into the asphalt-paved parking lot of the television station.

Several cars occupied the spaces in front of the flat-roofed building. Terra waited for him next to her SUV.

An hour ago, he had called to tell Terra that the woman in Denver responsible for filing a restraining order against Dane Reynolds had returned from her vacation and he'd finally spoken to her. Terra wanted to be in on the interview with the reporter, which was a good idea, but the thought of being with her still put a kink in Jack's gut. They hadn't seen each other in four days and had spoken by phone only twice. Once to touch base about this visit to Reynolds, the other so Jack could tell her that his checking had revealed Cecily did not have a prescription from her regular doctor for the sleeping pill, Halcion. But both Jack and Terra agreed Cecily could've gotten it elsewhere. He planned to follow up on that.

Terra looked trim and chic in a cinnamon-plaid jacket and cinnamon slacks. The short jacket, which zipped snugly atop a deep rust turtleneck, nipped in at her waist. Her fire investigator's badge nestled on a chain between her full breasts.

She wore her hair back today in a neat twist, drawing his gaze to her sculpted cheekbones and elegant neck. Midafternoon sunlight skimmed over lush curves. Jack swallowed hard as he got out of his truck and set his mind on the questions he wanted to ask the reporter.

"Hi." Terra's voice was friendly, but her green eyes were unreadable. Guarded.

Jack was willing to meet her halfway; he hoped he carried it off as well as she did. "Hey."

He had it under control. He even managed to smile as he held the door for her, allowing his gaze to trace her lean curves just once more.

A young woman with waist-length brown hair welcomed them into the reception area. The news channel's logo spread across the wall behind her. Jack pulled out his badge and told the girl they needed to speak to Reynolds.

Having called the station earlier, Jack knew the reporter was here. The receptionist paged the man and a few minutes later, Reynolds strolled through a door to Jack and Terra's right.

He sauntered over to Terra as if he expected her to fall at his feet. "Hello, Luscious. Change your mind about having coffee?"

Despite the way Jack's jaw tightened at the pet name Reynolds used, he suspected Terra's reaction would knock the guy down a peg or two.

She tapped her badge. "We're here to ask you some questions, Dane. I think you know Detective Spencer."

The man's gaze moved unwillingly to Jack. "Detective."

Jack pocketed his badge. "Would you care to talk in private, Reynolds?"

Even though the reporter shrugged, Jack saw his gaze flash to the receptionist.

"We can talk in the break room or outside, if you'd rather."

"Outside is fine," Reynolds said quickly.

He told the receptionist he'd be back shortly and pushed

through the door Jack and Terra had entered moments before.

Jack gestured for Terra to precede him to the shade of a tree starting to lose its gold leaves.

The reporter grinned at Terra, his gaze roaming down her body. "Interested in that interview now?"

Jack jammed a hand in his pocket. He didn't think the reporter's grin would look so perfect if he were missing a few teeth. "We're here to ask you some questions."

"About what?"

The overheated way Reynolds stared at Terra had restlessness charging through Jack. He shifted from one foot to the other. "We have information that you left your anchor job in Denver a year before your contract expired."

"Yeah. Is that a crime?"

"A woman named Nina Fontaine filed two complaints of harassment against you and obtained a temporary restraining order. That's not exactly getting along with your neighbors," Terra said.

The reporter arched his eyebrows. "That order was ridiculous."

"How so?"

Jack liked how his fire investigator got right to the punch. Reynolds gave that insolent shrug again. "She liked the constant attention."

"Evidently not." Terra crossed her arms.

A smile slid across the reporter's face. He leaned toward Terra as if confiding in her. "I only gave her what she wanted."

The look of disgust on Terra's face reflected exactly how Jack felt. "I've spoken to Ms. Fontaine at length, Reynolds. We know you made harassing phone calls, followed her after she broke up with you."

"I never harassed her." The man's icy gaze sliced to

Jack. "She filed that order as some kind of power play, to put me in my place. Nina liked making my life miserable."

"That's not the way she tells it."

"Do *you* understand women, Detective?"

Jack thought about his kiss with Terra and how unaffected she'd seemed when they decided to keep things strictly business.

The reporter's gaze shifted from Jack to Terra. "Why are you asking questions about Nina? I haven't seen her for almost two years."

"Have you been in contact with her?" Jack asked.

"I just said I haven't."

"You said you hadn't seen her," he reminded evenly. "No phone calls, letters? E-mails?"

"No. If she's saying I talked to her, she's lying."

"Maybe you should worry about what you need to be saying to us." Jack glanced at Terra and saw how intently she studied the other man.

Reynolds noticed, too. He gave her that smarmy smile. "Do you have any leads about this serial arsonist, Investigator? Are you looking at anyone?"

"Yes, we are," Jack answered with a penetrating stare.

"Seems you've got some pretty interesting things in your past, Dane," Terra said carefully.

"Don't you?"

"Nothing like having a restraining order filed against me."

Reynolds' gaze flickered away briefly. "I told you about that."

"So, why did you leave your job so quickly?" she asked.

"Because this one opened up. When I got the offer from Channel Four, I didn't see any reason to hang around Denver. I applied for this job several months before I heard anything.'' He flashed a smile at her. ''When they offered it, I took it. I had no control over the timing.''

''So, the job offer conveniently came at the same time the restraining order was issued against you?'' Jack said.

Reynolds crossed his arms and sent him a smug look. ''That order had nothing to do with why I left Denver.''

Jack stomped on the urge to drag the guy down to the station. ''Aren't people in your business bound by contracts?''

''Yes, but people do leave before their contracts expire. Mine stated if I did so, I couldn't work in a competing market for eighteen months.''

''Oklahoma City isn't a competing market?''

''The contract clause refers to a same-state or same-region area.''

''Then you moved here?'' Terra asked.

''Yes.'' Again, his gaze hop-scotched over her body. ''I've never been sorry.''

If the goon didn't stop looking at Terra as if she were his favorite snack, Jack thought there were probably a couple of ways he could make the reporter sorry. His voice came out rougher than he'd anticipated. ''Do you have a prescription for Halcion?''

''What's that?''

''A sleeping pill.''

Reynolds shook his head.

''Where were you the night of the fire at Harris Vaughn's house, before you showed up to cover the story?''

''When was that? About two weeks ago?'' Frowning, he glanced from one to the other. ''Am I a suspect?''

Jack thought the surprise that lit the reporter's eyes was genuine. ''Do you want to call a lawyer?''

''I don't need one.''

''Good. So where were you?''

"Home in bed. Alone, unfortunately. That fire was around midnight, if I recall." His gaze shifted to Terra. "How about if I answer your questions, you answer some for me?"

"That's not how it works." Jack struggled to diffuse the irritation burning through him.

The reporter pressed on. "If you went on the record with me, Terra, you'd get the word out and perhaps receive some useful information."

She had already talked to Jack about the idea, but neither of them wanted to tip their hand on any part of the investigation.

She considered Reynolds for a moment. "What kind of questions?"

Excitement lit the man's eyes. "What do you have on the investigation so far? How many fires has this guy set?"

"We were hoping you could answer that last one," Jack put in.

"I know of four, but I don't have all the information our lovely investigator does."

"I meant, perhaps you'd know from personal experience."

Surprise flared in Reynolds's eyes at Jack's bluntness. "You're just not going to let it go, are you?"

"Want a lawyer now?"

His gaze swung to Terra. "Do you think I started those fires, too?"

"You have been at every fire, Dane."

"So have you," he said archly.

She gave him a flat stare.

Jack knew he had no claim on her, but he couldn't stop the possessiveness that welled up inside him, the fierce urge to protect her. But he kept his hands and his thoughts to himself.

Reynolds glanced at his watch. "If that's all, I have an assignment."

"We may have more questions," Jack cautioned with a hard stare. More than once during this interview, he'd wanted to make it clear to Reynolds that Terra was Jack's territory and to stay the hell away. But she wasn't, and he hadn't.

Dane waved a dismissive hand at them. "I think I've been more than cooperative. Angel Face, if you change your mind—"

"She won't." Jack barely kept from snarling.

Terra frowned in his direction as she answered Reynolds, "If I decide to do an interview, Dane, I'll let you know."

"Thanks." He sent a stone-cold look Jack's way before turning and going back inside the building.

Jack's gaze shifted to find Terra studying him. "What?"

"Nothing. What do you think about Reynolds?"

"Love his alibi," he drawled.

"Yes, me, too. Home alone, can't be proven." She puffed out a breath as she retrieved her keys from the pocket of her jacket.

"What did you think?"

"He could smile the chrome off a bumper," Terra muttered.

Jack chuckled. "Or die trying."

A smile curved her lips. "Do you think he was telling the truth about why he left Denver? That it had nothing to do with the restraining order filed by Nina Fontaine?"

"It has a ring of truth to it," Jack admitted slowly. "We certainly can't prove otherwise. Yet."

"True. We're at a dead-end with Cecily right now, too."

"I plan to ask her friends if she ever mentioned Halcion and also see if anyone heard her threaten to harm Harris."

"I can ask the firefighters about threats, too."

"Good." The spicy-sweet scent of her drifted to him on the air and Jack's body tightened. He scrambled to keep his focus. "I'll see if I can learn anything else about Reynolds from Miss Fontaine."

"Keep me posted and I'll do the same."

"You got it." He waited until she'd driven off before he pulled out of the parking lot.

Reynolds set off Jack's radar. He didn't know if it was because his instincts screamed the reporter was hiding something or because he'd made his intentions toward Terra crystal clear.

Jack didn't much like either option. He'd made a deal with Terra that things between them wouldn't get personal, but he worked with a woman who made him ache and want and imagine. He wanted to get a helluva lot *more* personal.

It had been two days since she'd seen Jack, and Terra's body hadn't stopped humming. Anticipation was the only word to describe the low-level vibration inside her, but she had no idea what she was anticipating. She and Jack had agreed to keep things strictly business and so far, they had. In fact, she thought she'd handled things very well at the police station last Sunday and again at the television station on Thursday, especially considering that she hadn't been able to stop thinking about his kiss. Or wondering what his real reasons were for not wanting to get involved.

"I have a problem with your... Too distracting. You're damn distracting."

He had sounded as if he were going to say something else. Something that didn't have anything to do with her being distracting. He had a problem with *her.* Her...something. Her job, her hair, what?

She wasn't going to pursue it, but that didn't mean she could just switch off the attraction she felt for Detective

Yummy. She'd done pretty well about keeping him out of her mind, except when she was at home alone. Like now.

As she prepared for bed on Saturday night, she changed into her Presley Fire Department T-shirt and brushed her teeth. The guy could drive her crazy, if she let him.

Work around it. That's what she'd done and what she would continue doing. As she climbed into bed, she turned her thoughts to Cecily. She hadn't had any luck finding anything else that further incriminated the woman. The firefighters she'd spoken with so far couldn't recall ever hearing Cecily threaten Harris. Or even recall Harris mentioning the two of them had fought.

Harris had been an extremely private person. She and his two buddies must've been the only ones who knew how fractious things had gotten between him and his ex-wife. Cecily's friends would probably know something, but Jack had said he would talk to them. If he had turned up anything new, he would've called.

So far, their one-phone-call-a-day had been restricted to touching base about updates, of which there were none.

Terra felt as though she'd just gone to sleep when her pager buzzed. It was just before midnight and dispatch advised her of a car burning in the driveway of a middle-class neighborhood.

She dressed quickly in jeans and layered a sweatshirt over her T-shirt, jamming her feet into socks and tennis shoes at the front door. She reached the scene on the south side of town in about ten minutes.

As she stepped out into the cool fall air, she pulled on her turnout coat. Flames crackled and swarmed out of and around a small black compact. A firefighter stood in the middle of the street, videotaping the scene. The smell of gasoline hung heavy in the night, but she would run a careful check for other accelerants before drawing any conclusions. So far, this didn't appear to be her serial arsonist's pattern.

She pulled on her steel-soled rubber boots and made her way through the streams of water in the street over to Captain Maguire, who stood talking to a thin, young woman.

Terra stepped over the hydrant hose, noting that Station Four already had the fire contained. The woman with Captain Maguire gestured wildly toward the smoking car.

The burly man caught Terra's eye and motioned her over. "This is Investigator August. I want you to tell her what you've told me, okay?"

"Okay." The girl's voice shook as she turned toward Terra. Tears streaked her narrow face and she kept her arms crossed tight. A lightweight T-shirt and boxer shorts emphasized her lankiness.

Captain Maguire draped his turnout coat over the shivering girl. "Investigator, this is Lisa Perkins."

"Hi, Lisa." Terra smiled reassuringly. "Do you feel up to talking to me?"

"Yes." The girl glared toward her car. "I think I know who did this."

"You do?"

The Captain stepped back and mouthed to Terra that he would set up her portable floodlights.

She nodded, then gave her full attention to the woman.

"My boyfriend. I mean, my *ex*-boyfriend."

"What's his name?"

"Tom Estes."

"Did you see him do it?"

"No, but we had a fight earlier. I told him I wanted to break up and he was really, really mad."

"But you didn't see anything?"

"No, I was asleep. I heard a noise and woke up."

"What kind of noise?"

The girl paused thoughtfully. "Like an explosion, I guess."

"Are you hurt?"

"No. When I saw my car burning, I called the fire department and went out the back."

"Good thinking." Terra patted the girl's shoulder, feeling her shiver.

Tears trembled on the girl's lashes. "That car was almost new. I bought it two months ago."

"I'm sorry."

The girl nodded, her face pale and angry in the streak of strobing police lights from the black-and-white cruiser on the scene.

"Can you wait here while I take a look around?" Terra asked.

Lisa nodded and Terra walked over to the smoldering hunk of metal that had once been Lisa's car.

The bright white of floodlights bathed the area surrounding the car. The driveway was scorched, as were the branches of an overhanging oak. Firefighters squished through the grass on either side of the vehicle, rolling up their hoses.

Captain Maguire walked her around the scene and through the house. They both agreed there was no further threat to residents or the house, which had been spared. Terra retraced her steps with the captain and stopped in the street next to the firefighter who stood videotaping the scene.

"I've gotten every angle, Investigator," the man said. "I think I'm about finished."

"Keep it rolling for a while, okay, Poe?"

He nodded as Terra walked back toward the car, pulling on her heavy gloves and automatically sliding her hard hat onto her head. Firefighters moved around her, finishing up with the hose and stowing equipment. She glanced up in time to see Don LeBass stride toward her.

"It's been a whole ten minutes, Ace." His voice lashed at her. "Surely you've got this one figured out by now."

She met his gaze head-on, but didn't speak. Resentment flooded his features and he stomped off toward the ladder truck with an ax over his shoulder.

"Don't let him get to you, Terra." Rusty Ferguson stopped beside her, removing his hard hat to wipe at the sweat and soot on his forehead. "He's just sore about not getting the F.I. job."

"That was four years ago. He needs to move on."

Rusty shook his head. "No, I mean his latest try."

"His latest try?" Terra glanced at LeBass, who slammed a side door on the ladder truck.

"He was turned down about three or four weeks ago. Didn't pass his assessment."

Three or four weeks ago? Right before Harris's murder. Harris had been a consulting assessor for the Oklahoma City Fire Department, but as a former city employee, he wasn't allowed to assess candidates applying for positions to Presley's fire department. "Who gave him a negative review?"

"Harris Vaughn."

Terra's gaze swerved sharply to Rusty. "LeBass applied to OCFD?"

"Yeah. He figured you weren't going to retire any time soon. Plus with the budget crunch, who knows when we'll get another fire investigator."

Terra had been promised one in the next fiscal year, but maybe that wasn't soon enough for LeBass. Besides, he would've known she wouldn't welcome working with him and probably expected her to fight his application. She watched LeBass disappear around the side of the ladder truck. "I bet he was pretty hot."

"He did blow off some steam," the firefighter admitted.

"To Harris? Did LeBass make threats?"

"Who knows? He can be pretty mouthy when he gets going."

None of the firefighters Terra had spoken with so far had heard Cecily threaten Harris either, but it didn't mean the threats hadn't happened.

Harris's negative evaluation gave LeBass another motive for arson besides revenge against her, but murder? He certainly had the knowledge to do what had been done to Harris. She had to call Jack.

"Hey, you okay?" Rusty touched her arm.

"Yeah, sure. I better get busy."

"We'll stick around for a while. Captain said you want to keep the camera rolling."

Terra nodded as she picked up her tackle box and moved to the driver's side of the charred car. Broken glass crunched as she sloshed through puddles of water. Keeping an eye on LeBass, Terra pulled off one of her heavy gloves and unclipped her cell phone from the waistband of her jeans. She found Jack's home number, which she'd put in her phone's memory after he'd called her regarding the woman in Denver.

He answered on the third ring, his voice gravelly and sexy with sleep. Terra's stomach did a funny flip-flop.

"Sorry to wake you, but I'm at a fire scene. I wonder if you could meet me here?"

"Sure. What's going on?"

She didn't want to risk being overheard by LeBass or anyone else. "I'll tell you when I see you."

"Okay."

She gave him the address, then disconnected and got to work.

After about fifteen minutes, Terra concluded this blaze

wasn't the work of their serial arsonist. The drive and car reeked with the sharp odor of gasoline. Finding a length of cut garden hose under the car convinced her that gasoline, not cleaning solvent, was the accelerant in this case.

She didn't need her "sniffer" to identify the substance, but still, she took samples from the car's upholstery, carpet and paint. The odor of gasoline in the garden hose and a charred lighter bore out the scenario she was piecing together. She also spied a light-colored baseball cap stuck on a high branch in the overhanging oak tree.

Though it might be irrelevant, Terra collected the cap with the handle of her shovel. She carefully put it in a brown paper bag and walked over to the victim. "Lisa?"

The girl turned, the light from an approaching vehicle sweeping across her face. Terra recognized the black pickup that parked across the street and the low-level hum of anticipation which she'd managed to convince herself was gone.

As Jack walked toward her, she struggled to concentrate on the case at hand. He moved through shadow and light with a confidence that was lethally sexy. Though she couldn't see his eyes, she could feel his laser-sharp gaze on her. All over her.

A shiver rippled through her. *Work around it,* she reminded herself. She nodded at him, then turned to the victim.

Jack stopped a good distance away, giving her and the other woman some privacy. Terra opened the paper sack and, still wearing her gloves, carefully removed the hat she could now tell was light gray. "Do you recognize this?"

"Ohmygosh." The girl squinted hard at the hat emblazoned with a local lawn care company's name then shook her head, anger flaring on her face. "That's Tom's hat. I gave it to him last week."

"Is there any reason you can think of why it would be stuck in your tree?"

Lisa looked quickly at the oak. "That tree?"

"Yes."

"I have no idea."

"Okay, we'll talk to him. Thanks for your help."

"Thank *you*. You're going to arrest him, aren't you?"

"We have to talk to him first."

"Do I need to do anything else?"

"I'll want to talk to you again after I've talked to Tom."

Lisa nodded, her mouth setting firmly. "What an idiot."

Terra smiled in agreement. "Do you have somewhere you can stay tonight?"

"Yeah, I can call a girlfriend."

"Write down the address and phone number for me so I can get in touch with you." Terra pulled off one glove and reached inside the pocket of her heavy coat. "Here's my card. You call if you need to. For anything."

The girl took the card, swiping at the tears on her cheeks. "Thanks."

Terra squeezed her shoulder. "If you'll go with Captain Maguire, he'll get you a phone."

"All right."

The captain led Lisa to the police cruiser where she could sit comfortably.

Tugging on her glove, Terra stepped back up on the curb. Jack joined her. "What happened here?"

"I'm still putting things together, but it looks like a jilted boyfriend tried to get even."

"That's his hat?"

"Yes."

Jack's gaze traveled up the massive oak. "How did it get up there?"

"I've got an idea, but I need more information." She

tapped the bag which held the cap. "Not as good as a fingerprint, but we'll see where it gets us."

She looked around to see if LeBass were within hearing distance. He stood next to the ladder truck with Ferguson and two other firefighters.

The driveway and yard had been cordoned off with crime-scene tape. Terra ducked beneath it and Jack did the same. There were questions in his eyes, but he didn't ask them. She knew he was waiting for a signal from her that it was all right. She would feel better once LeBass left the scene, but she didn't know when that would be.

Two of the local news channels had already arrived, including Dane Reynolds and T. J. Coontz, his cameraman. Great. Terra knew it would be a while before she had any privacy, but at least the news media would be kept outside the crime scene tape.

"Walk with me," she said quietly to Jack, moving slowly along the driver's side of the car.

Wearing a black leather jacket and jeans, he looked like a rowdy biker. And sexy as hell. His blue eyes, midnight-dark in the night shadows, burned with intensity.

Warmth spread through her like honey. "Sorry for waking you."

"I figure it was important."

His crooked smile sent a shaft of heat through her. "I picked up some very interesting information about Don LeBass," she said in a low voice.

They stopped at the driver's side window of the scorched vehicle. Jack stood close enough that Terra could see the shadow of stubble along his jaw, smell the dark masculine scent of him. "Yeah?"

His gaze locked on her face and for an instant, Terra wanted to forget why she had called him. Anticipation strummed her nerves into high pitch. Good ever-lovin' grief, the man *was* yummy. And he tasted that way, too.

She cleared her throat. "Rusty Ferguson just told me that LeBass applied for a fire investigator position with Oklahoma City."

"Recently?"

She nodded. "His request was rejected three to four weeks ago because of a negative evaluation."

Jack's eyes narrowed. "From Harris?"

"Yes."

Jack's gaze sliced over the hood of the car to LeBass. "Well, well."

"Hey, Luscious, what do you have here?"

Reynolds. Before turning to face the reporter, Terra gave Jack a look. He tensed, but she stepped in front of him. "I'll release a statement when I know, Dane."

The reporter's gaze slid to Jack, then back to Terra. "I've been thinking about the conversation we had a couple of days ago."

"Oh, yeah?" Jack moved up beside her.

"I just know we can help each other, *Investigator*," the other man said silkily. "I scratch your back, you scratch mine."

"Dane, c'mon." T.J. bumped the reporter's shoulder with his camera. "Knock it off."

Jack planted his hands on his hips, his badge flashing dully at his waist in the dim light. "Buddy, I think Ms. August already made it clear that she's not scratching anything of yours."

"What about answering some questions, then?"

Terra sighed. "Like what? I already told you I haven't reached any conclusions on this scene yet."

"But you've probably reached some on the Harris Vaughn fire. Or the fire at the dentist's office. Or the photography studio." Dane stuck a microphone in her face. "Turn on that camera, T.J. Investigator, do you have any hard evidence in the serial arsons that have plagued Presley in the past couple of months?"

She wanted to strangle him. "Not at this time."

Beside her, she felt tension snap through Jack's body.

"Maybe you can tell the good people of Presley why you called in Harris Vaughn's widow for questioning. Is she a suspect in his murder and arson?"

What?! Terra barely kept from gaping. How had Reynolds found out about that? From the way Jack stilled, she guessed he was as stunned as she was. "No comment," she said.

"Investigator August, isn't it true that you *did* interview Ms. Vaughn at the police station?"

"She said no comment," Jack growled.

Dane aimed his mike at Jack. "Detective Spencer, are you speaking for the fire investigator?"

"This investigation is a joint effort between the Presley police and fire departments."

Oooh, good, Jack, Terra thought.

Dane smirked. "Would you say this 'joint effort' involves more than just the investigation?"

What a jerk. Anger erupted at his insinuation and Terra advanced on the reporter, but Jack beat her there. His handsome features were rigid and furious; he looked intimidating and downright dangerous. Terra wouldn't want to cross him in a dark alley.

He got right in Reynolds's face. "Investigator August has been a lot nicer to you than I'm going to be. She's not interested. She's pretty much spelled it out for you. Back off."

The reporter put his hands up in mock surrender. "Hey, take it easy. I'm just doing my job."

"Go do it somewhere else," Jack growled.

"C'mon, Dane." T.J. nudged the guy away from Terra and amazingly he went.

She realized T. J. Coontz had turned off the camera, thank goodness. She didn't want to speak until Reynolds was a safe distance away, but she wasn't sure she could find the words anyway. Part of her thrilled at the way Jack had put himself between her and squirrely Dane Reynolds. But another part of her was annoyed. They'd agreed to keep things strictly business between them. Jack's riding to the rescue didn't make Terra want to keep things platonic. At all.

"I could've handled that myself."

"I know, and no doubt you would've done it better than I did. But I'm sick of seeing Reynolds bird-dog you." He took her by the elbow and guided her none-too-gently under the crime scene tape and into the shadows of the house.

"Jack?" She glanced over her shoulder, relieved to see that no one seemed to be watching. Especially the reporter. The last thing she and Jack needed was to be shown on the morning news huddled together in the shadows.

He pressed her into the wall of the house, his body lean and hard against hers. He was plainly aroused and Terra's stomach dipped in reaction.

"Jack," she whispered, her hands going up involuntarily to grip his biceps.

"I can't stand to think about that guy putting his hands on you," he gritted out. "Not when that's what *I* want to do."

In the next breath, Jack's mouth came down hard on hers. Hungry, relentless, possessive.

Her world tilted. She gripped his broad shoulders, her legs turning to rubber. His mouth was hot and dark, his tongue stroking hers in a way that had her plastering herself against him. Her body trembled. She couldn't breathe, couldn't think. Didn't want to.

He pulled away, his breathing ragged, his eyes glittering like onyx in the hazy light. "I want to kill that guy for the way he strips you with his eyes."

Terra could barely get a breath. "I…thought…we were going to keep things professional."

"I can't." His eyes darkened with secrets, fire, promises. Terra wanted them all. "Can you?"

Her breasts rose and fell against his chest, the small friction causing an ache between her legs. Lips still moist from his, she looked into his eyes. The raw hunger she saw there, the want also burned inside her. In answer, she pulled his head down to her. "No."

She kissed him this time, but when he changed the pace, she let him. Her knees went soft as he slowly savored her. With one hand, he tilted her head back, the other he slid beneath her turnout coat, resting it just below her breasts. White-hot need clawed through her.

Twining her arms around his neck, she let herself sink into the solid-as-brick chest, the strong thighs splayed on either side of hers. She wanted more. All of him.

He lifted his head, eyes blazing. His breath mingled with hers. Then he kissed her again, softly, quickly. "I thought I was going to have to put some whup-ass on that guy."

She laughed, giddy pleasure and desire tightening her belly. Humor *and* yumminess. She liked that in a man.

Jack's hand slid down and hooked into her waistband. His gaze flared hotly as he murmured, "If there weren't so many people around, I'd show you what I really want to do."

"Same here." Her throat was so tight it hurt. Her gaze didn't waver from his, even though her nerves shimmered wildly.

He grinned, glancing out at the crime scene. He braced one arm against the wall over her head. "I think we should go to dinner tonight."

"Dinner?" she squeaked. "Like a date?"

He nodded, his gaze locking on her lips. "Like a date."

She swallowed. "Okay."

"I'll pick you up around six-thirty. All right?"

"Great." She was proud she could formulate a single word.

The sounds around them penetrated Terra's desire-fogged mind. Captain Maguire yelling at his crew. The deep gunning of a starting fire truck. The calm voice of Paul Lewis, the public information officer for Presley's fire department as he answered questions by Reynolds and his rival reporters.

"We'd better get back out there," Jack said.

"Yes." Terra felt dazed, her nerves jangling just like they had at her first fire. A date with Jack Spencer. After he'd said he didn't want to get involved.

After they'd both said they wouldn't.

This was probably a mistake.

She couldn't wait.

Chapter 9

Jack had a hard time focusing on his job all day. All he cared about was burning daylight so he could see Terra again. He thought about the way she had responded to his kisses. About how he wanted to get her somewhere private and finish what they'd started in the shadows of that fire scene.

But the last thing they needed was word getting out that he'd dragged her behind that house and made out with her like a teenager who had finally gotten past first base. If his common sense hadn't returned, Jack would've taken her right there against the brick wall.

And she would've let him.

The realization heated his blood all over again.

He'd told the truth when he'd said she was too distracting, but he was past caring. Last night, he hadn't given a damn about professional distance or who might have seen them. That was dangerous. It was also dangerous that he had reached the point where he would be more distracted if he *didn't* explore the attraction between them.

Watching Dane Reynolds sniff around her had slammed home to Jack what he had tried to get past. He wanted her. Wanted to know her, wanted to be with her, wanted her beneath him.

He'd been drawn to her from the first moment he'd seen her, but the perceived dangers of her job had kept him at arm's length. Working with her the past few weeks had shown him her job was like his. She was an investigator, not a firefighter. That common ground, and the mind-blowing kisses they'd shared, had erased the last of his reservations about becoming involved with her.

He was amazed to find himself counting the hours, then the minutes until he picked her up for dinner. Even so, he wasn't prepared when she opened the door.

"Hi," she said.

"Hi." His nerves charged as he took in the thick, golden-red hair swirling around her shoulders. Subtle makeup highlighted her sculpted cheekbones and elegant neck. The curve of her glossy coral lips brought memories of her mouth on his and his body tightened.

His interest in dinner right now was zero. He'd much rather stay here and have her. Which was why they should go on to the restaurant. "Ready?"

"Yes." She walked out on the front porch and locked the door behind her.

Despite the no-holds-barred participation Jack had gotten last night, her green eyes were guarded. He caught a glimpse of a gold sweater beneath her tan cashmere coat and brown slacks that hid the model-long legs he'd fantasized about most of the day.

His brother-in-law's sleek black two-door sat at her curb rather than his pickup truck. Jack opened the passenger door, his lungs filling with the provocative spice of her scent as she moved in front of him to slide into the passenger seat. Tracking his gaze slowly up her long, lean legs to her eyes, his heart kicked hard when her lips curved into a slow, lush smile. "Did you see us on the morning news?"

"Yes, and all through the day," she said dryly. "I really liked how Reynolds said there was no comment from either the police or fire department about the official interview with Ms. Vaughn."

"I noticed Cecily's attorney said the same thing."

Terra nodded. "The mayor called me four times today."

"I heard from him, too. I told him we were doing all we could, as fast as we could."

"Same here."

He walked around to the driver's side and got behind the wheel. Shutting himself in the car with her made his gut tighten in awareness of the scent of musky woman beneath the perfume. "I thought we'd go to Newberry's."

"That sounds wonderful."

Good to know she liked steak. And that the intimate atmosphere of the small Oklahoma City restaurant didn't have her going skittish. Sweat slicked his palms and he tightened his grip on the steering wheel. It had been a hell of a long time since he'd been out on a date. Since he'd cared about *being* on a date.

As he headed west toward Western Avenue, he decided if that sissy news reporter got a look at Terra right now, he'd sit up and howl like a coyote. Even if it made him a Neanderthal, Jack didn't try to squash the flare of satisfaction he felt that he, not Reynolds, was with Terra.

Her hair pooled in a thick satin mane across her shoulders, making him itch to thrust his hands into all that silk. The hot dark scent of her settled in his chest. He wanted to see her eyes go all dreamy and soft, the way they had last night.

Jack figured he'd better get a grip and shift his thoughts in another direction. The night was young. "What's the status of your car fire?"

"Case closed." She smiled, relaxing slightly for the first time since he'd picked her up.

"That was fast."

"I got lucky. Once I finished at the scene, I started looking for the boyfriend. Had Presley P.D. looking, too. Just before noon, I got a call about a burn victim at Baptist Hospital."

"He went all the way into central Oklahoma City, huh?"

Terra nodded. "The officer who called said the victim had reported being doused with gasoline in a drive-by, then the guys in the car had thrown a match on him. The name was the same one given to me by the victim so I went to talk to him. It took about an hour, but he finally confessed he 'lit up' his ex-girlfriend's car."

"And lied about being doused by drive-by attackers? I'm shocked." Jack chuckled. "What about the hat?"

"It was his." Terra turned toward him, leaning in slightly. "This is the hardest part for me to believe. The guy sucked gas out of her car tank with that length of garden hose I found, then poured it into the car. He tried to start the fire with lit pieces of paper, but it wouldn't ignite. The air-to-gas mixture was too rich for the enclosed car interior. But after a few minutes—"

"When the air had time to get to it," Jack put in.

"Right. He stuck his whole arm in the window with a lighter. Bam! It caused a minor explosion, which is what woke Lisa. Blew his hat up into the tree."

Jack couldn't help laughing. "Unbelievable."

"Isn't it? The guy's just lucky he sustained only minor burns to his arms and shoulders."

"Is the ex-girlfriend planning to press charges?"

"Yes, and even if she didn't, I would."

"Good."

The next fifteen minutes were spent talking about movies and music. She liked country music and he preferred classic rock, but they both liked thrillers and action-adventure movies.

Even though Terra seemed more at ease, Jack didn't miss the hint of wariness still in her eyes. He didn't blame her. He was a little wary, too.

Once inside the restaurant, the waiter seated them at a corner table in the back of the carpeted room. Muted lights from small tulip fixtures played over the glass-fronted bookcases that lined the walls. Dark wood floors lent to the studylike atmosphere. Rich, deep wine-and-navy upholstery kept the mood soothing and elegant. A string orchestra played faintly beneath the delicate clink of crystal and silverware. The music over the sound system accompanied conversation rather than drowned it out.

"I love this place, Jack."

"Great. I was hoping you would."

She removed her coat and Jack swallowed hard. A soft cashmere sweater the color of old gold cupped her full breasts and tucked neatly into a pair of dark brown slacks that showcased her long legs and firm rear.

"You look great," he said hoarsely.

"Thanks." Pleasure flashed in her eyes and in the flicker of the votive candles on the table, he saw color tinge her cheeks. "So do you."

He'd worn a suit jacket and tie. Until now, he hadn't been aware of what he'd put on, but at least it matched.

The waiter seated her then Jack took his chair. He moved

his napkin to his lap then to the table then back to his lap. Had he been this nervous on his first date with Lori?

In an effort to relieve the tension twisting through his neck, he fell back on work. "I followed up on that information from Ferguson and double-checked the assessment Harris Vaughn gave LeBass. LeBass was given the bad news the week before the Vaughn fire."

"And murder," Terra reminded quietly.

Jack hated the flash of pain in her eyes. He thought about taking her hand, but didn't.

She sipped at her water. "I appreciate you doing the leg work on LeBass's assessment. I didn't have time today, what with the car fire and all the mayor's calls."

"You're welcome. I also ran LeBass NCIC, but I turned up nothing." Terra knew as well as Jack that if LeBass had a record, it would show up in the National Crime Information Center's computer.

"I think we need to interview the guy," he said. "We know he worked the Vaughn fire, but we don't know about the other fires."

"We may have to do more than check his schedule. Even if LeBass didn't work the other fires, he could've stopped by the scene when he heard there was a call. A lot of fire-fighters do it. I know I did, when I was riding a rig."

Jack nodded, making a mental note. Cops did the same thing.

"We can view the fire scene videos again and see if we spot LeBass."

"Good. And his neighbors will be able to tell us how things are between him and his wife. If they've overheard any yelling or witnessed any domestic disturbances. We'll check into the Halcion connection for him, too. Both Cecily Vaughn and Dane Reynolds say they don't have a prescription. I don't have enough to get a search warrant to see if either of them are lying.''

''What about doing surveillance on Reynolds?''

''The victim's protective order against him might be enough to get my captain to okay it. I'll try. If we need to…follow other channels, we can.''

Terra smiled.

''We need to reinterview witnesses at each fire scene, see if they recognize LeBass, Reynolds or Cecily Vaughn. I'm not looking at any other firefighters for this, especially after the new information you picked up concerning LeBass's negative assessment from Vaughn.

''I haven't found anything remotely suspicious about any of the other firefighters. I've had all their backgrounds checked, just like the city did when they were hired. LeBass was the only one from Presley who applied for the fire investigator test in Oklahoma City.''

The waiter walked up and they both ordered steak. After the man left, there was a long moment of silence. Jack noticed Terra stroking her neck in what he'd come to recognize as a nervous gesture.

''Can I ask you something?'' she said.

''Sure.''

She glanced down, aligned her fork with her knife, then raised her gaze to his. ''I know you lost your wife. Do you ever talk about her?''

''Not usually.''

Terra nodded, brushing his hand with her fingers. ''Well, I'm very sorry for your loss.''

''Thanks.'' He paused for a long moment. ''It happened over three years ago.''

''You don't have to tell me.'' She started to draw away, but Jack curled his fingers over hers.

''It's okay.'' For the first time since Lori's death, he

wanted to talk about it. Somewhere over time, the pain had dimmed. There was still loss, a sense of emptiness about that part of his life, but now he didn't feel as if his heart were being ripped out just by saying his wife's name. "She was murdered."

Terra's hand tightened on his.

"She was a social worker. She was arranging to remove two children from their abusive father after he'd nearly beaten their mother to death. The guy found out where we lived and shot her in the driveway. Four times. Lori never had a chance."

"Oh, Jack. I'm sorry."

"Presley detectives caught the S.O.B. and now he's on death row at McAlester."

"Good." Terra's hand stayed locked with his.

He knew she understood the pain, the conflict of having to do her job in a circumstance where a loved one had been killed. Her quiet strength released something in his chest. As if he were finally able to breathe fully again for the first time since Lori had died.

"We had a good life. We were married ten years. Met in college and married a year after graduation. I'd gotten on with the department by then. Lori finished her master's in social work, then was hired by the state."

"No kids?"

"We tried, but it never happened. We were discussing adoption when she was killed. It was best in the end that we didn't have children. I would've been useless to anyone else dealing with her death."

"I don't believe that." Terra smiled at him, compassion and conviction burning in her green eyes. "You've helped me since Harris's death. You're not pushy, but you don't tiptoe around the subject either. I know if I want to talk, you'll listen."

Jack moved his thumb back and forth across her wrist and felt her pulse skitter. If it hadn't been for the stubborn support of his parents and sister, he probably would've eaten his gun at some point. And then he wouldn't have met his fire investigator. "So, what about you? You were married before, right?"

"He was a lawyer, as you know," she reminded wryly, drawing his mind back to the questions he'd asked about her in the hours after the Vaughn fire.

He grinned. "Keith Garcia."

"Yes. We met in college, too. I always thought we were lucky. We both had jobs we loved. Our marriage was good. At least it was until I couldn't spend the time with Keith that he wanted. He made partner at his law firm, which required more politicking, more parties, more out-of-town meetings the spouses were expected to attend. I couldn't take the time away and he resented it.

"He made it clear he wanted me to quit, but I couldn't. I'd already waited two years to test for fire investigations and by then, all the compromise had been on my side. When I received the promotion, he demanded I quit. I guess if I'd done it, I'd still be married."

"You'd be miserable." Garcia should've been glad Terra had moved off the front lines. "Plus you're damn good at your job."

"Thanks." Her hand squeezed his. "I thought I knew him so well, thought I knew our marriage. I didn't. My judgement was way off, but I did learn that I can't give up my job for anyone."

Taking note of the way her voice firmed, Jack nodded. "Me either. In the days after Lori's death, the job was all that held me together."

The waiter delivered their food and, after making sure they had everything they needed, left them alone. Jack's steak was great and Terra seemed to enjoy hers, too. She talked about her grandfather, Joe August, who'd raised her after her parents were killed in a car wreck. Jack told her about his parents and sister, who lived in nearby Edmond.

She touched him easily, a hand on his arm, their fingers brushing when they simultaneously reached for their wine. The sassy scent she wore drifted around him. He wanted to kiss her again, wanted to know if the rest of her skin was as silky as the hand that had curled into his for those few brief moments. Hot need drew tight in his belly and he cautioned himself to go slow.

As the evening passed, the pleasure in her eyes was plain. But so was the occasional cloud of wariness, the doubt he'd seen when she talked about misjudging her marriage.

After dinner, he held her coat while she slipped into it and found his hands lingering on her shoulders. She glanced back at him and smiled.

As he paid for their meal, Jack caught her watching him. Hotly. Curiously. The same curiosity burned inside him.

As he drove her home, they swapped a couple of war stories. His favorite was her most recent case involving the boyfriend and his fire-revenge-gone-bad. He couldn't recall feeling this relaxed with a woman in years. Both of them had been drawn into investigations because of their need to solve puzzles, to get to the root of a crime. He liked that about her, too.

He parked in front of her house and walked around to open her door. When she stepped out, her hair brushed his cheek. He inhaled the fresh, teasing scent of her shampoo and his throat tightened. Placing his hand lightly in the small of her back, he walked her to the front door. Their shoulders touched briefly, sharpening the hum of electricity Jack already felt.

Her porch light threw a shaft of yellow onto the sidewalk.

Terra took out her keys and unlocked her front door, then turned to face him.

"I had a great time, Jack. And thanks for telling me about Lori. I wish I'd known her."

"You would've liked her." His gaze traced her features, lingered on her lips. He was definitely going to kiss her; he just wondered if he could stop.

She edged closer, rested her hand lightly on his chest. "If you don't hurry up and kiss me, I'm going to sound the alarm."

He grinned and hooked an arm around her waist, pulling her into him. Even with her coat between them, he felt the curve of her breasts, her hips against his.

He threaded his other hand through her thick silky hair, slid his palm around to her nape and tilted her head back. Instead of kissing her lips, he kissed her neck. Nipped and laved her with his tongue. She gasped and tilted her head to give him better access. White-hot need slashed through him, but he forced himself to go slowly. He nibbled along her jawline, his body going rigid when she made a sound deep in her throat.

She slid her hands up his arms, over his shoulders. Her fingernails scraped lightly across his nape. He took her mouth, his blood hammering with a searing desire that fogged his thoughts. He focused on the need thundering through him, the woman in his arms who kissed him back with enough fervor to push him over the edge.

She fumbled for the door. "Come in, come in," she said against his mouth.

He did, functioning solely on the heat driving through him, the heady scent of the woman who slammed the door behind him and dragged him to her.

Each kiss went longer, deeper, hotter. He pushed at her

coat and she shrugged out of it. He kicked it out of the way. She tugged off his jacket, fumbled with his tie.

He yanked at it, loosened it while she unfastened the buttons on his shirt. Sliding his hands up her rib cage, he tugged the hem of her sweater from her slacks and peeled off her top. She felt like velvet and cream beneath his palms. She bent and pressed kisses on his chest, up to his neck as she spread his shirt wide.

Want drove through him in unrelenting waves. He backed her against the door, lifted her arms over her head so he could look at her. Lush breasts swelled over the top of a flesh-colored lace bra; rosy nipples peeked out at him.

With one hand, he kept her arms pinned loosely over her head. With the other, he touched her magnolia-smooth skin. Traced the valley of her breasts, skimmed the crest and dipped his finger inside her bra. She shifted against him, urging him on.

Heart thundering in his ears, his gaze locked on hers. She mouthed his name. For the first time since he'd met her, her gaze was totally open, vulnerable. Pleading.

He cupped her breast, his heart pounding so hard he thought it would blow through his chest. She pressed into him, dropping her arms to pull him to her. Her mouth—that gorgeously wicked mouth—closed over his, kindled an ache to have her kiss him all over.

He dragged his thumb across her nipple, teasing it to a hard peak. Sliding one bra strap from her shoulder, Jack leaned down to capture a pink nipple in his mouth. A breath shuddered out of her as she arched against him.

"Stay, Jack. Stay with me."

That was all he wanted. She dragged her fingernails down his back, cupped his flanks as her thigh slid between his legs and pressed hard against his erection. Then her hands found him, stroking him, urging him. Despite the barrier of his slacks, he felt her touch like a branding iron. He surged into her hand.

"Stay for tonight," she said. "Just for tonight."

It was then he realized how far they'd gone. And exactly what he wanted. Pleasure throbbed through his body on a sharp ache that edged into pain.

"Wait. Terra, wait."

"What is it?" She drew back, looking at him with heated eyes. Her face was flushed, her hair tousled. Her pulse pounded wildly in her throat.

"Are you sure?"

"Yes." She put her hand over his, hugged it to her bare breast. "Don't I feel sure?"

"I know you want me." His hands shook as he stroked a stray tendril of hair away from her face. "I want you, too. But I want more than one night."

She blinked up at him.

"You've got to be sure that's what you want." Biting off a curse at the tight pressure of his body, he gently took her hands between his. "This thing between us isn't going away and I don't want to move too fast. When we make love, I want you to be sure you want more than one night. Are you ready for that?"

Wariness flashed through her eyes before she masked it.

"I want you to be able to trust your judgement when you get involved with me."

"But I—"

"Do you?" He gently slid her bra strap back up, wondering if he was the biggest idiot ever born. She was vibrant and beautiful and sexy. And he was walking away. "There's no hurry. We have time, if you're interested."

"I'm definitely interested." She looked dazed, gathering the edges of his shirt and trying to button it. His tie hung halfway down his back. One shirttail was out, the other in.

Hard and aching, he bent and picked up her sweater. She took it, holding it to her breasts protectively. Shadows of doubt still clouded her eyes.

"You're right," she said. "I really can't think straight when you're kissing me like that. And I do need some time."

He hated the uncertainty he'd seen, the uncertainty he'd reinforced. He thought about saying to hell with it and taking her to the floor. "It's okay if you change your mind about wanting to pursue this, but I hope you don't."

"I hope I don't either."

For an instant, Jack thought he'd made the worst mistake of his life. But he wasn't cut out for one-night stands. He wanted Terra's trust as much as he wanted her body. Wanted her to believe getting involved would be the right thing. A good thing. "You let me know. I want you to be as sure as I am."

She nodded, her face still flushed, her lips still swollen from his kisses.

Despite the want clawing through him, he knew this was right. He wanted her to know, too. "Good night," he said hoarsely.

"Good night," she whispered, pressing a soft kiss on the side of his mouth.

She opened the door and he picked up his jacket, stuffed his tie in the pocket. He gently ran his thumb across her bottom lip then turned and walked to his car. Behind him, her door shut quietly. Hell, he *was* the biggest idiot ever born.

Jack couldn't sleep. A stop at the gym and five rounds with the punching bag hadn't relieved the frustration boiling inside him. Pure physical need. How long had it been since he'd felt this sharp gnawing ache for a woman? Too long to remember.

Exhaustion pulled at him, but his mind refused to click off. More than the razor-edge of need sawed through him. He'd never thought he would open his heart again, but Terra's spirit, her intelligence, even her hesitation to get involved had opened a place inside him that he would've sworn was irreversibly sealed.

Fighting the remembered feel of her breast in his hand, the taste of her, Jack tried to empty his mind and go to sleep. After long, futile minutes, he resorted to his most extreme sleep-inducer and turned on the television. He punched the remote until he came to one of those home shopping channels that always put him out.

Finally the tautness inside him eased and he drifted off. In and out mostly, caught between reality and dreams where green eyes still invited. Where the phantom feel of Terra's body finally soothed him.

A crashing noise jerked him awake. He automatically reached for his 9mm Glock and sat up slowly, his hand closing around the familiar steel. His breathing shallow, heart thundering, he tried to identify the noise as he moved silently out of his room, up the hall and toward the front of the house.

Before he reached the living room, a bitter odor drifted to him. Smoke? Just as he thought it, a thin wisp of black floated down the hall toward him. He thought he heard something crackle.

He drew even with the corner of the living room wall and— What the hell!

Flames shot up from his carpet. Bright orange, they stretched higher, longer, traveling across the floor and lapping at a chair leg, reaching for the sofa.

He'd been expecting a burglar, not fire.

Coughing, he started to run across the room and grab a bucket from his garage when a cracking noise sounded, this one in front of him. The window flanking the front door crashed inward. Something dark hit the floor twenty feet away from him, shattered, then exploded with an ear-splitting burst.

Jack reflexively threw his arm up to protect his face. In the half second before he turned away, he recognized the object as a bottle. A Molotov cocktail.

Eyes burning now, he hit the floor. Flames erupted, reaching out to gorge on the fire already racing along the floor. Dark gray smoke filled the room as if expelled by a rocket and he coughed. Heat seared his lungs.

The fire moved like a tide, washing over the sofa, flowing to the walls. He had only seconds before the thing reached him. Killed him.

Gripping his gun tightly, he stayed low to the floor, moving on his belly back to his room. Thick smoke obliterated his already limited vision, making him as good as blind. It didn't matter. His eyes watered too badly for him to see anyway. Every breath stung his lungs.

His hand finally curled around the doorjamb. His bedroom. Staying on the ground, choking on the smoke that chased him from the living room, he scrambled to his bed, slid his hand along the edge of the frame and groped for his nightstand. From there, he charged straight to the window.

He could hear the fire now, spitting and hissing, tearing its way toward him. Yanking up the mini-blinds, he fumbled for the locks and threw open the window. He punched out the screen. Turned and grabbed his badge and cell phone from the nightstand, and a pair of sweatpants from a chair next to the window.

Then he dove for safety like he was the next big-screen action hero. He hit the ground, jolting his shoulder painfully, but he kept moving until he was several hundred feet away from the house. He sucked in clean air, his lungs screaming. Chest heaving, he punched in 9-1-1 on his cell phone and gave his address, watching in shocked disbelief as flames snaked out of his living room window.

The damp grass chilled his feet and the sensation finally pierced his dazed astonishment. Jack jerked on his sweatpants and ran to alert his neighbor, Mr. Plumley.

What in the hell had just happened?

Chapter 10

Jack's hands were on her, stroking, teasing, torturing. Just as he peeled off her panties, a noise trilled in her ear. And trilled. And trilled.

She tried to hold on to the dream, but the annoying chirp ground it into dust.

Terra pushed up on one elbow as she registered the beep of her pager. Several seconds passed before her training kicked in and the sensual fog of her dream slid to the back of her mind. Her breasts, sensitive and heavy, were reminders she couldn't disregard as easily.

She rolled out of bed, struggled into her jeans, a long-sleeved T-shirt then a flannel shirt. En route to the scene, she called dispatch from her truck.

When Maria gave her the address, the lingering warmth of Terra's dream disappeared in a frigid swell of panic. "Repeat, Dispatch. Repeat."

"1718 Antelope Drive."

Jack's house? "Are you sure?"

"Yes," the other woman confirmed. "You all right, Investigator?"

"I'm on my way. ETA ten minutes."

"I'll radio the responding unit."

When Terra arrived at Jack's, the blaze was out, but her heart rapped painfully against her ribs. She parked up the street ahead of a ladder truck and rushed out of her SUV, sloshing through the water in the street toward the curb of the neighbor's drive. Black-brown smoke hazed the chilly night air, hanging like a veil over the trees of the older subdivision. Anxious to find Jack, her gaze skimmed the blackened front porch, the sodden yard, the driveway.

"I want to know, dammit!" Jack's voice sliced through the air.

Terra turned in time to see him slam Dane Reynolds up against the back end of Station Two's ladder truck. Relief that Jack seemed all right collided with apprehension. What in the world was he doing?

She darted across the pavement toward the two men. A turnout coat covered his broad shoulders and he wore steel-soled rubber boots like hers. "Jack!"

A female police officer raced from the other direction. Terra reached him and Reynolds, saw the reporter straining on his tiptoes in an effort to escape Jack's grip.

Reynolds's eyes were slitted, fervid with anger and uncertainty.

"Jack, let go. What's going on? Let go!"

He didn't seem to hear her. He pinned Reynolds to the fire truck, one hand wrapped around the man's throat. "You got here before the first officer on the scene. Why is that?"

"I...heard it...over the scanner," the reporter rasped out. "I wasn't...far away."

"You never seem to be far away."

"Jack, please. Let go." Terra put her hand on his arm. He felt like a solid block of steel.

The female officer, red hair tucked into her uniform cap, moved over to Jack's other side. "Spencer, take it easy. Let the guy up for air."

"Jack, tell me what's going on." Terra kept her voice low and steady, but her heart hammered like a hyped-up junkie.

He looked over at her, a flicker of recognition in his eyes.

"Let go." She kept her gaze locked on his, trying to penetrate the raw fury she saw there. She pulled at his wrist in an effort to ease the vice grip he had on the reporter. "Jack, please."

He stared at her for a moment, refusal making his eyes obsidian hard.

"Come on, Detective." The female officer shouldered her way between the two men and stared Jack down.

His gaze shifted back to Reynolds. His blue eyes burned with a hard light Terra had never seen. She didn't think she wanted to see it again.

He jerked his hand off the reporter's neck, saying to the other officer, "Get him out of here, Russell."

Reynolds bent at the waist, dragging in deep breaths and coughing. After a few seconds, he straightened, holding his throat protectively. "Your commanding officer will hear from me, Spencer."

Jack succinctly told him where to get off.

The reporter bristled and Terra tightened her hold on Jack's arm, afraid things would start all over again between the men. Officer Russell slapped a restraining hand on the reporter's chest. Finally, Reynolds walked off with her.

Jack pivoted and stalked toward the front of the truck. A breath shuddered out of Terra. Reassured that Dane was fine, she followed Jack around Station Two's ladder truck. "Jack?"

Head bowed, shoulders heaving, he didn't look up. She laid a hand on his back.

He turned, eyes smoke-reddened and swollen in the shadows. "Sorry."

Had the smoke done a number on him? Or had Reynolds? "What happened back there?"

Jack stepped over, staring down the street at the reporter who stood readjusting his jacket. "Clark Kent got here before the first officer. Almost at the same time as the fire trucks."

"And?"

"Why?" Jack braced his hands on his hips, his features cold and hard. Intimidating. The coat parted to reveal his bare chest again. "Why was he the first one here? Why has he been first at *every* scene?"

"I don't think you're going to get answers by beating him up. You can't just go wild like that. We'll have to interview him."

"What if he's our arsonist?"

"What if he's not?" Terra countered. "We don't have any proof yet."

"He stuck that damn mike in my face and asked me how I got out. Not 'how did the fire start?' or 'did I have any comment?' No, he asked how I got out."

"It's a little odd, Jack, but it doesn't prove anything."

"I know." He shoved a hand through his hair then shook his head. "I looked up from that fire and there he was. I lost my cool."

He'd gone after Reynolds with the unleashed force of a guard dog. She'd feel more calm if she got Jack as far as possible from the reporter. "Let's go talk to Captain Sandusky."

"I'm okay. You can trust me to stay away from Reynolds."

"I want you to come with me. Please."

After a moment, he fell into step with her.

She caught a glimpse of his hard, bare chest, a shadow of hair there. Sweat pants hung low on his hips. "Nice outfit," she said. "Did you get that somewhere special?"

"Quit lusting after me, August. People will talk."

Relief ached in her chest. She ducked under the crime scene tape and waited as he did the same. "Are you all right?" she asked in a low voice.

"I'm fine." He ran an unsteady hand through his hair, knocking loose some ash. Soot streaked one cheek.

"Are you burned anywhere?" She wanted to throw herself on him, hold him tight so she could feel every inch for herself, but she contented herself with a squeeze of his arm.

"Detective, are you okay?" Captain Sandusky from Station Two caught up with them. The wizened veteran stood about five foot eight and had the wiry strength of weathered leather. He gave a loose, two-fingered salute. "Hey, Terra."

"Hey, Captain. What do we have?"

"Stations Two and Three both responded since Detective Spencer lives on the northwest border of Quadrant Two. The fire was contained within three minutes and completely doused inside of fifteen. They stopped the flames before they spread out of the living room."

"Good. What areas are most affected?"

"The living room, edge of the kitchen and hallway." He hooked a thumb toward Jack. "The detective and his neighbor were already working on putting out the blaze when we arrived. He still hasn't let the paramedics check him out."

Terra peered more closely at Jack. Was part of his eyebrow singed? The sharp jab of concern in her chest was unexpectedly severe. Police car headlights brightened Jack's yard and illuminated one side of his face. She didn't spot any soot around his nose or mouth, but it might be a couple of hours before some indications of smoke inhalation appeared.

"Are you burned, Jack?" she repeated the question Captain Sandusky's arrival had interrupted.

Coughing, he turned the back of one hand toward her. "My right hand. It's just a blister."

"Are you nauseous? Having trouble breathing?"

"No. My throat's sore. I feel like I swallowed a ball of fire."

He would bear close watching over the next forty-eight hours. "You're not sleepy or light-headed?"

"No."

"Confused?"

"Hell, no. Someone tried to kill me tonight. I'm real clear about that."

She turned him so the light fell on the other side of his face. His hair, eyebrows and eyelashes didn't appear to be singed. His blue eyes were lucid, but tired and smoke-reddened. She spied a raw burn the diameter of a pencil eraser on the side of his neck. "I'll make sure he gets medical attention, Captain," she said to Station Two's leader, then asked Jack, "Has anyone given you a damage report?"

"A firefighter named Fox saved my nephews' drawings from the fridge and she said my truck seemed all right."

Terra made a mental note to thank Shelby Fox for her thoughtfulness.

"But I lost my boxing gloves autographed by Joe Frasier." After another spasm of coughing, he continued, "My sister practically hocked her car in high school to get those."

Terra hated that he had lost a prized possession, but she

was thrilled he was all right. She knew his sister would be, too.

"Nothing's been moved," Captain Sandusky said. "You may be able to figure out things pretty quickly."

She glanced at Jack, trying to ease the panic that still lapped at her. "Did you see anything? Hear anything?"

"I heard crashing glass. That's what woke me up. I followed the sound to the living room and saw flames." He cleared his throat. "Then a bottle came through the front window and exploded."

"Bottle?" She frowned in the direction of the house. "Molotov cocktail?"

"That's my guess. I'm sure you'll know more once you get inside and do your hocus-pocus."

She smiled, jotting down Jack's answers in her pocket notebook. "Any of your neighbors see or hear anything?"

"Detective Spencer has already canvassed the neighborhood," Captain Sandusky put in with a chuckle. "No one saw or heard anything until he made it over to his next door neighbor's house and told him about the fire."

"Mr. Plumley. He lives there." Jack pointed to a gray brick house on the south side of his. "He's talking to the fireman with the video camera."

"I'll touch base with him."

Captain Sandusky clapped Jack on the back. "Detective, I need to get my crew rounded up here. I know I'm leaving you in good hands."

"Thanks for your quick response."

"Sure."

As the other man walked off, Terra studied Jack. His face appeared calmer; his eyes did not. They were stormy and cold as his gaze lasered in on Reynolds.

"You sure you're okay?"

"Yes." He coughed again, his gaze fixed on the street

now teeming with rescue personnel, neighbors and news reporters.

Tension vibrated from him. Even in the dim light, she could see the muscle in his jaw flex.

Terra glanced at the street and saw Reynolds start toward her with his cameraman. After a few steps, he halted, his gaze locking on Jack. Reynolds's gaze flicked to Terra then he pivoted and walked back to the street, motioning T. J. Coontz to follow.

T.J. rolled his eyes, hefting his large-lens camera up to his shoulder as he made his way carefully behind Reynolds.

Terra's gaze shifted to the big man beside her. Another glimpse of his bare chest had her wondering if he felt the cold at all. "Jack, I'm worried about you."

"I'm mad as hell." He stared at his splintered front door, the broken windows. "Was this some kind of prank? Or someone trying to get even?"

"Has one of your collars recently been released from prison?"

"Corrections usually lets me know when someone gets out, but some do slip through the cracks. I'll check in with them."

Hands braced on his hips, he stared through slitted eyes at his damaged home then turned away as if he couldn't bear to look any longer.

Terra's heart ached for him. Around them, firefighters squished through the yard, rolling up their hoses, storing a couple of axes in the trucks.

Jack's voice sliced through the night air. "What the hell is *he* doing here?"

Terra followed his gaze and spotted LeBass.

"He doesn't work out of Station Two."

"No, he doesn't." Terra studied the fireman whom she'd just learned had a reason to be very angry at Harris. Angry enough to kill. "I'll find out why he's here, but it looks as if he's definitely working this fire."

"Call me paranoid, but I don't like seeing two of our suspects show up at a fire at my house."

"I don't either."

He rubbed his neck, looked into her eyes. "It's probably just the arson making me hinky. It's not every day I get a Molotov cocktail thrown through my living room."

"You're entitled."

He coughed again, rubbing at his eyes with the heels of his palms.

"You really need to let the paramedics check you out."

"And you need to get to work."

She squeezed his arm, wishing she could do more. "Can I call someone for you?"

"I called my sister. Didn't want her or the kids to hear about this on the morning news. She's going to call our parents."

"Do you want to spend the night with me? I mean, do you need a place—"

"Got a one-track mind, Investigator?" Despite the exhaustion etching his handsome features, he winked. "Wanting to pick up where we left off?"

"You wish." She grinned.

"Absolutely." Their gazes met as the memory of their heated kisses played through Terra's mind.

"Thanks for the offer of a bed, but my sister's on her way over to pick me up. I'll stay with her tonight. I'll figure out something else tomorrow."

"Okay."

She discreetly slipped her fingers through his, hiding their hands between the bulky turnout coats they wore. "I'm glad you're all right," she said softly, surprised at the clutch of pain in her chest.

"I am, too, sweetheart. You're not getting rid of me that easily. Remember what we talked about earlier."

"As if I could forget." She wanted to kiss him right now, tell all these people to go away so she could take care of Jack herself. "Will you call me when you get to your sister's? Just so I'll know you made it there all right?"

He tugged on the hem of her coat, drawing her marginally closer. "Yes."

"Do *not* leave here without letting the paramedics check you out." She motioned over one of the guys watching from the street.

"Sure. Whatever." His gaze softened and he squeezed her hand hard. His eyes promised *later.*

"There's my sister." He pointed to a white minivan that stopped two driveways down. "I'm glad I returned my brother-in-law's car tonight instead of waiting."

"No kidding. I'll call you about the fire as soon as I know something."

"I managed to save my cell phone, and my sister's in the book."

"All right."

He squeezed her hand one last time and ducked under the crime scene tape, following the paramedic over to his ambulance.

Terra watched him, struggling to level her racing heart. Seeing him in the middle of the sodden yard, surrounded by arson remains had jammed her breath painfully under her ribs. Thank goodness he hadn't been hurt. Or worse. Jack's close brush with death brought home just how much he'd come to mean to her. He was right to go slow with their relationship, but she was definitely interested in exploring the feelings between them. She'd make sure he knew that.

Her throat burned with sudden tears, but she fought them

back. She had work to do. She was going to find out who'd torched Jack's house, and why.

Sitting at his desk the next morning, Jack felt like hell, inside and out. His throat was as raw as scalded flesh and his chest hurt from coughing all night, but he knew it could've been a lot worse. So far, he had exhibited none of the symptoms of smoke inhalation that the E.M.T. had described.

He'd spoken to his parents briefly last night, then for about half an hour this morning. Two hours with his sister had netted him a place to live until the repairs were finished at his house. Plenty of work stacked his desk, but Jack's thoughts were squarely on last night's fire.

Since being jerked awake by crashing glass right before midnight, a cold fury had settled inside him. He hoped Terra's investigation yielded a good jumping-off place to start tracking the S.O.B. who'd started the fire at his house, but it didn't matter. Jack would find whoever had done it. If it had been Reynolds, the reporter would need reconstructive surgery before he ever got back on the air.

Had last night been some kind of prank? Or had Jack been targeted by some do-wrong he'd put away in the past? He hung up from the Department of Corrections. None of his collars had been released recently and he hadn't received any threats lately. Besides this homicide investigation with Terra, Jack had three more open cases on his desk, but carjackers and sex pervs typically didn't send threats to the investigating detective.

Knowing he'd need more information before he closed in on the slimeball who'd tried to kill him, Jack decided to continue his check of Don LeBass. Terra's information that LeBass had received another negative assessment from Harris Vaughn just two weeks before the retired fire investigator's murder was reason enough to return to Harris's neighborhood and see if anyone recognized LeBass.

Just after ten-thirty, Jack arrived at the quiet residential section where the fall-splashed beauty was marred only by the blackened remains of Harris's house. Jack had cut out a picture of LeBass from this morning's newspaper article about the fire last night and he wanted to see if anyone recognized it. Since the photo was considered public domain, Jack could show it to whomever he wanted.

Forty-five minutes later, the widow in the house across the street from Harris gave Jack a sweet piece of information. Hoping to get more, he continued to interview the neighbors and had just finished the houses on one side of the street when his cell phone rang.

He recognized Terra's office number on the readout. "Hey, you." His voice was still raspy from smoke. "What's going on?"

"Could you please come to my office?"

"Sure, I'm almost finished with my canvass of Harris's neighborhood—"

"Could you come right now?"

The eerie stillness of her voice made the hairs on his neck stand up. "I'll be there as soon as I can."

He used his siren and reached the old brick building inside of ten minutes. What had happened to put that grim, flat note in her voice?

Darla looked up from her computer when he walked in. "Go on back. She's waiting for you."

"Thanks." His gaze shifted to the window of Terra's office. She stood with her back to him, looking down at something on her desk. Her body was rigid, her hair gathered up in a loose ponytail. His shoulders tensed. What was going on? Trouble with the mayor? The investigation?

He stepped into her office and saw the burst of fresh color in the middle of her desk. Red roses.

She looked up, her gaze dark and troubled.

"What is it?"

"You got here fast."

"I've never heard you like that." She'd sounded shaken, off balance.

She carefully held out a piece of paper and he noticed the latex gloves she wore.

A hard slam of certainty told Jack that it was from the arsonist. Fishing his own pair of gloves out of his jacket pocket, he pulled them on before he took the note. "The Molotovs were a nice change of pace, weren't they?" he read aloud, his gaze meeting hers. "So, it was definitely Molotov cocktails. And it *was* our serial arsonist."

"That seems to be the claim."

"But Molotovs aren't—"

"I know. There was no lightbulb plant. You weren't drugged. The pattern doesn't match, but an arsonist's main craving is fire. And this torch is obviously sending a message."

"Why me?"

"Because we're getting close."

"I wish we knew who we were close to. Cecily, Reynolds, LeBass. Or someone else."

She nodded, her features pale and tight.

"If it is Reynolds, he's got brass ones for showing up at my house right after he did this."

"Think about it, Jack." Her gaze locked on his. "The arsonist knows where you live."

He laid down the note before he crumpled it in his fist. "That means he or she has been watching other places in addition to fire scenes."

"Watching one or both of us."

A hot wave of protectiveness surged through him. "I went straight home from your place last night. They were either watching your house when I picked you up or when we returned from dinner."

She nodded, gripping the edge of her desk until her knuckles gleamed white. Her eyes glowed in her face like hot stones.

He cursed. The icy rage that had settled in his chest since last night grew sharper. "Are you all right?"

"Yes. We have to catch this torch." Fury made her voice as brittle as his. "And fast."

He didn't have to tell her they were working as fast as they could. She knew. But it reminded him of what he'd been doing when she called. Just as he started to tell her about the information he'd learned from Harris's neighbor, an irate voice boomed behind them.

He and Terra turned at the same time. Don LeBass marched toward them, his face florid with anger.

Darla jumped out of her seat and hurried behind the fireman. "I said you have to wait for her. She's busy—"

"She'll see me." LeBass stopped at Terra's door, his eyes flashing. He barely looked at Jack. "What the hell do you think you're doing, August?"

"What's this about?" Jack asked.

"It don't concern you." The burly fireman stabbed a finger toward Terra. "You been asking questions about me. I wanna know why."

Jack shifted until he stood partially in front of Terra. "Stop yelling."

"What's the matter, Ace? Can't find your arsonist so you're looking to hurt me?"

"Hardly, LeBass. I only wanted to know why you worked with Station Two last night."

"Ray Emery had to go to the Emergency Room with

kidney stones. He called me from there and asked if I'd work his shift.''

''I'm sure your friend will back up your story.''

''Hell, yes. Why is it any of your business?''

''I didn't like seeing you at my house last night,'' Jack put in.

The fireman drew up short. ''I put out that damn fire and this is the thanks I get?''

''I wanted to be sure you didn't start it.''

''Start it! Why the hell would I do that?''

Jack decided to see what kind of reaction he could surprise out of LeBass. ''We just found out you applied to the O.C.F.D. for a fire investigator's position and Harris Vaughn gave you a negative assessment.''

''This is about Vaughn?''

''Isn't it true that you got those results about a week before his murder?''

''You think I'd kill him because of that?''

''Weren't you furious?'' Terra asked.

''Yes, but I wouldn't kill anybody.''

''Hadn't Harris given you *two* negative assessments over the years?'' Jack watched the man carefully.

LeBass clamped his mouth shut, glaring at Terra.

So far the fireman hadn't let anything slip, but Jack had one more tidbit. ''I have a witness who saw you at Harris's house the night of the arson and murder.''

Beside him, he felt Terra start, but he didn't take his gaze from the other man's face.

LeBass stilled and panic flared in his eyes. ''I went there to talk to him about the assessment. See if I could get him to change his mind.''

''How far were you willing to go?'' Terra asked.

''Not that far.''

''If you did it, LeBass, we'll prove it,'' she said.

"So what if I was there? You can't prove I *didn't* go just to talk to him. He wasn't even there so I never saw him that night."

"Where did you go after that? Looking for him?" Jack asked.

"I went home. I was there the rest of the night."

Terra gave an exasperated sigh. Jack was getting as frustrated as she by these "home all night" alibis. "You know we'll check that out."

"Go ahead."

"When was the last time you saw him?" Jack asked.

"If you want to know anything else, talk to my lawyer." His hateful gaze drilled into Terra. "Do your job, Ace, and stop wasting time on me."

With a final glare, he stormed out.

Jack waited until the front door closed behind the fireman. He turned to Terra, glad to see a bit of color high on her cheekbones. "You all right?"

"Yes." She huffed out a breath, looking tired and wan.

"Sorry. I didn't have time to brief you about what I learned during my canvass this morning. The widow who lives across the street from Harris told me she saw LeBass the night of the fire."

Terra frowned. "How did she know it was LeBass? Did she describe him?"

"I showed her the picture of LeBass that was in the newspaper."

"A picture?"

"It was in this morning's edition with the caption Firefighters Save Cop's House or some rot. Sure made LeBass nervous."

"Still, he's right. We can't prove why he went to Harris's."

"We may not have to."

"Yeah." She crossed her arms, her mouth tightening. "We're just going around in circles, Jack."

"No, we're not. We're weeding through things. We'll get this torch."

She was quiet for a long moment and when she looked up, tears brightened her eyes. "What if you'd been killed last night? What if you hadn't gotten out?"

"Hey, I did get out." He nudged her chin up with one finger. "I'm okay. Don't I look okay?"

She smiled tremulously. "You look great."

"Well, there ya go."

Terra dabbed at her eyes. "Sorry about that. It just kind of hit me all at once."

"No problem." He cupped the side of her face, stroked his thumb across her cheekbone. "Does this mean you're still interested? In us?"

"Very interested." She closed her fingers around his wrist. "*You* haven't changed your mind, have you?"

"Not a chance. Want to go out with me tonight?"

"What did you have in mind?"

"There's a dinner dance for outgoing District Attorney Gibson. I have to make an appearance."

"Sure, I'd love to."

"Great. I'll pick you up at seven-fifteen. The dress is 'after-five.'"

She nodded. "I'll be ready."

"We're not going to talk business all night, either," he warned.

"All right."

He wanted to kiss her, but he was aware that Darla looked on. Turning, he picked up the note that had been delivered with the roses and put it in an evidence bag he fished from his jacket pocket. "I'll take these things to the lab, see if I can get any prints. Then I'm going to visit this florist and see if I can get a description of who ordered the flowers.''

"I'll see you tonight. I'm looking forward to it."

"Same here."

The smile she gave him hinted at a secret, flicked his nerve endings to heated life. He carefully picked up the vase of roses and started out the door, but that smile demanded he do something. Hell, he didn't care if Darla *was* watching. He stopped. Turned.

Terra moved up beside him. "Everything okay?"

He leaned over and kissed her softly. Her lips parted in surprise, then invitation. Leaning into him, she lifted one hand to his chest.

Jack's grip tightened on the glass vase. He pulled back and winked. "Now it is."

She gave him a slow smile, promises smoldering in her green eyes. His body hardened and he strode out of the room. Hell, he didn't know how he'd last until tonight.

He walked past the secretary's desk. "See ya, Darla."

She grinned and gave him a thumbs-up.

He chuckled.

Chapter 11

Silverware clinked against china as the last of the dinner dishes were cleared away by waiters and waitresses in crisp black suits and white shirts. This was the first time Terra had been to the Cowboy Hall of Fame since the name had changed to the National Cowboy and Western Heritage Museum. This banquet room, called the Special Events Center, looked fantastic.

A live band in a far corner started a medley of dance tunes. Soft light showered over the round table for eight where Terra and Jack sat. People at dozens of the same linen-covered tables surrounded them.

She politely listened to the female attorney on her left, but her thoughts were on the sexy homicide detective who draped his arm loosely across the back of her chair.

Jack Spencer had gotten under her skin, managed to erode her stubborn resistance to another relationship. If she needed any proof, it was in the cold panic that had knifed through her heart last night when she'd been paged to the fire at his house. And the fact that his presence had calmed her nerves today after she'd received the chilling note from the arsonist along with the now expected roses.

The fear that had clutched at her upon realizing the serial arsonist had been watching them—stalking them—had since turned to anger. The arsonist might have watched Jack or her this afternoon. Could be watching even now during the black-tie dinner dance.

Her gaze cut through the throng of people in front of her and scanned the magnificent oversized banquet room. Several reporters and cameramen lined the back wall where one of five giant, three-piece paintings of Western landscapes at sunset hung.

Bright camera bulbs overpowered the soft fall of light from the chandeliers overhead. The D.A., who'd given a farewell speech during dessert, stopped to have a few words with each reporter.

Terra didn't know whether to be grateful or suspicious that Dane Reynolds wasn't among those covering the dinner. Was the reporter on another assignment? Or was he somewhere watching them? They had no proof he was the arsonist, but too many things about him didn't add up.

The fire at Jack's was a plain warning that they were closing in on the arsonist, but who were they closing in on? Jack was looking hard at Reynolds, but LeBass couldn't prove where he'd been the night of Harris's murder, just as Cecily Vaughn couldn't, either.

As Terra responded to the attorney's questions about her job, Jack's easy, frequent touch drove all thoughts of the investigation to the back of her mind. During the drive down to the museum, he had brought her up to speed on the case. Since nothing new demanded her attention right now, she was determined to enjoy herself.

He sat to her right, talking to a cop buddy. Clay Jessup

was a lanky hunk of man with sandy blond hair and green eyes. Occasionally, Jack touched her knee under the table or fingered the hem of her black cocktail dress. She wanted to get closer to him, feel his hands on her the way she had the other night.

Something had changed for Terra after the fire at Jack's. The man had come to mean more to her than she'd ever expected. As a result, she'd been a little nervous and giddy about their date tonight. She was used to controlling her feelings, but right now she wasn't sure she could control so much as a sneeze.

His hand felt incredible on the bare skin right above the low back of her dress. When he leaned forward to better hear something Clay said, his thumb stroked the base of her neck. A shiver danced through her.

She wanted him to touch her all over, wanted to touch *him* all over. Draped in the heat of his body she felt more protected and turned on than she had ever felt with a man.

A sudden rush of impatience made her restless. There were too many people in here, too much noise. She wanted him all to herself. When she could politely do so, she wound up her conversation with the attorney and waited for a lull in his chat with his cop buddy.

She laid a hand on Jack's granite-hard leg, curled her fingers lightly against the inside of his thigh. Beneath her palm, his muscles jerked and she smiled into his eyes. "Detective, what about that dance you promised me?"

"Yes, absolutely." As he stood and held her chair, he said to his friend, "Got a better offer, Jessup."

"Can't argue with that." The other man lifted a hand as they walked off. "Nice to meet you, Terra."

"You, too."

Jack swept her onto the crowded dance floor for the end

of a quick tempo song. Completely ignoring the jazzy beat, he held her close and moved slowly.

She melted against him, looping her arms around his neck. "I'm not the greatest dancer," she said.

"You feel pretty great to me."

They swayed together, her thighs teasing in and out of his. The occasional brush of his erection against her belly set off the heat already smoldering inside her. He held her close, his touch burning through her dress. The measured friction of their bodies hardened her nipples and set off a chain reaction in her nerves.

Jack's hand moved up to the center of her back, his thumb resting on her bare skin. "You look gorgeous."

"So do you." She pulled back and gave him an admiring look. When he'd shown up on her doorstep, his dark handsomeness had sent a jolt through her system.

The black suit and white shirt emphasized his lean good looks, the chiseled features. Blue eyes had seemed to pierce right through her. He was clean-shaven and his woodsy scent made her think about the night he'd backed her into the shadows and kissed her as if it were his last day on earth.

His heated gaze roamed over her halter neckline and down to the hint of cleavage revealed by the shallow V-cut bodice. "I like the dress, but I don't know if I have the strength to beat off all these guys who obviously like it, too."

She laughed, enjoying the way his gaze stroked over her bare shoulders. She had definitely needed her coat on the way in, but Jack was keeping her plenty warm now.

The music changed to a slow dance, matching the rhythm he had set all along. Their bodies locked and unlocked, moving together fluidly like muscles in the same body.

Terra laid her head on his shoulder, loving the hard strength of his arms, the feel of him against her.

"You smell great." His voice rumbled in her ear, sending a ripple of sensation through her.

She turned her head and brushed a kiss over the small burn on his neck.

His hands tightened on her waist. "What are you thinking about?"

That she'd found someone who understood her dedication to her job, who was just as dedicated to his. After her mistaken belief in her marriage, she'd never thought to find that. Never trusted that she would. "How much I enjoy working with you. I think we make a great team."

"I agree." His hand slid down to the small of her back, pressed her tighter into his hips.

Her body draped his like silk. "I feel as if you think I contribute. That I'm valued."

"You are." His gaze fixed on hers. "You're a damn good investigator, Terra. When you're not busy in my fantasies."

She playfully pinched his shoulder. "That you respect what I do means a lot to me. My ex thought my job wasn't as significant as his, and for a while I wondered if he was right. I know he wasn't."

"No, he wasn't. The idiot."

She grinned, feeling as if they were floating. Her nerves buzzed with every warm brush of Jack's hand on her back, the whisper of his breath against her cheek.

Intoxicated by his touch, any hesitation she had about him crumbled. She slid her hands to his shoulders, brushing her thumb back and forth across the lapel of his jacket. "You're sure you're all right? Still no signs of smoke inhalation?"

"I'm great." He maneuvered her around an older couple. "Wishing you could've done mouth-to-mouth on me?"

"I would've let Rusty do it," she teased back, but when

she looked up at him, her smile faded. "Jack, I was scared to death when I got that page to your house last night. I couldn't shake it until I saw you were all right."

He rested his forehead on hers as they swayed on the edge of the crowd. "I like you, too."

His words touched her. He'd been right to wait on their relationship until she was sure about what she wanted. She might not be prepared for another brutal heartbreak, but she was definitely ready to risk it again. "I didn't expect to care this much about you."

"How much?" he asked with a grin.

She cupped his cheek and said lightly, "A little."

"You know what scares *me?*" he asked.

"What?"

"That you might send me to that rent house alone tonight. After the fright I had last night, I don't think I can handle it."

"Well, we can't have that, Detective." The roguish grin he gave caused a tickle in her belly. She pulled back slightly so she could look into his eyes. Those beautiful blue eyes. "I've thought about what you said the other night. About what I want, about letting you know when I'm ready."

"And?"

Her gaze traced his features, lingered on the lips that had kissed her senseless. "Let's get out of here. I don't want to wait anymore."

He hesitated for all of one second. Fierce hunger flared in his eyes as he took her hand and led her off the dance floor. They stopped only long enough to pluck her coat from her chair and say goodbye to Clay.

Her heels clicked against the tile floor as they hurried down the wide corridor then veered left toward the front doors. Jack helped her on with her coat, which was a good thing because her hands were shaking so hard it would've taken her three tries to get it on.

Crisp fall air nipped at her as she held tight to Jack's hand and hurried with him across the parking lot. They quickly reached the low-slung black car he'd again borrowed from his brother-in-law.

He opened her door, then tugged her to him. "Come here."

His lips covered hers and she slid her arms around his neck, wanting to completely surrender. Always before, his kisses had been a measured seduction. Slow and sweet, chipping away at her resistance. Now they were urgent and reckless. His tongue swept inside her mouth and he plundered her. Terra's head spun. The want that had flickered off and on all night now ignited into a full flame.

The kiss went on and on. She clung tighter to him. She didn't want it to end, but eventually he lifted his head.

"Well," she breathed. "Hello, Detective."

He took her lips again in a dizzyingly fierce kiss. When he lifted his head, his eyes blazed with raw hunger.

A shiver danced through her. "Hurry," she whispered.

By unspoken agreement, he headed to her house. The drive was the longest blur of her life. Anticipation strung her nerves tight. She was aware only that Jack's hand burned through her dress, branding her thigh. That he smelled like primal male and sex and a new beginning. She kissed his neck, traced his ear with her tongue.

Sometime later—minutes or seconds—they turned onto her street, the scent of wood smoke drifting from the houses they passed. She leaned over, tugged on his earlobe with her teeth then laved the side of his neck, trying to be careful of the raw burn there.

His hand clenched on her thigh. "Did you move? This is taking too long," he growled.

"Two minutes." When her house came into sight, she pulled a remote from her purse. "Park in the garage. The front door has three locks."

Jack whipped into her driveway. The overhead door slid open noiselessly and he guided the car inside then killed the engine. She was out and had the door leading into the house open by the time he met her.

He stepped into the laundry room right behind her, punching the button to close the garage and shutting the house door. As the darkness settled around them, he slid his hands around her waist and pulled her into him. He was hard against her bottom and she pressed into him, a low driving pulse throbbing between her legs.

He moved his hands to her shoulders, slid off her coat and draped it over his arm as she turned. She found his face in the darkness, then his lips.

Cupping her rear, he held her tight, tempered chest against her breasts, the warm bulk of her coat at her back. He ravaged her mouth. Her knees went soft as desire spread like hot honey through her, flicking all her nerve endings to life.

His mouth left hers, trailed tiny love bites down her neck.

"This is for more than tonight," he rasped against her flesh. "Tell me."

"Yes."

He lifted his head, took her chin. In the dim light, she focused enough to see the hard glitter of his eyes. "Take down your hair."

Her hands were shaking as she lifted her arms. In the shadows, his eyes glinted dangerously. Terra had never thought to feel this way again. Sexy and wanted. Necessary.

As she worked loose the French twist, she backed her way into the kitchen. Desire sharpened his features, made his eyes gleam like blue steel. He draped her coat over the back of a bar stool. She slid two pins out of her hair, then unbraided it and shook out the heavy mass so that it brushed her shoulders.

He reached out and cupped her nape, twining his finger in her hair. Pulling her close, he buried his face in her neck. "I've waited a long time for this."

"I have, too." She hadn't realized just how long until tonight. She toed off her heels while unknotting his tie.

He pressed hot lips to her neck, his hand leaving her hair to trail over one bare shoulder. "What do you have on under here?"

She gave him a coy smile.

He grinned with wicked purpose and slid his hand to her nape to flick open the clasp holding up her dress. She let the top fall, her pulse spiking at the raging need in his eyes when he saw her low-cut strapless bra. "I've got to have you."

"Please."

He found the zipper at the middle of her back and palmed off her dress. She helped him with her hose, then stood before him clad only in the black bra and high-cut panties. His gaze scorched her. His hands skimmed every curve, teasing, molding. She gripped his shoulders and closed her eyes, riding the edge of pleasure that seared her.

He finally kissed her lips again. She reached for him, her nerves jumping as he hauled her hard into him.

Need clawed at her. "You've got on a lot more clothes than I do, Detective."

"Let me have a little fun, sweetheart. You're more than I ever imagined."

He lowered his head and nudged down her bra, taking one aching breast into his mouth. Sinking into the vortex of sensation, she arched her neck. His tongue flicked over sensitive flesh, drew her nipples into hard buds while his other hand slipped between her legs.

He cupped her through the silk of her panties and she gasped his name.

His touch ignited the wild fire that had been slowly burning. She reached out and fumbled open the buttons of his shirt, tugged it down his arms.

He yanked his T-shirt over his head and hauled her to him. "I want you. Now."

"Yes." Her knees trembled so violently she had to grip his arms.

She met his demanding kisses with her own. He lifted her, his mouth going to her other breast. She wrapped her legs around his waist. His belt buckle dug into her inner thigh, but she didn't care.

"Bedroom?" he said against her mouth.

"End…of the…hall. Straight ahead."

Somehow, despite their constant kissing and touching, he found it. Her blood was so hot Terra thought she would burst into flames.

At the edge of the bed, she unlocked her legs and slid down his body, resting her hands on his chest. The feel of supple flesh, warmed by her own, made her heart clench. Her hands went to his belt buckle and he unclasped her bra, peeled off her panties.

He had her on the bed before she finally got him naked.

"I wanted to go slow." He slid a finger into her silky heat. "But I can't."

"We can do slow later." She pulled his head down for another kiss.

Together, they fumbled a condom down his length. He entered her in one smooth thrust and Terra caught her breath. He felt perfect inside her. And then he began to move. Mind-numbing pleasure rolled over her in stormy waves. Clutching at his hard-muscled back, she matched his insistent pace.

He grasped her hips, guiding, giving. Tension coiled inside her, tighter and harder, then unraveled. She reached the peak quickly, but even as she thought she'd outpaced him, he moved faster. Reached some deeply buried core of passion she'd never known existed.

Jack drove her higher and higher. When he pushed her over the edge, control shattered. His body stroked hers to another blinding climax. His shoulders bowed and her hips arched with his. She cried out his name.

She'd never felt such a soul-deep connection, layers beneath what she'd ever shared with any other man. As they both shot into oblivion, Terra knew she never would. Only with Jack.

Wow. For a moment, that was all Jack could think as he rolled to his back and pulled Terra next to him. A fine sweat slicked his chest. He shouldn't have an ounce of strength left, but still he wanted her. He'd never craved a woman like he did Terra, never been so single-minded about a woman.

She rolled toward him and dropped a kiss on his collarbone. Light from a streetlamp outside filtered through the blinds. Pale shadows danced across her sheets, the slender leg that lay atop his.

"It's a good thing I didn't know what I was missing the other night," she said drowsily, "or I wouldn't have let you leave."

He grinned, his thumb stroking the velvet of her arm. Complete male satisfaction filled him, but it took him a moment to realize what was different. *He* was different. The part of him that had only ever been linked with Lori was still there, but now it was separate, as if it had been carefully packaged and stored.

The pain over the loss of his wife had at last given way to acceptance, enabling him to care about someone else. It had happened without him being aware, but he couldn't miss it now. Terra August was definitely in his life, and for more than a roll in the hay.

He'd spent weeks telling himself he couldn't be involved with a woman like her. Wouldn't be. Now he was. It wasn't the first time he'd been wrong.

"If you thought this thing between us was distracting before, what about now?" she teased, trailing her nails across his stomach, low on his hips.

Desire hooked into him. Her scent, soft with flowers and his aftershave, drifted around them. "I can't decide if you're more distracting at the job or like this. I imagine neither one of us will get a lick of work done now."

"Maybe we could just stay in bed." She traced his nipple with one fingernail.

"Works for me."

They lay there for long moments, the silence comfortable and cozy around them. She was so still Jack thought she'd gone to sleep, but suddenly she looked up at him. "You're not having regrets, are you?"

He covered her hand with his. "No, not at all. Are you?"

"Not one."

But something was bothering her. "What's wrong?"

"You're just…quiet."

He went with his instincts and pulled her on top of him, framing her face with his hands. "You're the first woman I've *wanted* to be with since Lori's death."

"Really?" She smiled softly, locking his heart up tight.

"I've been with a couple of others, but I was trying to

forget. They didn't interest me. And I don't mean just the sex."

She traced his lips with her finger. "I'm still not sure I should trust my feelings, but I can't seem to help myself. I'm glad I'm here with you."

"I am, too." He stroked a hand down the petal-soft skin of her back and murmured into her hair, "At least I don't have to worry about you walking into some life-threatening situation."

"Like your wife?"

He nodded.

A small frown puckered her brow, then she pressed a kiss to his lips. She gave a contented sigh and laid her head on his chest.

Jack held her as she slept. When she woke a couple of hours later and looked at him, he read the want-to in her eyes. She touched him and his body hardened. They came together this time without words, their hearts beating in perfect rhythm. She rode him, but Jack went slow, the way he'd wanted to before, showing Terra with his body that he was ready to move on.

Maybe this attraction would grow into something strong and lasting. He was willing to find out. Because of his first impression about her job, he'd kept her at a distance for as long as he'd been able. Seeing her in action made him realize she faced the same risks he did and that was something he could handle.

Early in the morning, when the sky was still black, Terra stirred and woke him. He must've dozed off after they'd made love again.

She pressed kisses across his chest, on his lips. "I'm starving. Are you?"

He reached for her, but she swatted at him. "For real food."

She got out of bed, taking the sheet. Grinning, he grabbed it, enjoying the sight of her lean curves as she tried to wrestle the linen away from him. She goosed the inside of his knee, causing him to loosen his grip and lunge for her. She snatched the sheet and danced away from him, leaving him naked on the bed.

"Hah." She wrapped the pink linen around her as she walked out.

He followed her, stopping to grab a towel from the hall bathroom and wrap it around his hips. By the time he reached the kitchen, she had a carton of vanilla ice cream and a bottle of root beer on the cabinet.

"How about an ice-cream float?" She dipped large spoonfuls of ice cream into a tall mug, then poured in the root beer.

They shared the foamy treat. Jack couldn't recall ever eating ice cream in the middle of the night. Certainly not with a woman who turned him inside out. Her breasts swelled over the sheet she'd knotted sarong-style around herself. Her tousled golden-red hair and swollen lips immediately gave away that she'd been thoroughly loved. By him.

An unfamiliar warmth pushed through his chest.

"What are you smiling at?" She scraped out the last large bite of ice cream.

He leaned in and kissed her, lips now cool from the dessert. "You. And I think that last bite is mine."

"I don't think so, Spencer." Eyes sparkling, she lifted the heaping teaspoonful to her mouth.

He reached for it and she quickly gobbled at the bite. Root beer and ice cream dripped down her chin and onto her front.

"Oooh," she squealed, jerking in reflex. "That's cold!"

She turned to get a rag from a nearby drawer, but Jack hooked an arm around her waist and pulled her to him. "I'll get that."

"Oh?" She wiggled suggestively against him.

He dipped his head and swiped his tongue over her chin,

then flicked his way down her neck. His blood heated at the taste of her mixed with the sweet ice cream. He kissed and nibbled his way over the curve of her breast.

Her hands speared into his hair and she held him to her. "Take me to bed, Jack."

He lifted his head, thinking he could get lost in the dark want of her emerald eyes. Scooping her into his arms, he carried her back to the bedroom. She looped her arms around his neck, nipping at his earlobe, breathing urgent words in his ear.

He laid her on the bed and unwrapped the sheet, staring down at the pale perfection of her body. Her breasts quivered under his gaze, causing his erection to throb painfully. Levering himself down on both elbows, he kissed her. She opened to him, mouth and body, making a sound deep in her throat that shot pure fire through him.

Passion and playfulness mixed on her face. "I've never done this three times in one night before."

"Neither have I," he said wryly. "Let's hope I can."

She laughed, reaching between their bodies. "Oh, I don't think you're going to have any trouble, Detective."

He caught her bottom lip between his teeth, parted her legs. Suddenly she froze.

Jack frowned. "What is it? Did I hurt you?"

"No. Listen." She turned her head toward the window and Jack did the same.

The streetlamp cast short fingers of light through the window, not enough to see by, but enough to distinguish between shadow and darkness. Something moved in front of the window. A crackle of underbrush sounded.

"Damn!" Jack popped up off the bed, scrambling for his slacks.

Terra was right behind him, grabbing her robe off the back of the door as she raced down the hall. He snatched up his suit jacket, running behind her as he felt for the backup gun he carried in the coat's inside pocket.

By the time he reached the entryway, his 9mm Glock was nestled in his hand. "Let me go first. I'm armed."

She opened the front door and waited as he stepped out on the porch. Cold concrete chilled the soles of his feet, but after the first sting of discomfort he ignored it. He stepped onto the sidewalk then into the grass.

"Wait." Terra disappeared, then returned in a few seconds with a flashlight.

"Good idea." He took the light and with her pressed to his back, they scanned the perimeter of the yard.

They saw no one around her two large maple trees. The branches were half-stripped and too sparse to hide anyone. Jack shone the light on Terra's bedroom window. Followed the line of brick down to the ground. The short evergreen bushes seemed undisturbed, but he thought he saw a dark shape in the grass.

"Over there. Let's be careful."

Together they moved up until the thin strip of light fell flush on the spot. He cocked his head. "Looks like a footprint."

"Yes." Terra glanced at the grass around the spot. "There's a pretty heavy dew tonight. Is there more than one print?"

Jack shifted the flashlight so that he illuminated a patch of yard, the grass looking streaked. "I can't be sure if it's a shoe print, but it looks like something went through the grass."

"Somebody was here. Outside my window." Terra gripped his arm.

"We can't be sure."

"You know it, and so do I, Jack." She stared unflinchingly into his eyes. "It's the serial arsonist."

He moved over to examine the drag marks in the grass, already fading because of more accumulating moisture.

"We don't know who it was." He put an arm around her.

"Let's go back inside. There's no one out here and you're freezing."

By the time they got inside, her teeth were chattering. "You last night, me tonight. Why *wouldn't* it be the arsonist?" she asked.

"I admit it looks that way."

"We can't afford to think otherwise, Jack. Not after the Molotov cocktails in your living room."

He shut the door, thumbed on the safety of his gun and laid it on a decorative table in her entryway before pulling her to him. "You're right. We need to be careful, but if the arsonist was going to do something tonight, he or she had the chance to do it."

"There's no telling how long he was at the window before we heard him."

"Right." He hugged her close, feeling the chill of her body through her light robe. "I don't think he'll be back tonight, but just to be safe, I'm going to call it in. See if a patrol car can sit outside the rest of the night."

"It's almost four o'clock."

"I'll feel better if we get someone over here."

She nodded.

"You okay?"

She hugged him tight. "That was creepy."

Very creepy, he thought later as he stood at the window in her bedroom. She'd finally gone to sleep, but he hadn't been able to close his eyes. He didn't know if his insomnia was due to the noisy lurker, or because of what had happened between him and Terra.

Chapter 12

A week after the incident at her house, Terra and Jack still had no leads on the prowler. Jack had canvassed her neighborhood and asked if anyone had seen or heard anything that night, but no one had.

The note from the last delivery of roses had yielded no prints. Neither had the vase. And the florist couldn't remember who had placed the order.

Terra hated the thought that she and Jack appeared to be targeted by the arsonist, but it meant they were close to something. They had met with the mayor and briefed him about the fire started by the serial arsonist at Jack's house. But all three of them agreed not to release that information to the media yet.

Their lack of progress had Terra ready to chew nails. Not only because they had no leads from the last flower delivery, but also because they couldn't prove why LeBass had gone to see Harris the night of the murder. They couldn't connect the Halcion to him, Cecily or Reynolds. They couldn't bust a single alibi.

The only thing going their way seemed to be their relationship. Jack was an attentive and generous lover, plus he made her laugh, which her ex-husband hadn't been able to do very often. But she sensed a reserve in him, some deep place he hadn't shared with her. She wouldn't push it. He would share with her when he was ready.

That Wednesday night, after dinner and a session of languorous lovemaking, Terra and Jack decided it was time to take a different tack in the investigation. She would call Dane Reynolds and let him know she was ready to grant an interview. Putting out a public plea might net them some new information. The exposure might also push the arsonist's buttons.

She was on her way home when a call came over her radio. A blaze had been reported in a poor residential area, less than three minutes away. Estimated arrival time for the closest responding unit was between eight and ten minutes. She radioed in that she would answer the call and to send the unit.

She pulled onto the street lined with small frame houses. All of the fifties-style A-frames had shallow porches and one-car garages. Only the paint colors differed. Orange flames shot into the sky over a yellow frame house and Terra slammed on her brakes in front of the cracked driveway.

Several people huddled in the street. A young black man trained a puny stream of water from a garden hose through the front door. Terra grabbed her turnout coat, slapped on her helmet and boots then snatched her ax from the back of her Explorer.

"Presley Fire Department." She rushed up carrying her air tank, mask and flashlight. "Who's in the house?"

"Mrs. Allison," the young man said. "And my dad, Frank Isaacs. He's trying to get her out."

"What's your name?"

"Travis." Sweat beaded his face. The front of his long-sleeved shirt was soaked. His eyes were already red with smoke.

"Travis, keep the water coming." Terra shrugged on the straps of her self-contained breathing apparatus, adjusting the thirty-plus-pounds weight on her shoulders. "The fire department will be here shortly. Don't go in. I'll have my hands full finding your dad and Mrs. Allison in this smoke. I can't come looking for you, too, okay?"

Fear strained his features, but he nodded, making an obvious effort to remain calm.

She smiled and pulled her mask up over her face. Ducking inside, she fell to her belly on the floor, swallowed up by smoke and darkness and heat.

Jack didn't remember driving to Presley Medical Center. After Terra had said "injured" and "concussion," his brain had seized up. Panic and dread cut straight to the bone.

He kept hearing her voice on the other end of the phone, swearing she was all right. She'd said something about rescuing someone from a fire, but he couldn't remember. All he cared about was seeing her, making sure she was safe.

Somehow he reached the hospital without having a wreck. He pushed through the revolving door and walked into a room dominated by a nurse's station. A clutter of people and noise assaulted his senses. Crying children, moaning adults. Medical personnel gave firm directives as they moved around the room, checking for the most serious cases. Several soon-to-be patients filled the chairs along the wall. Some stood.

Jack told a short, gray-haired nurse behind the desk who

he was looking for and she directed him to the last curtained cubicle. He thanked her, walking quickly down the hall. The smell of antiseptic underlined the scents of air freshener and sickness. A child cried out in a cubicle as he passed. Just being here dredged up the same numbing fear he'd felt when he had gotten the call about Lori.

Telling himself the situations were different didn't settle his nerves. They were as raw and exposed as if someone held a switchblade to his throat. Terra had said she was all right, but he had to see for himself.

How had this happened? Why had she been anywhere near a fire?

He tried to reason away the churning sickness in his gut. Just an hour ago, he'd known his world, his woman, felt secure in that knowledge. That phone call had ripped through him like shrapnel. Right now, he felt as if he'd been dropped blindfolded into a foreign country.

As he neared her cubicle, Jack slowed. The buzz of voices drifted from the other side of the curtain. She had visitors.

He stopped at the sound of her voice.

"I thought that ceiling was going to collapse before I got her out."

"It did, Terra," a woman said wryly. "Your head is just harder than a roof beam."

"You guys sure took your time getting there," Terra joked.

Jack ran a hand over his face, surprised to feel sweat. She sounded hoarse, her voice almost buoyant.

"You charged in there like the Lone Ranger," a man said. "Don't think you needed much help."

"Yeah, you glory hound." This time the voice came from an older male voice. "You've still got it, Ace. You can watch my back any time."

She won't be watching anyone's back, Jack thought savagely.

"If I eat all this ice cream you guys brought, watching is about all I'll be doing."

They all laughed.

"Good job on that lady, Ace," the older man said. "She and the neighbor would've been lost if you hadn't acted so quickly."

"I'm glad I was nearby."

"And didn't forget how to use your equipment," the younger man teased.

"Ha ha," Terra said. "You all know it was luck as much as anything. With all the smoke and heat, I couldn't tell what was what until I got right to her."

Jack detected a thread of exhaustion beneath her light reply. He struggled to level out his emotions. This was probably her way of decompressing after the all-out adrenaline rush of a rescue, but he couldn't listen to any more of this.

The people in her room were too accepting of what had nearly happened, the danger Terra had faced. Oh, he knew the drill. Cops were the same way. Joking helped release the stress that followed after facing death or a risky situation. It was all part of the job. The problem was Jack hadn't counted on Terra still doing the job of a firefighter. She was an investigator. She wasn't supposed to be on the front lines anymore.

Using all his years of experience as a cop, he blanked his face and stepped inside the small room. "Hello?"

Three firefighters surrounded the stainless steel hospital bed, filling the boxy exam room to capacity.

"Jack, come in." Terra's eyes lit up and she motioned him over.

He moved behind a man in full firefighter gear and stepped up to the bed. Jack recognized the red-haired man, but couldn't name him. A bandage glared white against her temple and his heart clenched at the raw scrape showing beneath it. She wore a soot-streaked white T-shirt and jeans. Her tennis shoes and a long-sleeved denim shirt were in a chair in the corner. A grimy turnout coat and boots lay on the floor. Propped up with pillows, she looked fragile. Vulnerable.

He swallowed around a hard lump in his throat. "How are you?"

"I'm okay." Her gaze met his, trying to reassure.

She didn't look okay to him. Still he nodded, trying to keep his emotions in check.

She glanced at the firefighters. "Do you guys know Detective Spencer?"

He recognized the woman and nodded. Shelby Fox had fought the fire at his house.

The older of the two male firefighters cleared his throat and stuck his hand across the bed. "Detective, I'm Jerry French. I worked the Vaughn fire."

"Yes, I remember." Jack shook his hand. "How are you?"

The man next to Jack, Rusty Ferguson, nodded at him. Shelby extended her hand.

"Hi, Shelby. Nice to see you again."

"Looks like you made it all right after the fire at your house."

"Yeah, thanks."

"Glad to hear it."

Jack glanced back at Terra, itching to touch her. *Get these people out of here.*

A half-gallon carton of chocolate ice cream sat open on a wheeled table next to the bed and he raised an eyebrow. "Ice cream?"

"Shelby brought it." Terra gestured to two brown paper

bags on the floor next to her bed. "Rusty and Jerry brought some, too."

"Ice cream is a big deal at the station," French explained. "Kinda like cops and donuts."

Jack's smile felt forced and brittle. He couldn't stop checking her pale perfect skin for bruises or burns. That he saw only one bandage was a small relief.

"What's the prognosis?" he asked, trying to keep the hard edge out of his voice.

"She's gonna live," Shelby joked.

Jack stiffened.

Terra slid a hand into his and squeezed in silent understanding.

Rusty grinned. "We'd better get out of here before we're thrown out."

"Thanks for coming," Terra said. "Tell Captain Maguire I'm fine."

"Will do," Shelby said as she walked out with the men.

Finally alone with Terra, Jack battled to keep his jaw from clenching up.

Easing closer to the bed, he glanced again at the dressing on her temple. He wanted to touch her, but didn't know if he should. "Are you hurt anywhere else?"

"No, just my head. I'm really okay, Jack. Promise."

"What did the doctor say?"

"I have a mild concussion and a knot on my head." She touched the bandage. "I'll be good as new as soon as you kiss me."

She lifted her face to his. Shadows of pain lingered in her eyes; the blacks of her pupils edged out the beautiful green.

He kissed her gently. "I can bring some of your stuff from home."

"No thanks. The doctor is filling out my release papers. I shouldn't be much longer."

"You're leaving tonight?"

"The doctor said I could."

"Doesn't he think you should stay overnight? What if something happens?"

"He wouldn't let me leave if he thought there was a chance of that," she said softly.

"You didn't bully him into it?"

"Me?" She fluttered her eyelashes at him.

He didn't see how she could be so relaxed.

"Jack." She tugged him down to her eye level. "I'm fine."

Her eyes were red rimmed, but lucid. Though pale, her skin wasn't waxy. She didn't appear weak or as if she were about to pass out. The vise around his chest eased. "Can I get you something? How about some root beer for a float?"

"That sounds wonderful, but maybe later. I've had enough ice cream for tonight. It doesn't really help my headache, but I didn't have the heart to tell the guys."

"Anything else? I'm at your beck and call."

"Too bad I can't take advantage of it right now." She caressed his hand.

The thought that she might have been seriously injured—or worse—squeezed his heart painfully. The room pressed in on him, cut off his air. "Let me check on the doctor."

"Thanks. It's Dr. Laird. One of the nurses will probably know where he is."

Jack needed some space before he put his fist through the wall. He had to get out of here. A few minutes later, he returned with the middle-aged physician whose Looney Tunes tie was spotted with blood. Jack wondered if any of it belonged to Terra.

As much as he hated being in this room, hated that *she* was here, he wouldn't leave.

The doctor checked her pupils and asked her a couple of

questions before turning to Jack. "She was unconscious for less than a minute. She has a slight headache and enlarged pupils, but no memory problems, no confusion or nausea."

Jack nodded.

"She did sustain a bruise to the temple. I've done a CAT scan and an EEG. Everything looks good. She can go home, but someone must stay with her for the next twenty-four hours." He glanced at his watch. "Until ten o'clock tomorrow night."

"Yes, sir. I can do that."

"Good." The doctor gave him a sheet of typed instructions and the symptoms that would demand medical attention.

He patted Terra's hand. "This could've been much worse. You're one lucky lady."

"Thanks, doc."

Jack clenched his fists.

"I think you'll be fine, but follow my orders to the letter."

"All right."

He looked at Jack. "Call me if you notice any of those signs, Detective."

"I will."

"You're released, young lady. Watch where you're going next time."

She grinned. "Thanks."

Once Terra had her shoes and denim shirt on, Jack pulled his truck up to the emergency room entrance. She insisted she was able to get in on her own, but he picked her up and settled her in the seat himself.

She kissed his cheek, her lips curving.

Her smile tore at something deep inside him. His pulse finally returned to normal, but as he drove to her house, he realized he'd been kidding himself.

Getting that call out of nowhere had shredded the illusion he'd created for himself. For them. She'd automatically gone into that fire, putting herself in harm's way. She could have been killed.

The thought of losing her just as suddenly as he'd lost Lori made Jack nauseous. He didn't have it in him to relive the helplessness, the rage or the brutal heartbreak that had ravaged him after Lori's death.

Getting involved with Terra had been a mistake.

By the time Terra showered off the smell of smoke and got to bed, it was nearly three in the morning. She slept until after noon with Jack waking her every two hours to ask what day it was and if she remembered what happened. She did, which the doctor had said was a good sign that her concussion was mild.

The worst part was the dull headache settled at the base of her skull. She hadn't popped this much acetaminophen since her days as a frontline firefighter.

Jack took great care of her. When she tired of her bed, he fixed a cozy place on the sofa and found an old John Wayne movie on the television. He settled in the leather recliner next to the sofa as they watched together.

By the time she finished the light supper he'd prepared, Terra felt more steady on her feet than she had all day. While he cleaned up the dishes, she called Presley Regional to check on the people she'd rescued last night. The neighbor, Mr. Isaacs, had been released, but the elderly woman had been admitted due to breathing problems.

Just as Jack walked back into the living room, she hung up. ''The nurse said Mrs. Allison is improving quickly and will probably be released tomorrow. It's lucky I was so close last night.''

"I'm glad she's better." He stood behind the recliner, flipping television channels with the remote.

"That kid I told you about, Travis? He was great, just kept fighting that fire with all he had."

"Do you need more acetaminophen?"

"No, thanks." She smiled, curled her legs under her as she looked up at Jack. Why wouldn't he look at her? "It's been a while since I've had that adrenaline rush. You know, after you've rescued someone. At first, you operate on instinct and training. Then things calm down and you're just…high. Exhilarated. Know what I mean?"

"Did you get enough to eat? I can fix something else."

"No, it was plenty." In the hours since the accident, she'd been aware of the concern that had darkened his eyes, but now his features were tight. Closed off.

"How's your head?"

"I think the pounding is gone." His behavior needled at her, though she didn't know exactly why. He was being perfectly sweet. Perfectly accommodating. Perfectly…distant. As if she hadn't touched every inch of his body. Just the way he had her.

"I can't remember the last time I made a fire rescue," she mused. "It had to be before I was promoted to fire investigator. A lot of our calls aren't too serious."

"Don't need too many serious ones," he said tightly.

She took in the penetrating stare, the worry lines carved between his eyes. "Jack, what's going on? Has something happened on our investigation?"

"Other than you getting whacked on the head by a burning rafter? No."

"So, it's the accident?" He was afraid for her. That was all.

"We can talk about this later." He turned toward the kitchen. "Let me get you something to drink."

"I don't want anything. Please tell me what's going on."

"Not now, Terra. You have a concussion, for crying out loud."

"You've been great since we got home, but you're keeping me at arm's length. I feel as if you're punishing me for something."

He came to her, his eyes full of turmoil. "I'm not trying to hurt you."

"I know that." She took his hand, squashed the sting she felt when he stiffened. "Just talk to me."

"No. This is the worst possible time."

"I get the feeling there isn't going to be a good time."

"You should rest, concentrate on getting back to a hundred percent."

She let go of his hand and stood. Anger and fear combusted inside her. "What am I supposed to think here? I don't understand why you're putting this distance between us. Things have been going so well."

"I hate seeing that bandage on your head."

"I admit it's not my best look—"

"You could have been killed last night. Don't make light of it."

Her throat tightened. "You were afraid for me."

"Hell, yes. And you should be afraid, too."

"I was," she said softly. "But I got through it. Just like you would've done."

"We're not talking about me. At least I know when I might be called into a dangerous situation."

"You don't always know." She frowned. "Do you have a problem with my job? You know what I do. You've always known."

"You're supposed to be an investigator."

"An investigator who has to fight fires on occasion."

Irritation burned beneath her hurt and apprehension. "And I'm fine. I'm arguing with you, aren't I?"

"Don't brush it off." He took her shoulders, his gaze lasering into hers. "You're fine now, but what about next time?"

"Jack, I hardly ever take rescue calls."

"But you will if you have to, and you should."

Maybe she did have a serious concussion because she was lost. "I don't understand what you're saying. If you know I might have to go on rescue calls, then what's the problem?"

"I'm not angry that you help people." His hold gentled and he lifted one knuckle to stroke her cheek. "Never. But I can't live knowing that some night you might go into a fire and not make it out."

"The same thing could happen when you get a call."

He stared at her for a long moment, creating a huge bubble of doubt and dread inside her. "I thought I could do this, but I was wrong."

The haunted words sent a warning to her brain. "Do what? Be involved with me?"

"Yes." His voice cracked, but he held her gaze.

"Why not?" Her voice trembled with emotion. This was just like Keith all over again. Jack couldn't accept her job, couldn't accept her.

"I'm sorry. I can't handle it. It's not you. It's me. I want you, so much that I allowed myself to believe you weren't a firefighter anymore. But you are."

She tried to staunch the swell of panic in her chest. "We can talk about this. We can get through this."

"I can't explain it, Terra. Hell, I'm not saying it even makes sense. I just know I can't deal with it. I don't have it in me to lose someone else the way I did my wife."

"Is it just me or did we have something special going on here?"

He didn't answer.

"You're the one who said you wanted more than one night. I thought you meant a *lot* more."

"I'm sorry."

"So, because that horrible man killed your wife—"

"On the job. She died *on the job*."

She took a deep breath, holding on to her restraint by a thread. "Because the same thing could happen to me, you want to forget what we've been building?"

"Your job is even higher risk than hers was. Chances are greater it could happen to you."

"It could happen to you, too, Jack. I didn't want to let you in either. If I went from my past experience, I would never have believed that what we had was real. It's very real and I took a chance in order to find that out. If I can do it, why can't you?"

"I just can't, Terra. I can't lose someone so close to me again. My whole life was blown apart and I thought I'd never rebuild it."

"You think you're cutting your losses now?" Her heart, which had begun to open again, shriveled shut. "I don't. It hurts just as badly and this time you're the one causing it."

"You can't hate me any more than I hate myself."

"I thought I'd finally found someone who understood my job, who accepted it. Someone I could trust when they said they wanted our relationship as much as I did. I've been through pain, too, Jack. Loss and loneliness, but I decided to take a risk. Like I thought you had. I can't change your mind, but I think you're making a big mistake."

"I don't think so."

"Do you think I'm not scared?" Frustrated tears stung her eyes. "Do you think I don't wonder what could happen to you or me? It's not just the job, Jack. It's life. We have something special. I don't know how often that happens, but I don't think you get to pick and choose when it will. You have to grab it when the chance finds you.''

"I'm sure you're right, but it doesn't change the fact that I can't give what you can to this relationship. I can't give what you deserve. That's not fair to you, Terra.''

I want you! Anger and rejection slashed at her, but she wouldn't beg. Defeated, she didn't trust herself to speak for a few seconds. "So what about the case?"

"It's my case." His eyes narrowed. "I'm not turning it over to someone else.''

"Neither am I. I can handle working together if you can." She couldn't, but hell would freeze over before she told him that.

"I can handle it," he said quietly.

"Fine. I'll contact Reynolds about the interview. I'll let you know how that goes.''

"Where will you tell him you want to meet?''

"My office. Just in case he's our—I mean, the arsonist, Darla will be there with me. He won't try anything with a witness.''

"That's good. Smart.''

Smart wasn't what she felt right now. She felt foolish and hurt and even a little used, though neither she nor Jack had made any promises. She gestured wildly toward the door. "You don't have to stay. Only three more hours left anyway.''

"I'm staying. I said I would.''

"No. I'll call Robin or Meredith to come over.''

"Terra—''

"Just go. I'll be fine.''

"You're not supposed to be alone.''

She stared at him until he swore and looked down. Biting

her bottom lip, struggling to keep the tears out of her eyes, she walked to the phone and called Meredith. Her friend said she'd be there in less than half an hour.

Terra put down the phone and gave in to the anger roiling through her. "I wish you'd told me you felt this way before I...slept with you."

She'd nearly said *fell in love with you.* The thought caused her jaw to lock. She was *not* in love with him.

"I'm staying until she gets here."

"Do whatever you want." Her heart clenching with pain, she turned and walked to her bedroom.

Chapter 13

Two days later, Terra's headache had returned and it had nothing to do with the concussion. It was all thanks to Jack Spencer. Her evening interview with Dane Reynolds, out in front of the fire investigator's office, only increased the dull throbbing behind her eyes.

Reynolds had predictably asked her out before the cameras rolled, then shot questions at her like a string of firecrackers. At the end of the session, she gave out the phone numbers for hers and Jack's offices, asking anyone with information to call.

Afterwards, she went into her office, wrapped up all her paperwork on the fire at Jack's house and sent him an e-mail about the interview. She didn't have it in her to talk to him yet. That would come soon enough. As soon as they got a lead from this interview, she'd be talking to him plenty.

It was late when she got home. The headache, not to

mention the hurt she felt at Jack's rejection, had drained her. After eating a bowl of cereal, she headed to bed.

The last conversation she'd had with Jack played over and over in her mind. What made her as mad as anything was that she couldn't even argue with his reasons for walking away. He simply wasn't ready for another relationship and there was nothing she could do to make him ready.

That frustrated helplessness gouged as deeply as the pain. Whatever had been between them was finished. She climbed into bed and squeezed her eyes shut. She'd done all the crying she was going to do. Forcing herself to focus on her breathing, she put her mind and body into a state of relaxation that she hoped Jack Spencer couldn't invade. And she prayed as hard as she could that sleep would come.

Her pager beeped, jerking her awake. She fumbled for it, noting dispatch's number on the back-lit readout. Pale yellow light from the streetlamp wedged through her blinds. The time on the clock glowed five-twelve.

She dressed quickly, throwing on clothes and tennis shoes, racing out the door to her truck. A call to dispatch got her a familiar sounding address on the south edge of Presley and the news that there was one fatality.

Clicking off her radio, her mind zeroed in on the address. It was in the same strip mall as the site of the first serial arson, a janitorial supply store. Before she could do more than wonder about that, her cell phone rang.

"Hello."

"Terra?"

"Jack?" Her pulse cartwheeled and she reminded herself he couldn't be calling for personal reasons. Something must have happened on the case.

"I'm at a fire scene."

"I'm on my way to one now. On the south side—"

"Near the janitorial supply store?"

"Yes."

"That's where I am."

She went still inside, automatically guiding her car around a corner. Why was Jack the officer assigned to her fire scene? "Dispatch told me we have one fatality. Who is it?"

"Dane Reynolds."

Terra started, completely taken aback. "Dane? But I just saw him."

"I know," Jack said quietly. "I thought you'd want to be prepared."

"I appreciate it. I'm on my way."

Dane Reynolds? As her initial disbelief faded, Terra's mind raced. If he was their arsonist, had he torched himself? If he wasn't the arsonist, was his death related to their case? She wouldn't get answers until she arrived at the scene, but the questions still circled through her mind.

Almost twenty minutes after getting the page, she reached the strip mall. In front of her, sirens screamed as an ambulance turned into a large parking lot which serviced the mall.

Along with the supply store, an alterations shop, a shoe store and a family-owned grocery comprised the mall's businesses. Terra followed the ambulance into the lot. One patrol car guarded the entrance, its red and blue lights flashing through the dusky night. After she showed her badge, the officer waved her in. She parked a couple of hundred feet away from the janitorial supply store.

Station Four had the blaze out. Smoke floated overhead. A van, its white paint charred and peeling, squatted in the hazy yellow floodlight like a crippled bug. On this side of the vehicle, only one of the four call letters remained. The channel number and other identifying marks had been scorched away.

She bailed out of her truck, slinging her camera around

her neck as she wove her way around another police car and the line of firefighters dragging back the main line which was attached to a hydrant on the curb. The burn pattern was most intense on the front doors of the van, not from under the hood or from the back near the gas tank.

Despite the hum of activity around her, her gaze went straight to Jack. He stood three to four car lengths away, directing a patrol officer who stretched crime scene tape around a square area about one hundred feet from the van.

"Roll that back!"

Terra glanced toward the familiar voice and saw Don LeBass at the head of the nozzle, dripping wet and moving the main hose to the truck. If he'd shown up with the crew, could he have started this fire? Neither she nor Jack had found anything to clear LeBass. Or Cecily, either.

She saw Captain Maguire speaking to two firefighters and she walked over. He turned to her. "I told them to leave the body as is for now. The guy never had a chance. This was a fast burn, Terra."

She nodded.

"You should be able to get to the van in a few minutes. Want my guys to set up your lights?"

"Yes, please. They're in the back of my truck. Who's taping the scene tonight?"

"Williams."

"I'll talk to him in a few minutes."

He gestured toward the burned vehicle. "The vic's a reporter. That one who's always bugging you."

"I heard." Thanks to Jack, she'd had time to wrap her mind around this. "Who was first on the scene?"

"Either Detective Spencer or the patrolman." Maguire pushed off his helmet and swiped at the black water running down his face. "I'm not sure."

"Thanks, Captain."

She might as well talk to Jack and get it over with. He still stood to one side of the cordoned-off area. As she passed a clump of firefighters, she heard one of them say, "That guy in there is toast. Doesn't look like he even tried to get out."

She glanced at the soaked, charred van. *Why* had Reynolds been here?

The sweep of headlights across the parking lot caught her attention. An SUV from Channel Five and a van from Channel Nine pulled up and stopped behind Station Two's rescue truck. It hadn't taken long for word to get out.

Shoulders tense, she sloshed through the water glistening on the pavement. This was the first time she'd seen or talked to Jack since that night at her house.

He watched her, his steady gaze causing a flutter in her belly. She resisted the impulse to run her gaze down his body, to replay the memory of their nights together. Forgetting all that lean power, the incredible way he'd made her feel would be difficult. The closer she got, the more her heart ached. She'd missed him. "What do you make of this?"

His blue gaze stayed fixed on her, setting off a nervous skitter in her pulse. She wanted to ask how he was. At the same time, she wanted to give in to the hurt still sawing at her and freeze him out. But this was all about work. He wanted only a partner; that's what he would get.

"Hello," he said quietly, his gaze flat and remote.

"Hello." The word felt thick in her throat and sweat clammed her palms inside her gloves. "Looks bad," she said. A brilliant observation. "Were you first on the scene?"

"Officer Pope was. He was driving this area and saw the flames. I heard it over the radio and got here a couple of minutes after he did." His gaze searched her eyes. "I wanted to call. I know you met with Reynolds tonight."

"I appreciate the heads-up. I don't think I would've handled it too well if I'd just shown up and found him like this with no warning."

The grim set of Jack's mouth, the bloodshot eyes had her wondering if he'd had as much trouble sleeping as she had.

"Since I seriously doubt Reynolds would torch himself, I think we have to conclude he isn't our arsonist."

"Unless guilt took over and he did himself in."

"True," Jack said.

"But not likely."

"Reynolds getting torched and being involved in our case is too much of a coincidence. I'd say this means we're down to two suspects," Jack said. "Despite his past, he wasn't our guy."

"Probably not, but we'll know more once I get the toxicology report. I want to know if there are any drugs in his system. From the fast burn of the fire and no evidence of an attempted escape, I suspect that he was probably unconscious when the blaze started."

"You've got to be thinking the same thing I am—our serial arsonist is responsible."

"Yes. We have no proof yet and the pattern is different, but something tells me this is the work of our torch." The sick feeling in her gut was the result of that hunch and not over the differences between her and Jack. "I'll take samples to see if the same accelerant was used as in our other fires."

"Why would Reynolds come here?" Jack asked. "This is the scene of the first arson."

"I think he was doing some background work on the case. Today during the interview, he asked several questions about this fire and the second one, at the photography studio. He kept checking his dates carefully against something in his notebook."

"How was he the rest of the time?" His gaze flicked over her. "Still trying to put the moves on you?"

Terra knew she should tell him to mind his own business. "He was his usual self."

Jack's jaw tightened and Terra wondered how he'd react if she told him the reporter had tried to back her against the office building and kiss her.

The air between them hung stilted and heavy. Her mind was able to separate from the last time she'd seen him, keep up a mental guard, but her body ached for his touch. She shifted, restless and annoyed.

He pointed to several reporters who circled the officer guarding the front line of the crime scene. "Wonder where Reynolds's buddy is? The cameraman?"

She looked over her shoulder, hating how uncomfortable she felt around Jack. "I don't know. He wasn't with Reynolds during our interview either."

"I thought they always worked together."

"So did I. I asked about him, and Dane said that he wanted someone on the camera other than T.J."

"Maybe T.J. was shooting another story."

She didn't think she could stand this close to Jack much longer. Smelling the sexy earthiness of his aftershave, remembering how his muscles rippled beneath her hands, her lips. "I guess I should get started."

"Me, too. That means I need to ask you some questions."

"Me?"

"From what I've gathered so far, you were one of the last people to see him alive."

Her head came up. "Just like Harris."

"Just like Harris," Jack repeated grimly. "Both murders happened within hours after you were with these men."

The watching, the stalking. It had been about *her,* not her and Jack. "The Molotov cocktails at your house."

"A murder attempt?"

She nodded. "Because you were with me?"

"It could be. If we go by body count, the theory is that the arsonist knew you were with Harris, knew you were with me, knew you were with Reynolds."

"But why kill *them?*"

"And not me?"

"That's not what I meant," she said crisply. "Why kill them at all? I wasn't involved with Harris or Reynolds. At least not the way I was with you."

Jack looked away, a muscle ticcing in his jaw. He rubbed a hand over his face. "What are motives for arson?"

"Revenge. To hide a crime."

"Attention."

"He or she has been getting attention," Terra pointed out. "Television, newspaper, radio."

"Maybe they want *your* attention."

She swallowed around a hard knot in her throat. "This can't be because of me. No."

"We've got to look at every angle, Terra. This is one we haven't seen before."

The thought that these men might have been killed simply because she'd spent time with them sent a chill through her. "I probably didn't spend thirty minutes total with Reynolds. Why him?"

"I'll start retracing his last steps. Maybe we can figure it out."

The thought that Jack could have been killed because of her cut her breath. Maybe he'd broken up with her just in time, but he could still be in danger. The arsonist had no way of knowing Jack had walked away from her. From *them*.

"What time did Reynolds leave your office?"

"Around six-thirty. I stayed and worked until a little before ten, then went home.'' She wanted to ask what he'd done all day, but she didn't.

"You say T.J. wasn't present at the interview. Who was?"

"Another cameraman. I think Dane called him Lonnie. And Darla was there. She stayed until after they left."

"Okay." Jack scribbled in his pocket notebook. "I'll go talk to these people. See if Lonnie knows why Dane might have come here. I'll also find T.J. and ask if he saw Dane tonight or knows why Reynolds might've come here."

Terra tried to shake off her distress about Reynolds's death. Her forced closeness to Jack wasn't helping. Still, she had a job to do. Popping the lens off her camera, she prepared to take pictures of the burned van.

"Let me know when you get the tox results."

"I will." She turned to walk away, relief and disappointment mixing that she was finally getting some space from Jack.

His voice stopped her. "We can't prove that Cecily and LeBass were at every fire scene, but we can prove Reynolds was."

She glanced over her shoulder, wondering at his thoughts. "Right."

"As much as Dane worked with Coontz, it's likely the cameraman was at all the scenes, too."

"But his alibis checked out."

"They didn't send up any red flags," Jack admitted, "but it can't hurt to check them again. Besides, Coontz's connection to Reynolds is something we should definitely explore further."

Terra faced him. "Are you thinking Coontz could be the torch? You saw photos of him at his cousin's wedding the night of Harris's murder."

"True." Jack thought for a minute. "He could've slipped

out during the wedding, shown back up at the reception and had his picture snapped.''

''So maybe there's a crack in the alibi he also gave for the night of the arson at the photography studio, when he said he was out of town.''

''Right.''

''This scene may take me several hours.''

''I plan to check in with all the florists this morning. If the arsonist stays true to form, you should be getting a flower delivery sometime today. I'll show Coontz's picture along with Cecily's and LeBass's. Maybe we can get an identification this time.''

As much as anything, she would miss working with Jack, figuring things out. How could standing in this damp cold air at the crack of dawn talking about a torch make her want him? ''Sounds good.''

''I guess I'll get started.''

Under the lights, his eyes were dark, unreadable. Yet something held her there, something provocative and powerful. ''I'll keep you posted.''

''Good luck finding what you want in the lab tests.''

''Good luck getting an ID.'' This was ridiculous. One of them had to walk away sometime. ''Please be careful, Jack. If this arsonist is killing people because of their involvement with me, he may not know we're...over.''

Fierce heat flared in his eyes. His face hardened and for a moment, Terra thought he might say something. Change his mind about them. All he did was give a curt nod.

She walked away, pressing a fist to her chest to stave off the stab of pain at what they'd given up.

Over. Yes, he and Terra were over. It had been at his insistence. He had no right to feel angry or irritated, but he did.

Rubbing his face, he tried to shift his gaze from the graceful sway of her hips as she moved off, then gave up. He didn't like their splitting up to follow different leads, especially not now that they had a hunch the murders had been committed because these men had spent time with her, but she'd be safe enough here. Pope would be here and so would the other officer guarding the crime scene. Jack would just have to take comfort in that fact, brush off the irritating knowledge that someone besides him would be protecting her.

The best thing he could do, especially if the arsonist was trying to get her attention, was to solve this case as quickly as possible. A cleared case would also wipe out the fog of desire and need affecting his mental equilibrium. Just being around her made him second-guess the decision he'd made. The only decision he *could* make.

Tearing his gaze from her long-legged stride, he forced his thoughts to the investigation and mentally laid out what he needed to do. Stopping at the television station to ask who'd last seen Dane Reynolds was first on his list. He'd follow the bread crumbs from there until it was time for him to appear in court this afternoon.

Terra stood near one of her high-powered floodlights, her hair a warm glow of color in the drab night. He had to get to work before he did something stupid like grab her and tell her he'd made a huge mistake.

He'd done the right thing by putting the brakes on their relationship. Even if he couldn't stop thinking—dreaming—about the green-eyed woman who seemed to have effortlessly made herself a permanent part of him.

As he watched her snap pictures of the van, Jack wondered darkly if walking away from her had been the biggest mistake of his life. It didn't help his disposition that a voice inside his head screamed back "yes."

* * *

All that morning and into the afternoon, Terra told herself to focus only on the work. The sooner this case was solved, the sooner Jack Spencer would be out of her life. That thought had her gripping the steering wheel tight enough to cramp her hands. Seeing him at the scene of Reynolds's murder had made her realize that she'd been waiting these past two days for Jack to tell her he'd made a mistake, see if they could try it again. But she knew now that wasn't going to happen.

It had also made her realize something else. She'd fallen in love with him.

Despite thinking she'd never go there again, despite knowing he didn't love her back. She loved him enough to risk getting her heart broken, enough to risk him walking out on her.

Tears tightened her throat and she took a shaky breath. Jack was out of her life. He'd made that clear. She had to move on and forget. Somehow.

Work would help. Dane's death was awful, but perhaps it was just what they needed to finally get a break. She had worked the scene thoroughly, finishing up about eight-thirty that morning. Rather than send her samples to the lab in Oklahoma City, she drove them there, and told the chemist she'd like to wait for the results. It was urgent.

The tests took a few hours, but Terra put the time to good use. She made exhaustive notes, drew a timeline and began to plug in what she knew about T. J. Coontz and her arson dates. Several phone calls netted her the information that T.J. had registered for the out-of-town training seminar he'd given as an alibi for the date of the photography studio arson, but had never picked up his name badge. The seminar chairwoman didn't remember seeing him at all.

For lunch, she had half a sandwich and a cup of coffee

from the vending machine in the hall. Shortly before noon, the head chemist gave her toxicology and accelerant reports.

Now, hours after Dane Reynolds had burned to death, she read the results, satisfaction sweeping through her. Paper in hand, she called Jack's cell phone.

When he answered, she said excitedly, "I've got news."

"Let's hear it."

After telling him that Coontz's training seminar was unverified, she said, "Test results show the accelerant used to torch the news van is the same as the alcohol-based cleaning solution used at Harris's house and the other three arson sites. Also the toxicology report reveals high levels of Halcion in Dane's system."

"Enough to have rendered him unconscious and unable to get out of the van," Jack said.

"Yes. So we're definitely dealing with the same arsonist here, even though the pattern is different."

"One link is the same. You."

The knowledge put a queasy knot in her belly.

"I've got some news, too." He sounded tired, but determined. "You and Lonnie were the last ones to see Dane. No one knows why he went to the janitorial supply store. Coontz wasn't at the studio when I was there, nor was he at home. We need to talk to him."

"Together."

"Absolutely. I did find a florist who thought T.J. was in her shop this morning buying flowers. She wasn't one hundred percent on the ID when I showed her his picture, but she definitely remembered a Channel Four van driving away. I decided to come to your office. I wanted to be here if the roses were delivered, and they were, right before you called."

"Is there a note?"

"Yeah." Jack didn't want to read it, felt his whole body

pucker up. But his personal feelings had no place in this investigation. Not anymore. "It says, 'I guess I wasn't clear last time. No other men.'"

"Ohmygosh!"

The tremor in her voice had Jack's hand tightening on the phone. "Are you all right?"

"Yes," she whispered. "I just can't believe these men were killed because of me. How sickening."

He couldn't argue. He also couldn't protect her, at least not from here. "I think it's Coontz."

"I'm afraid you might be right," she said dully.

His heart ached for her. He wanted to solve this case and he knew she did, too, but she'd never once suspected the cameraman. Hell, neither had he. "I've got to go."

"Please be careful, Jack." Her voice trembled, reaching through the phone to twist in his gut. "He could go after you next, just like he did Harris and Dane."

"You've got to be careful, too. I'm sending someone over to watch your house. We don't know where he might show up."

"What about you?"

"There's no sense having anyone watch the place I'm staying. No way would the lieutenant okay the manpower for someone to sit on an empty place. I'll make sure no one follows me. You need to do the same."

"I will."

"Damn, I've got to be in court this afternoon and you won't be able to reach me on my cell phone."

"I'm sure I'll be fine. If I find out anything else, I'll leave a voice mail on your phone."

"I'll check it as soon as I can. We can interview Coontz tonight, once I'm out of court."

"All right. I'll meet you at your rent house. What time?"

"Six. I should definitely be finished by then."

"I'm going to stop by each of the arson sites and talk to the owners and managers. See if any of them can identify T.J. or give me some kind of connection. I want to have as much information as possible when we interview him tonight."

"That's good. I've got the department secretary running a check on him. I'll let you know if I turn up anything. Watch your back, Terra."

"You, too."

She hung up, apprehension suffocating her. Fingers crossed, they would have their serial arsonist and murderer by tonight.

An hour later, Terra was certain T. J. Coontz was her torch. How could she have missed him? He'd been in plain sight the whole time, but so unsuspicious.

The owner of the burned photography studio recognized the picture of T.J. immediately. Randy Wates told her that Coontz had been a part-time employee and done a fine job until he'd started misplacing orders. After dozens of missing orders and two reprimands, Wates had no choice but to fire T.J.

Terra's second stop, at the dental office, reaped more compelling evidence against Coontz. She called Jack's cell phone and left him a voice message. "Jack, T.J. has to be our guy. I've found connections between him and the photography studio *and* the dental office. I'll meet you at your house at six o'clock. Be careful."

I love you, she wanted to add, but she bit off the words. Jack didn't want to hear them. He'd made that perfectly clear.

All afternoon, while Jack sat impatiently in court and waited his turn to testify, he kept seeing the hurt in Terra's eyes the other night, the way her face had paled. She had tried to reason with him, but obviously he'd been insane, driven crazy by fear. He'd let fear push her away. And now he couldn't shake the sense that his future had flashed right past while he worried about getting hurt.

He'd been so sure that breaking things off with her was the right thing. Which, of course, was why he couldn't concentrate worth a damn. He couldn't stop thinking about her. Couldn't breathe when he realized that the end of this case would signify the finality of their relationship.

He wasn't going to get over her.

He was crazy in love with her.

He didn't need his sister telling him—three times today—that he was an idiot for walking away from Terra. He'd figured it out all by himself.

And he was going to tell her tonight as soon as she got to his house. He would do whatever he had to, including grovel, to win her back.

After the longest hours of his life, Jack finally gave his testimony and court was recessed until Monday. A glance at his watch told him he had almost an hour before Terra arrived at his house. Enough time to stop for some flowers, maybe some root beer and ice cream.

As he slid behind the wheel of his truck and left downtown Oklahoma City, he called the department secretary. "Wanda, it's Jack. Did you find what I was looking for?"

"You betcha. That boy, Coontz, has a juvenile record. For arson."

Arson. There were still questions to be asked, pieces to fit together, but he and Terra had found their arsonist. Listening to the voice mail she had left confirmed for Jack that Terra knew it, too.

After they nailed this sicko, Jack was going to beg her forgiveness. Ask her to give them another chance.

He stopped at a florist's shop, then the grocery. Careful to make sure he wasn't followed, Jack drove on to the older stone house he was renting until the repairs on his own were finished. He got out to lift the wooden garage door, then nosed his truck inside. After opening the door that led into the utility room, he leaned back into the vehicle to get his purchases.

A shuffle at his back had him turning, then pain exploded in his head. He crumpled to the floor, his vision blurring before everything went black.

Chapter 14

Terra parked her Explorer in Jack's driveway and sat there for a moment, psyching herself up to see him. Working with him scraped across her bruised and raw nerves like a blade.

She hadn't expected their split to hurt this much or to feel like she'd lost a part of herself. It would pass, she thought. Sometime in this century, please. Keith and her failed marriage had taught her she couldn't commit to anyone who wasn't willing to take her as a whole. Still, Jack's rejection and the lost promise of what she thought she'd found with him opened a wrenching emptiness inside her.

Taking a deep breath, she slid out into the chilly evening. She could do this. Just go in and tell Jack what she'd learned about Coontz, then go with him to interview the man. All business. All about the case.

Terra walked up to the wide porch of Jack's rented house and rang the doorbell someone had painted over. The modest neighborhood boasted small, well-maintained yards. Yellow and red leaves scattered across the grass and into the street. Where was Jack? His truck sat inside the open garage. She rang the bell again. And caught an acrid, familiar scent. Smoke.

Glancing down, she saw a wisp curl out past the screen door. ''Jack!'' She pounded on one of two vertical windows that flanked the door. ''Jack!''

No answer.

She jerked open the screen, but the heavy main door wouldn't budge.

Alarmed, Terra sprinted off the porch for her truck. Jerking open the back door, she grabbed the first available tool, her shovel. She flew to the porch and jabbed the shovel into the window. Glass shattered. Smoke plumed out.

Early stages, her mind catalogued as she stuck a hand inside the splintered window. She unlocked the door, glass stabbing into her wrist. She could detect no noise or movement from inside. The sting of pain was nothing compared to the fear closing off her throat, her air.

She turned the knob and rushed inside. Jack lay in the fetal position on an area rug in the middle of the small living area's wooden floor. Grimy rope bound his hands and feet. His eyes were shut. He didn't move. A dark stain marred the collar of his camel-hair jacket.

Panic clutched at her. What had happened? Gripping the shovel, she hurried to him. A pile of rags burned several feet away. Clear liquid puddled near his feet. She took in the alcohol smell of lighter fluid. Once the rags ignited the floor and sucked up the liquid, the blaze would feed and rush them like a rabid animal. She had to get him out of here.

''Jack, can you hear me? Jack?''

He moaned.

''Come on, come on.'' She fumbled with the rope around his ankles. The knot gave. ''Jack, wake up.''

His eyelashes fluttered.

"Get away from him, Terra."

She jerked toward the voice. T. J. Coontz stood behind the front door. "T.J., listen to me. I don't know what happened—"

"Get up." His face hardened into something sharp and almost unrecognizable. "You can't save him. It's too late."

The odor of burning cloth and fire smoke spiked her already frantic pulse. She grabbed for her shovel.

"Don't."

He pointed a gun at her, some kind of semiautomatic. Held out his other hand. "We have to get out of here. I won't hurt you."

Jack's finger moved against her knee. Though elated, Terra kept from looking down.

"Now. We don't have much time," T.J. pleaded.

Praying Jack had given her a signal, she stood. Hesitated. She didn't have a plan, but she wasn't leaving Jack in here to burn alive. Even if T.J. shot her.

"Terra, please."

Acting on pure instinct that the cameraman wouldn't hurt her, she swung around and grabbed Jack under his arms. Turned him on his back. "I'm not leaving him! If you don't want the death penalty, you'd better help me."

Grasping Jack under the arms, she tugged. Flames climbed out of the burning rags, snaked toward the lighter fluid.

"Get away from him," T.J. yelled.

"No!" She tugged, hoping Coontz would come closer.

He ran over, waving the gun in her face. "There's no time."

"Then help me." *Go down by Jack's feet. Please.*

Fire ate the fluid in one gulp, crawled toward Jack. Terra pulled hard, felt him tense as if he might try to get up.

Agony sharpened T.J.'s eyes. He looked at her, then the gun.

"Help me," she urged again. "I'll go with you after you help me."

He moved to Jack's feet.

Jack's legs punched out, caught the other man square in the chest.

The gun flew from T.J.'s hand as he stumbled back, one foot landing in the fire. Flames snatched at his pant leg like greedy beggars. He screamed in horror.

Jack pushed himself to one knee, tried to rise. "Get out of here!"

"Not without you—"

T.J. launched himself at Jack. Both men dropped like cement blocks.

Jack's hands were still tied. He fended off a flying fist with his shoulder. T.J. landed a blow that cracked against Jack's jaw. Fire skipped up T.J.'s pants, licked at the floor beneath Jack.

Terra grabbed her shovel. T.J. brought his arm back to hit Jack again.

She swung.

Outside, Terra turned her attention to Jack. "Are you okay?"

He nodded, dragging in lungfuls of air. "Yeah. Are you?"

"Yes. I'll be back." Leaving Jack sitting in the cool grass beside the still-unconscious T.J., she sprinted to her truck and called dispatch.

A woman from the next yard ran over. "I saw smoke and called the fire department. Is everyone all right?"

"I think so." Terra breathed in deep draughts of air, cold sweat trickling between her breasts. "Thank you."

She heard the distant scream of a siren. Hopefully the guys would arrive in time to save most of the house.

The woman looked at Jack, then at the man crumpled on the ground. "What on earth happened?"

"Police business, ma'am." Jack leaned over and pulled a pair of handcuffs from his belt, slapping them on a motionless Coontz.

"Oh." The woman took a few steps back, joining other onlookers from the neighborhood.

Station Two's rescue truck pulled up with their ladder truck not far behind. Captain Sandusky saw her and hurried over. She gave him a brief rundown of what had happened and arranged to talk to him later. After she'd checked on Jack. She knew what had happened so she didn't need to investigate this blaze.

She turned to the woman who'd called the fire department. "Please be available to give your statement to Captain Sandusky, all right?"

The woman nodded, her eyes huge as she took in the firefighters spilling out of the rescue truck. They fell into place with the military precision of trained soldiers. Hose out, hydrant connected, marching forward. Another siren chirped under the roar of pressurized water and Terra saw a black-and-white pull up.

Coontz stirred, moaning.

Looking pale and weak, Jack touched the back of his head. Blood smeared his fingers. He got to his feet, unsteady enough that Terra moved quickly to his side.

Until now, she had acted, not thought. But now fears rushed in. Was Jack really all right? What had Coontz done to him?

He planted one booted foot on T.J.'s back and motioned to the patrol cop. "Get this guy in your car."

While the officer half dragged, half carried Coontz to his

black-and-white patrol car, Terra turned to Jack. She started to reach for him then dropped her hand. Seeing him laid out by Coontz had shaken her to her core. She wanted to touch him, kiss him. Her hands curled into fists, pressed against her thighs. Her voice was uneven. "You need to see the paramedics."

"So do you."

"I'm fine."

Watching her warily, he gently picked up her hand. Her gaze followed his. A cut across her right wrist oozed blood and she remembered the jab of pain when she'd reached inside the broken window.

Jack's eyes darkened with fury, sending a shiver across her shoulders. "He would've hurt you, whether he meant to or not."

He started for the patrol car.

She followed. "Please let the E.M.T.s check you out."

"I want to talk to Coontz first."

"After that, will you let them look at you?"

"Yes."

He stalked over to the car. Coontz sagged half into the back seat, his feet still resting on the pavement.

"Don't kill him," Terra said, hoping to ease the rage on Jack's face. "We don't have any proof yet it was him."

"Oh, it was him." Jack planted a hand on the car's roof, leaned down into the man's face. "Wasn't it, Coontz?"

Blood trickled from T.J.'s ear and down his neck. His gaze, though dazed, focused on Terra. "I would never hurt you. I only wanted you to notice me."

"You murdered people, you scumbag. She sure as hell noticed that."

Terra shot Jack a warning look. She didn't want Coontz clamming up.

"Investigator August, Coontz here had a juvenile record for arson. You might as well talk, T.J."

The cameraman's lips flattened. Terra wondered if she would be able to get anywhere with him.

"A juvenile offender, T.J.?" She stepped up to the car, residual shock and adrenaline making her voice tremble. "You killed Harris and Dane, didn't you?"

He hesitated, then nodded.

Pain plunged through her like a blade as she thought of Harris. "Why?"

"This was between you and me." He looked confused, as if he thought she should already know. "They had no place in it."

Terra shook her head. He didn't come off as crazy, but this made no sense. "I thought you and I were friends. Harris and Dane weren't going to take away from that."

"We can be more than friends. I would be good for you. But you never noticed me, even when I set all those fires."

"How many, Coontz?" Jack's voice was hard, vibrating with tightly leashed anger.

"Five." He stared at Terra with adoring eyes. "Dane was so pushy. I knew you wouldn't like that."

"I didn't."

"He kicked me off your interview last night. He told me you didn't want me there, that the two of you were going out afterwards."

"You surely knew better than that."

"I did. I know you so much better than he did."

"Is that why you killed Reynolds?" Jack asked. "So he couldn't be with Terra?"

T.J. clamped his jaw tight.

"Why, T.J.?" she appealed quietly.

He hesitated then said, "He figured out I was setting the fires."

The information Terra had uncovered that very afternoon clicked in her mind. "He knew you were fired from Wates Photography Studio, didn't he? And that you dated the hygienist from the dental office you torched? Is that how he put it all together?"

"At first, Dane only knew that I'd worked at the photography studio, which is what got him nosing around. Then he found out about the hygienist at the dental office dumping me."

"Why burn the janitorial supply store? Did you steal the accelerant from there? You always used the same fire starter."

"I knew you'd figure it out." A smile etched his soot-streaked face. "You would've noticed me much sooner if those guys hadn't distracted your attention from me. From us."

Setting the fires had been T.J.'s way of getting her attention without risking rejection. How sad. And horribly twisted.

"I knew you would be the one investigating, since you're the only fire investigator in town." He looked so proud, so perversely pleased with himself that Terra's stomach turned.

"But you didn't count on me, did you, Coontz?" Jack shifted, his face sallow in the wash of streetlight. Shadows cut a jagged streak across his cheek.

She thought back over the summer, all the fires. "The first fire. It happened three days after you loaned me that camera."

"Yes. That's when I knew we'd be good together." He glared at Jack, hatred making his eyes glacial. "I saw you with him. On the porch at your house. I tried to warn him, but he was too stubborn."

"People throwing Molotov cocktails into my house tend to hack me off," Jack bit out.

The other man looked pleadingly into her eyes. "He can't make you happy, Terra. I can."

"I had to move out of my house after you threw your fire bombs." Jack straightened, rubbed at his eyes. "How the hell did you find out about this place?"

"I have a buddy at the utility company."

He threw the guy a disgusted look.

Terra's nerves were raw. She wanted to wrap this up, get as far from T.J. as she could. "You were outside my house on another night, weren't you?"

"Yes." A fierce frown snapped his brows together. "I knew what you two were doing in there. I couldn't stop it, but I couldn't let it go on."

"So you ambushed me tonight, beat the hell out of my head and tried to burn me alive," Jack growled. "We'll have more questions later." He turned to the patrol cop. "Get him out of my sight."

"Come with me, Terra." T.J. reached for her.

She shook her head.

"Please—"

Jack stepped in front of her, shoved Coontz's legs into the car and slammed the door.

She wrapped her arms around her waist, watching the police officer drive away with Coontz. What a sad and twisted man. And how pathetically ironic. He hadn't wanted her and Jack together; thanks to Jack, they weren't.

She should leave now, but she couldn't until she knew he was all right.

He turned, his gaze steady on her face. She pointed to the firefighters waiting next to the rescue truck.

"We need to talk," he said.

"*After* you see them. I'm worried about your head. What else did he do to you?"

"He hit me with a pipe or something. That's all."

"Let's go."

"I will. *If* you agree to hear me out afterwards."

Her lips firmed. She couldn't imagine what he wanted to say. If he was going to repeat how wrong they were for each other, she'd gotten it the first time.

His eyes glinted stubbornly. "That's the deal. Please."

"Okay."

About fifteen minutes later, the cut on his head had been bandaged and so had the one on her wrist. His lungs were clear, as were hers. He thanked the E.M.T. and stepped onto the curb as the rescue truck pulled away.

"I'm glad you're all right," she said stiffly, hating the fact that she still wanted to throw her arms around him. She turned to leave.

"Terra, wait." The soft ache in his voice stopped her.

"I'm tired, Jack. You've got to be, too."

"This is important."

"We can wrap up tomorrow. I need to talk to Sandusky."

"I don't blame you for wanting to go," he said. "But could you give me just a few minutes?"

She bit off the retort that she'd been prepared to give him a lot more than that. As the adrenaline drained out of her, exhaustion crept in. His close call, coupled with her waning self-control, meant she couldn't fight with him right now. "Okay."

She finally turned. Uncertainty clouded his eyes, the shadow of fear. Surely she misread that. Jack Spencer afraid?

"Will you come with me?"

She glanced around. The fire was out. Water gurgled into the street grates. The crew had their hoses packed and were loading onto the ladder truck. "Where?"

"The garage."

She frowned, but walked across the grass and up the

driveway with him. Once inside, he stopped next to the driver's side door.

Lines of pain creased his forehead and fanned out from his eyes. His head must hurt like the devil. The part of her that couldn't dismiss him surfaced. "I'm so sorry, Jack. That's quite a knot on your head. If it weren't for me, this wouldn't have happened at all."

"My head isn't what's bothering me."

"What is?" Her gaze took him in, hungrily if she were honest, as she looked for other injuries.

He stepped closer and she stiffened, lifting her head to look him in the eye. Warn him off.

"I made a huge mistake by telling you I didn't want to be involved. I do."

She blinked.

He opened his truck door, pulling out bunches of tissue-wrapped flowers and a grocery bag.

"Flowers?"

"Three kinds." He handed them to her, a riot of gold, purple and burgundy. "No roses."

"Good idea." She took them reluctantly, feeling herself being drawn into those blue eyes.

"And…" He reached into the bag, pulled out a carton of ice cream and a liter of root beer. Vanilla ice cream dripped down the side of the container.

Her gaze challenged his. "That's melted."

"It wasn't supposed to be."

"You were going to give me flowers and ice cream?" She clutched the bouquets tight, uncertain about where he was going. Not sure she wanted to know.

"Flowers and ice-cream floats. To start working on your forgiving me."

Despite how she'd tried to protect herself, her heart cracked open a tiny bit. "You were planning to bribe me?"

"I was desperate." He grinned, making her knees soft. "I'm willing to bribe or beg."

"Is crawling part of your plan?"

"Sweetheart, I'll crawl on my belly if that's what you want."

"I don't know about this, Jack."

He took her hand, sliding his thumb across the pulse in her wrist. Earnest blue eyes sought hers, urgent and determined. "I'm sorry for hurting you, Terra. It wasn't your job that had me backing away. It was panic. I was afraid of losing you."

Though she should probably pull away, she kept her hand in his. "My job hasn't changed, Jack." She swallowed, saying the words even though they ripped at her. "It's not going to."

"And it shouldn't. I wouldn't ask you to do that."

She bristled. "No, you certainly won't."

"I'm trying to tell you…I'm an idiot. I thought I could walk away, but it was already too late. You're part of me, Terra. I can't go five seconds without thinking of you, wanting to talk to you, needing you."

A surprised breath shuddered out of her. "But you said—"

"Don't remind me." He moved another step closer and cupped her shoulders. "When I saw you in that hospital, all I could think of was losing you the way I lost Lori. How it felt to love her, then lose her in a flash, with no warning, for no reason. I couldn't let myself go there again. But I was already there. With you. And I panicked."

His warmth wrapped around her. The clean earthy scent she loved was mixed with smoke. Her heart softened. "I was afraid, too, Jack."

"I thought I'd never find another woman who would make me want to take a chance again, but I did. You're that woman, Terra August.'' He rested his forehead against hers, his breath warm against her skin. Weakening the guard she'd worked so hard to raise against him.

''I never should've walked away from you. Please say you forgive me.''

''I can't argue with your reasons for walking away, Jack. Something could happen. To either one of us.''

''I know that, but it would be a bigger loss to turn my back on what we have. For however long it lasts. I'm afraid I've ruined the best thing to ever happen to me. I know we can make it work. Since you're still listening, I'm hoping you'll give us a chance.

''I love you, Terra,'' he said fiercely. ''Both the fire investigator *and* the firefighter. I know you're not one without the other. I want all of you.''

''I have to be both those things, Jack.''

''I know. I know going into this that you're a gutsy, sexy lady who may have to fight fires on occasion. But don't blame me if I hope it isn't very often.''

Could she believe him? Trust that he wouldn't change his mind later? ''Are you sure?''

''Absolutely. For always.''

He'd taken the risk, finally. How could she not? Her last wall crumbled as emotion tightened her throat. ''I love you, too.''

His eyes turned smoky and he kissed her, slowly, tenderly.

She twined her arms around his neck, melting against him. Long moments later, he lifted his head and nuzzled her neck. ''I don't know what I would've done if you'd said no, but I wouldn't have given up.''

Touched, she pulled back and looked into his eyes. The tenderness she saw there started a slow burn inside her. ''Let's go to my house.''

"Wait. Since I'm on a roll, I want to know...will you marry me?"

Her eyes widened. "Are you planning to bribe me for that, too?"

"If I have to. What's it gonna be? Ice cream or flowers?"

"Actually, your idea about crawling is good."

His head came up; his eyes narrowed. "On my belly?"

"How about on me?" she whispered, her body humming in anticipation.

Grinning, he ran his hands down her arms and flicked a heated look over her body. "Now that's some crawling I can handle."

She hooked a finger into his waistband and pulled him to her. "Get busy, Detective."

* * * * *

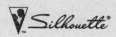

INTIMATE MOMENTS™

KYLIE BRANT's
miniseries
The Tremaine Tradition
continues with

Truth or Lies
(IM #1238)
on sale August 2003

To catch a criminal, detective Cade Tremaine turned
to Dr. Shae O'Riley, the beautiful surgeon who had
caught the eye of a suspected drug runner. But
neither Cade nor Shae expected the spiraling path of
danger and corruption they faced. And they didn't
anticipate finding love....

The**Tremaine**
Tradition

*Where unexpected assignments
lead to unexpected pleasures...*

Available at your favorite retail outlet.

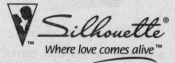

Where love comes alive™

Visit Silhouette at www.eHarlequin.com

SIMTOL

eHARLEQUIN.com

The eHarlequin.com online community is *the* place to share opinions, thoughts and feelings!

- Joining the community is easy, fun and **FREE!**

- Connect with **other romance fans** on our message boards.

- Meet your **favorite authors** without leaving home!

- **Share opinions** on books, movies, celebrities…and *more!*

Here's what our members say:

"I love the friendly and helpful atmosphere filled with support and humor."
—Texanna (eHarlequin.com member)

"Is this the place for me, or what? There is nothing I love more than 'talking' books, especially with fellow readers who are reading the same ones I am."
—Jo Ann (eHarlequin.com member)

Join today by visiting
www.eHarlequin.com!

INTCOMM

If you enjoyed what you just read,
then we've got an offer you can't resist!

Take 2 bestselling love stories FREE!

Plus get a FREE surprise gift!

Clip this page and mail it to Silhouette Reader Service™

IN U.S.A.
3010 Walden Ave.
P.O. Box 1867
Buffalo, N.Y. 14240-1867

IN CANADA
P.O. Box 609
Fort Erie, Ontario
L2A 5X3

YES! Please send me 2 free Silhouette Intimate Moments® novels and my free surprise gift. After receiving them, if I don't wish to receive anymore, I can return the shipping statement marked cancel. If I don't cancel, I will receive 6 brand-new novels every month, before they're available in stores! In the U.S.A., bill me at the bargain price of $3.99 plus 25¢ shipping and handling per book and applicable sales tax, if any*. In Canada, bill me at the bargain price of $4.74 plus 25¢ shipping and handling per book and applicable taxes**. That's the complete price and a savings of at least 10% off the cover prices—what a great deal! I understand that accepting the 2 free books and gift places me under no obligation ever to buy any books. I can always return a shipment and cancel at any time. Even if I never buy another book from Silhouette, the 2 free books and gift are mine to keep forever.

245 SDN DNUV
345 SDN DNUW

Name	(PLEASE PRINT)	
Address	Apt.#	
City	State/Prov.	Zip/Postal Code

* Terms and prices subject to change without notice. Sales tax applicable in N.Y.
** Canadian residents will be charged applicable provincial taxes and GST.
 All orders subject to approval. Offer limited to one per household and not valid to current Silhouette Intimate Moments® subscribers.
® are registered trademarks of Harlequin Books S.A., used under license.

INMOM02   ©1998 Harlequin Enterprises Limited

Coming in August 2003

Back by popular demand!

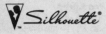

I N T I M A T E   M O M E N T S™

proudly presents RITA® Award-winning
and RWA Hall of Fame author

KATHLEEN KORBEL

Enjoy her latest Kendall Family title

Some Men's Dreams
(IM #1237)

Genevieve Kendall had devoted her entire
life to caring for others, all the while hiding
the pain of her own childhood. Now, to help
single father Dr. Jack O'Neill's little girl, she
must finally reveal her most personal secret.
But if she risks herself to save his daughter,
will Jack be there to mend Gen's broken heart?

*Don't miss the other emotional Kendall Family titles,
available only from Silhouette Books.*

JAKE'S WAY IM #413
SIMPLE GIFTS IM #571

Where love comes alive™

Visit Silhouette at www.eHarlequin.com   SIMSMD

COMING NEXT MONTH

SIMCNM0703